The Glory Days of Aimée Bonnard

A NOVEL

MARIA ELENA SANDOVICI

ISBN: 9798581025833

Edited by Mandy Schoen

With invaluable input on
Galveston Island's history
by Margaret Doran.

All mistakes and
inaccuracies are my own.

DEDICATION

To Bob and Rosa Pollard

FOREWORD

It is called the oldest profession in the world, but often overlooked is the fact that prostitution both originated and continued out of necessity. Until the second half of the twentieth century, prostitution was one of the only viable professions available to women in the U.S. and one of fewer that allowed financial autonomy. This paradox was amplified during the Victorian era, when the rigid societal expectations thrust upon women intensified and caused the demand for prostitution to skyrocket, resulting in a marked expansion into mass prostitution by way of densely populated red-light districts that emerged in cities across the country. I discovered these bleak but undeniable claims about American history while writing *Galveston's Red Light District: A History of The Line* (The History Press, 2018), but historical facts do not always elicit empathy or even understanding—sometimes, it takes fiction to do that.

I first met Elena Sandovici through mutual friends we shared within Galveston's eclectic community of artists, activists, small business owners, and dreamers of all varieties. Although originally, I knew her only as a visual artist, I soon became acquainted with her written works that possess strong themes of feminism and self-actualization. Still later, I learned about her background which includes giving up a tenured position in academia to pursue an artistic career and living in parts of the world where prostitution is neither illegal nor considered taboo. I was certain then that she was the perfect author not only to personify and illuminate a facet of history that modern women can scarcely imagine, but also to do so in a way that shines a delicate spotlight on the commonality between then and now, between us and them: our innate desire for freedom and the courage to become the truest version of ourselves.

This was the same goal I had when I produced *A History of The Line*, and I was deeply honored when Elena told me that my perspective of these sullied women of history—as women of purpose, acumen, and poise rather than downtrodden, listless victims of circumstance—was an inspiration for Aimée. However, examining societal inadequacies and their subsequent evolution from an academic perspective is one thing. It is an entirely different notion to plunge yourself, as Elena has, into an unknown world to reveal the emotional life of an unapologetic woman who is both a consummate professional and wholly human, subject to the fears, elations, triumphs, and trials of life.

Swept up in a whirlwind of intrigue, calculated seductions, and phantoms of her past existence, Aimée maneuvers the politics and personalities of the country's most famous red-light district with a grace and sophistication that belies her occupation, only to learn that the most daunting task she faces is that of self-discovery. By her side, we learn that redemption is found only after we first forgive ourselves. Love is more than a romantic feeling, rather a force of nature that is always on the side of truth and justice. And when we inevitably become disillusioned with the world, its demands, and the sacrifices that chisel away at our dreams, life will remind us that we cannot put a price on freedom.

Kimber Fountain
Author, Historian, Speaker
www.KimberFountain.com

CHAPTER 1
GLORY DAYS

Galveston 1898

Nobody comes to a brothel seeking a true story. It's what I tell myself each morning, sipping the coffee devoid of chicory I'm still getting used to, letting the breeze come in through the open window of my hotel room, inhaling it for courage. Galveston smells of two things: salt air and money. It's a good reminder of why I'm here. With its bustling port, the Cotton Exchange, its glorious mansions and never ceasing activity, this bountiful barrier island in the Gulf of Mexico is an excellent place to reinvent myself.

I weave together the highlights of a story that's more enticing than it is believable. I play at disguising or enhancing the hint of French in my accent. I opt for enhancing it. I write my own letter of reference. I am no longer Yvonne, the prostitute who fled New Orleans after her best friend's death. I am Aimée Bonnard, and here in Galveston I will find a new benefactress among the local madams.

I prefer to pretend I have never been to the Crescent City. I've never been to Madame Rouge, never met a girl of the night called Marie, never seen that alluring birthmark on her lip, never danced with her in the Vieux Carré, never followed her into a hotel suite I should never have been in. For all intents and purposes I am not Yvonne LaCroix. I don't even look like her, or so I hope. With my bangs cut short, my hair combed differently, and never wearing her signature fragrance, it's easy to forget I've ever been her. It's not her face I see when I look in the mirror. I abandoned her the moment I fled New Orleans. As the steamship approached Galveston and I embarked upon my new life here, I chose a new name, a new identity for myself.

3

I am Aimée Bonnard. I come from Paris, where at the famous Chabanais, I've sampled supreme vices. I'm twenty-two years old to Yvonne's twenty-five. It cost me a few sleepless nights, but I was able to convince myself it's all right to spin a tall tale. Clients and madams alike are looking for an alluring persona, not the real woman behind it. And as glamorous and successful as Marie was, nobody would take too much trouble investigating the death of a prostitute – especially if it means ruffling the feathers of important men who cannot afford such a scandal.

I could, of course, take my savings and keep running. I could live modestly. Abandon silks and fine meals along with the chicory I so miss. I could make my way slowly to some dusty Texas town and rent a room there, become invisible. But I was meant for greatness, and the knowledge that nobody stands to profit from finding me emboldens me to try my luck again, here in this bustling port town, where there is wealth unmeasured and the houses of prostitution are very fine indeed.

The hotel itself is decadent enough to remind me of the life I want. I chose it for that reason. I picked the most expensive one, not only because I am spoiled – which I am – but also because I knew a fine establishment would motivate me. The view from my windows is my favorite feature of this room. The masts of ships visible behind the roofs of buildings, the cries of seagulls and the salt air wafting in with the breeze, the voices of people outside in the bustling commercial district, it all energizes me. I know in coming to Galveston I have come to the right place. And though at twenty-five many a girl has seen her glory days already past, as Aimée I am only twenty-two, fresh as a rose, and I am in a new town, a wealthy lucrative environment.

My glory days are only just beginning.

Before I start calling on the madams, I make a list in my mind of my requirements: the money and the creature comforts I wish to obtain in exchange for my services. They respect you more when you ask for more. And I will demand of the madams and their households higher standards still than I do from this hotel where I'm paying dearly. I dismiss the notion of asking for chicory coffee though. It might give me away. Why would a girl from Paris ask for such a thing? A less intelligent person might not think of details such as this, but I do. I've never traveled away from New Orleans before, but I have entertained men from many places, and I've listened to their stories. Likewise, I've followed Madame's advice to read widely – the paper and a great many books. For educated girls make better listeners, and it's the best listeners that make the most money.

4

Of course, while I don't think it's plausible that the police or any vengeful private person will investigate Marie's death too deeply, I'm also not a fool, and I know it's best to be cautious. It's ironic given my line of work, that what I've truly lost in this unfortunate debacle is my reputation. You'd think a fallen woman would not have a reputation to protect, but a pedigreed prostitute is a prize horse, not a mere piece of meat.

Forced to leave behind my track record at Madame Rouge and assume a new identity, I have no proof that a night with me is worth one hundred dollars, when this port town is full of pretty young girls willing to offer sailors a quick thrill for a small fraction of that. What I aspire to is not a sordid situation where I rent my body by the quarter hour in a stingy little room with a sad little wash basin. If those were my prospects, I'd rather live modestly off my savings for the rest of my days.

What I am looking for is an elegant house, a house of sophistication and refinement. A room of my own other than the one I entertain clients in. Beautiful dresses of the finest silk. Fragrances. Rouge in tiny crystal jars, rouge so subtle I look like a blushing rosebud instead of a painted lady. Embroidered petticoats. Silk stockings. Chocolate. Good coffee. But most of all, a chance at something grander and more thrilling than most respectable people can aspire to.

So I must find a way to capture the attention of the local madams. The assets I can use to advertise my profitability are my appearance, my allure, and the fake letter from France I took the liberty of writing myself, not even altering my handwriting because there is no reason why the local madams would recognize it. The beauty of this letter is that its proof of authenticity will lie as much in the Galveston madams' own desire to believe me as in my appearance and demeanor, my ability to show on the spot that I am an unparalleled seductress and entertainer. To that end I shall have to seduce and entertain the madams themselves. And that is a difficult task, because a woman who has mastered the art of fooling men should be a difficult creature to fool. But we all ultimately believe what is most convenient to us and madams are no exception. If only there were a way to make myself believe that I was not at fault in Marie's death. Will my guilt and remorse haunt me forever?

Marie was young, too young to die. She was younger than me and fairer. Marie had blonde hair to my black curls, she had a voice like a nightingale, she had the thinnest waist of all of us at Madame Rouge, the prettiest dresses, and she earned more than I did – but I don't know by how much. Marie was more accomplished in some ways, yet scrappier in others.

Her musical talent was evident and she picked up the piano without much effort. Yet she spoke not a word of French. She could remember the lyrics to every song, yet it took much practice to get her to say at least a few phrases that were *de rigueur*. The only clients that didn't prefer her to me were the French speaking ones. The girl could spin a tale. She understood just like I did what Madame Rouge taught us about entertaining men beyond just the carnal. She took it to heart, and rumors had it that she was the most successful prostitute of us all.

I envied Marie. I envied her in a way that is more of a mortal sin than all the other sins I've committed. How I wish I could change that now. How I wish I could change every interaction we had until that unfortunate night, and how I wish I could change, above all, the actions that led to that poor girl's demise. I'm trying to tell myself I never wished her dead, but it's not entirely true. And for that I shall repent for all eternity. If I'm not captured and dragged back to New Orleans to go to jail, I shall return for sure after my death and haunt the corridors of that hotel where Marie died. I wonder if she will too. I wonder if as ghosts we'll meet. If I'll get the chance to tell her I'm sorry. Like a bucket of cold ice thrown in my face, I have a vision of Marie slapping me. And I'm chilled to the bone because I know for certain that if we are to ever meet again on the other side, she will never forgive me.

But no, I cannot think about that now. I cannot think about Marie's eternal anger or even the damnation of my soul. For now I am very much alive and I am here in Galveston where I have one more chance to embody the talented courtesan Madame Rouge has taught me to be. This time I will do things right. This time I will not let my emotions interfere with my vocation. This time nobody will end up dead.

First though, I need to find the right madam. I will not go calling on them like your average girl. I want them to notice me. I want them to covet me. I'll find out who these women are and where they shop, where they have their dresses made. Once, in a different life, I was a dressmaker's apprentice. The only thing I learned in that capacity is that connections between women who trade in desire are often made while one of them is being fitted for a dress.

So I will find out where local madams buy their silks, and where they have their gowns made. I will make a point of showing up and looking good. I will be accompanied by hushed whispers and a general sense of awe. I will create my own advertising by fueling gossip. They will hear rumors about me before they set eyes on me. By the time I grace their doorsteps coming to inquire as if I am a customer trying to decide if a resort is up to snuff, they will be thrilled to see me.

But first I need information. I need accomplices. Spies. A shopgirl amenable to the occasional extra coin, but also a loose-tongued one, greedy for gossip and speculation. A shopgirl or a seamstress. Seamstresses love to talk. So do servants. There have to be loose-tongued maids in this hotel. And a bellboy. A bellboy who might perhaps be a little infatuated with me. I smile. I'm already feeling better.

Over the next few weeks, I select my confidantes and tell them stories about Le Chabanais – the most famous brothel in the world. I describe the girls, the bedrooms with their intricate décor, the bathtub full of champagne – all details I've collected from the stories of Madame Rouge. Like me, she'd never been to Paris, but she was fascinated by the allure of this legendary establishment. Occasionally, we'd meet a client who claimed to have visited Le Chabanais. We gathered anecdotes like pearls, and though I suspect some might be embellished, that never dulled their charm, but rather enhanced it. Now, I use these pearls like a trail of breadcrumbs that will hopefully lead the right madam to me.

"There is a room at Le Chabanais, where the walls are coated in this type of silk," I tell a shopgirl at Garbade, Eiband, & Co, running my finger over a wine-colored fabric with subtle purple gleams. "The insulation of their rooms is superior. Excellent privacy, if you know what I mean."

Her eyes are curious and confused. "Of course," I add, "I shouldn't talk to a nice girl like you about such things. It just reminded me. That place, it's impossible to forget. Its luxury is overwhelming. I doubt Galveston has such houses. It seems so… wholesome and serene."

I continue this game in my dealings with shopgirls, hotel maids, milliners, and seamstresses. I bring up a life of luxury and sin, then occasionally ask questions about the local madams, the local prostitutes. I ask for discretion about these inquiries, pay for it, in fact. Make them swear on all that is sacred they won't tell anyone that I'm a fallen woman looking for a fine house where I can sell my body for a fortune. Requiring secrecy is meant to embolden them to talk more. If you want people to gossip, ask for their discretion. The rumors that would ruin a decent girl are my advertising campaign.

I only hope the hotel will not start persecuting me. A silent lobby and judgmental glances are quite satisfying, an indication that the rumor mill is working. Cold coffee, on the other hand, cold meals, no fresh towels, or God forbid, an eviction notice would be quite unsavory. And if the news of such persecution should spread, I would lose my advantage in my negotiations with the madams. No matter my beauty or other accomplishments, my dresses, and all my anecdotes of Le Chabanais, a madam can smell the slightest whiff of desperation on a girl. When a madam becomes a savior instead of a business associate the girl can be sure she will not fare well. The most dangerous is a madam who appears to genuinely care for the girl's welfare. The motherly types are the most brutal.

For once in my life I am lucky. For as much as the rumors spread, for as much as respectable ladies in their boring dresses in boring colors avert their eyes as I pass, as much as the hotel staff whispers and giggles in the hallways, and as many hushed silences as I experience when I enter stores, my biscuits are served warm each morning, my coffee scalding, and my bill, which I pay immediately, is presented each week without a trace of threat about imminent eviction. Fresh soap appears in my bathroom next to a stack of clean towels each afternoon when I return from my walks and shopping expeditions. Someone takes the trouble to clean the hardwood floors, leaving behind traces of lemon scent. My room is aired out in my absence, fresh fruit and flowers arranged on the table, a paper delivered each morning with my breakfast.

While respectable Galvestonians start crossing to the other sidewalk when I pass, I'm thoroughly enjoying myself, as if on vacation on this beautiful island. I discover that I love the beach, its salty smell, its crashing waves, even the occasional wading into the water outfitted in a bathing dress, bathing stockings, and shoes – though I try to avoid too much exposure to the sun as freckles are most unbecoming. Also, I can't swim. Still, I acquire a glow that makes the careful application of rouge thoroughly redundant. I eat alone and eat lots of shrimp. I shop for new fabrics, then feed my chatty dressmaker and even the attendant of my bathing machine choice morsels of scandal about Le Chabanais.

The bathing machine is a funny contraption, most clever and delightful. It's like a movable little house in which one changes into one's bathing suit and other accoutrements in order to go into the water. There is a person inside responsible for transferring the movable house from the beach to the water. The person cannot see me, to preserve my modesty, but after being treated to several stories of Le Chabanais, they take it upon themselves to warn me that should I get funny notions such as bathing in a men's suit or taking off my shoes, I will be fined by the police.

The dressmaker, a Miss Poole, shows more promise in advancing my agenda and helping me advertise my talents and experience to the local madams. Miss Poole is an expensive dressmaker. I have chosen her because I have it on good authority that she also caters to Mrs. Harden, a local madam I've heard promising things about. I saw this Mrs. Harden a few times at Garbade, Eiband & Co. A plump, well-dressed woman with smooth skin that doesn't show her age, she has the air of a creature enjoying a life of comfort bordering on indolence. Perhaps one can afford to sit around eating confections when one has corralled other girls into doing the actual work of amassing one's fortune. But I should not be too quick to judge and dismiss Mrs. Harden, as she might hold the key to my own good fortune and my own future of indolence – in which I shall be more mindful not to gorge on bonbons and perhaps learn how to swim, wearing, of course, a proper women's suit, shoes, and stockings.

Rumor has it Mrs. Harden used to be a prostitute herself before a wealthy patron bought her a house of her own. He tired of her eventually. But she kept the house and hired girls to work for her, in a brothel that rises above the fray for Galveston. Though after walking by once or twice to see it from the outside, I have my doubts it's as decadent as Madame Rouge's establishment where I learned the trade. As to Le Chabanais... well, *non*. There is not bound to be a Moorish salon, a Japanese room, a bathtub full of champagne, or a private bedroom for a European prince in this three-story clapboard house with shady porches and blooming hibiscus in front. It looks almost idyllic.

Still, Mrs. Harden sounds like a prospect. Her girls are rumored to be well-bred and expensive. I've seen some of them around town. Her clients are most exclusive, and I was told the girls entertain the men in private dining rooms over a decadent meal before taking them into the bedrooms. That certainly sounds civilized. I decide that Mrs. Harden is worthy of my talents. I must meet her and charm her and secure a place in her house.

But there are mornings when, enthralled with the Island's beauty and the wholesome joy of walking, reading, and experiencing good food and lovely nature, I wonder if, given unlimited resources, I would still care to be a prostitute at all. I do require entertainment and excitement, but there's a part of my heart I have never before explored, a part that might be happy with more quiet pleasures. Could I buy a small cottage on this island and live my life in peace? Then I remind myself that I love long walks at sunset and reading books and sipping coffee as long as someone else brings my paper, replenishes my towels, bakes biscuits, and sews dresses for me. Yes, nestled into a life of expensive luxury, I do love taking the time to enjoy simple pleasures and am surprisingly well entertained by them. But waking up in a shabby bed in a shabby room, having to sweep and scrub and brew my own coffee, having to walk to the market and cook my own food, having to mend my dresses when they fall apart, would surely dull the charm of my long walks and would probably diminish my appreciation of sunsets, flowers, and misty mornings.

I tell myself that if I work the few more years my looks will allow, I shall with skill and luck amass enough of a fortune to live for the rest of my life in the way that I've been living these past few weeks. And if nobody pursues me over the death of Marie, perhaps I shall even stay on this island. I had considered moving farther West after a few months, changing my name again, but I'm growing fond of this place. There's something wistful about its salty breezes, its blooming oleanders, its palm trees swaying in the wind. And while I know I cannot afford to be sentimental, and I resolve to rule over my emotions with an iron fist, I also know that this is what I'm saving for.

Once I am thirty, once the first lines start showing on my face, I shall buy a house and employ servants, and I shall allow myself feelings, if not for people, then for animals, for nature, for this beautiful place. For the sea and its energy. If I am still capable of feeling things by then. But surely, whatever I forget, the ocean will help me relearn. At that thought, a tear rolls down my cheek, salty like sea water, and I am shocked, for I have not cried in years, not cried even when I fled New Orleans with fear and regret in my heart.

An unexpected sadness fills me at the thought of leaving my beautiful room, my peaceful life, my tranquil walks. Don't be silly, I tell myself! You will still have occasional peace! You will still go for walks. But never in the mornings. No, as much freedom and luxury as my life as a prostitute might allow – for I am not one of those unfortunate girls who have to entertain several men a day – I will lose the pleasures of mornings. I will lose the freedom of reading in bed at night. It's true that I am most fortunate to only entertain one client each evening, and to meet the most interesting men, to be presented to them in the most beautiful silk dresses, to be unwrapped like a present and savored over long hours much like the finest meal. But nights will be long – enjoyable, but long. I shall remain awake, I shall remain engaged and good-humored for as long as the client wishes. And most men can talk into the wee hours. Once they leave me, I shall retire to my own private quarters. I shall hear morning birds as I wash up, and I shall fall exhausted into my own clean sheets. I could not bear to sleep in a bed where I've entertained like most girls do. But I will sleep the day away, and only if I'm lucky, after a late afternoon coffee and breakfast, I might have time for a short walk before I'll need to start my toilette for the evening ahead.

I remind myself that it's an interesting life. I remind myself there are many joys in it. Dresses and fragrances, flowers from clients and other choice gifts. The money I share with the madam, my own room and bathroom, leisurely baths reading the paper – the only times I get to read as a prostitute, and trust me that reading the paper is essential to carrying on good conversation – the evening's frivolity, the entertainment in the parlor, the glances of admiration and even envy from other girls and their clients, and then my *tête a têtes* which often include exquisite meals, interesting gossip, political talk, all spiced with laughter, flirting, and pleasures of the flesh. There is suspense, there can be adventures, for a difficult client is nothing but a challenge, a riddle to solve. I remind myself that my thirtieth birthday will arrive before I tire of it all. But today I can't convince myself that my life as a prostitute is all that exciting. I wonder if Marie has cursed me. I wonder if I've lost my most important talent, the talent for genuinely loving what I do.

CHAPTER 2
MRS. HARDEN IS NO FOOL

My meeting with Mrs. Harden is precipitated not only by my own desire to advance in my plans and the unavoidability of moving forward if I am to resume my lucrative trade, but also by what I have already set in motion and now can no longer stop. For I have fueled local gossip and created the opportunity to discuss my prospects with the madam, and now it appears that I'm no longer the only one interested in engineering our encounter.

"Your dress will be ready on Friday," Miss Poole, the dressmaker, says one afternoon, taking the pins out of her mouth and fastening them so close to my skin that I fear being scratched. "Come at five thirty. I will be closed, but I will let you in. And you will meet Mrs. Harden, whom you've asked so much about."

"It's too tight," I say, refusing to show gratitude or excitement. If I show myself appreciative of Miss Poole facilitating the meeting, she'll expect something in return. Besides, it's political to let everyone believe it's the madam who stands to gain from meeting me, not vice versa.

"It's not too tight," she retorts. "You need a maid to lace up your corset properly and it will fit just fine. Show off your figure while you still have it."

I ignore the jab. "A girl still needs to breathe," I say. "And if I have to have it altered…"

At this she relents. It's good to remind them who's paying. And to show I don't feel the least bit indebted to her for her introduction to the madam. My face in the mirror remains impassive, but inside the too tight bodice of the new red dress, my greedy heart is alive with anticipation. I'm so close to reaching my goal, so close to reclaiming my life. I can already envision myself entertaining wealthy clients in this new dress, can already imagine taking it off for them, ever so slowly. My fingers dance on its tiny buttons. "Make it so that I can breathe in it, and it shall do just fine," I say.

On Friday I make a point of being late, but the madam is later still. By the time she arrives, I'm standing in front of a mirror in my corset and chemise, supposedly to make sure once and for all the dress fits me. But in reality I know that I'm standing here undressed for my body to be evaluated as if I were a heifer brought to market.

The madam makes no pretense of being interested in a dress herself.

"So you are Miss Bonnard, whom I've heard so much about," she says by means of introduction. She stands a little too close, her perfume sweet, not unpleasant but perhaps too insidious. "Turn around," she says, assessing me.

"Excuse me?" I ask, feigning outrage. Then I think better of it and start to laugh, do a little pirouette and a curtsey.

"A girl with spirit," she says. "I like that."

"Everyone does. But do you like it to the tune of sixty dollars a night?"

"Not one for small talk, are you?"

"*Au contraire.* I excel at small talk when I'm paid to do so."

"Good to know. Is sixty then how much you charge? I'd say it's rather steep."

"I charge one twenty." I'm hoping actually for one hundred, even eighty if pressed. "But I figure we'd split it evenly."

"That's a bit much for Galveston. I like your optimism, but it's just not the standard."

"I'm not your standard girl."

"I'd say." She reaches over and touches first my arm, then my breast. Instead of recoiling, I take her hand and guide it, wiggling and purring like a cat, looking into her eyes and smiling as if she were a client. Her face shows pleasure – not sensual pleasure at the touch of my body, but appreciation, from one professional to another.

"How old are you?" she asks.

"Old enough to be an expert of my trade, yet young enough to still perform it."

"Ha! Still, dear—"

"Will you examine my teeth next?"

"Why do I even bother asking? But your face is fresh and your flesh quite firm. You have a few more good years. I'll admit you're a beautiful girl. And you have presence. Where were you before?"

"Paris."

She laughs. "The hell you were."

"Have you heard of Le Chabanais?" I whisper as if letting her in on a secret. I reach over to my purse, fish out the fake letter of recommendation, and hand it to her.

"You're a good writer," she says. "Lovely penmanship too. Shows a certain level of *je ne sais quoi*… And I do appreciate a girl with imagination."

"So will your clients," I say, undeterred by the fact that Mrs. Harden is no fool.

"I can see that while you've created a rather unbelievable fiction, the descriptions of your talents are promising. You seem to know a good deal about desire and about some of the other things men want when paying to be entertained. But a hundred and twenty dollars…"

"I might settle for a hundred if I like the house I'm working in, but I will not take less."

"I'll need to ask around and see. If men here in Galveston are amenable to paying such an outrageous fee, we might discuss it further."

"I have a few requirements," I say.

"Of course you do. Miss Poole intimated you're fussy. Let's see first if you have any clients before you start making demands. I need a week or two to make some inquiries. If I succeed in finding clients willing to pay a fortune for an encounter with a high-end kind of girl, one with claims at an exotic past, no less, I will communicate it to Miss Poole and she will let you know. You can then come see me and we'll negotiate our terms."

She turns to go, then pauses, looks at me again, and says, "And Miss Bonnard, it's one thing that you weave a tale of an interesting past to tell your clients – using the appropriate irony, I would hope. But should we enter a business arrangement together, and should there be the slightest evidence of you trying to cheat me or of you being untruthful... Well, I don't care what you wished to escape in your past life, but it will be a joke compared to what will chase you out of Galveston."

I look at her with big innocent eyes.

"A jealous man, Mrs. Harden. A man who tried to hurt me. It's not a secret, just not a pleasant story to tell. I don't mind you knowing my past, but it will not amuse our clients. And I trust you to protect me from such situations in the future. It's why I wish to join your house."

"Smart girl," she says, her voice now warmer, though I'm not sure she believes any of it. "I can assure you I do not allow violent men. It's why you're wise to seek out my protection. I cherry-pick good, decent clients for all my girls, even the less expensive ones. It's a pure horror what can happen in houses where the madams don't have such high standards or as many friends in high places. And yes, I agree, clients do not wish to be bored with anything unpleasant."

That she's not eager to accept my so carefully imagined past is somewhat disappointing, maybe even alarming. But nothing is ever ideal, and the madam's intelligence might serve me in the end. A cunning woman is likely to find good clients. She's also likely to protect me once I prove profitable. And she is not insisting on learning more about me, so I choose to elegantly deflect.

"Nobody does, least of all I," I say. "In fact, I would much rather talk about my clients then about myself. Men love attention."

"Everyone does. It's why the world belongs to women like us, women who'd rather listen."

"I feel like I could learn a lot from you, Mrs. Harden."

"Save the flattery for the clients, dear." But now I'm sure she likes me, and the validation reminds me once more that there is pleasure and power in what I do, pleasure and power of a nature I can't resist. I'm eager to be back in the game. Yet a small part of me mourns the imminent loss of my simple freedoms, of mornings full of sunshine and evenings in the company of books.

CHAPTER 3
VOCATION

Be careful what you wish for, for it may just come true. In no time, Mrs. Harden does indeed secure clients eager to meet me. Her house proves satisfactory. My red dress is ready. And soon enough, my vacation at the hotel is over. I am about to return to my vocation. I am about to become the best paid woman in Galveston.

My last day before moving into Mrs. Harden's is bittersweet. I try to enjoy my last leisurely breakfast, but its joy is tinted with sadness. I try to enjoy morning birds, my walk through town, and then my evening walk on the beach. I try to enjoy packing my books and my dresses, and the anticipation of evening entertainment in the new madam's parlor. But I am overcome with dread.

The next night, as I descend the grand staircase at Mrs. Harden's wearing the red silk dress Miss Poole made for me, mercifully altered to where I can not only breathe but actually sway, curious glances envelop me. I smile the kind of smile that shows I'm happy to be there, yet not entirely approachable, not entirely open. The secret to being a successful courtesan is to never give yourself away completely. You need to know how to withhold, as people want above all what they can't have. So I descend the stairs like a queen, my smile both warm and cold, my willingness balanced carefully with my reserve. I pause at the halfway point, giving the guests and girls assembled downstairs one more chance to look at me, giving myself a chance to take them in too. Seeing my eyes upon them, measuring them openly – another trick to make people desire your admiration – they fall silent.

There are ten people downstairs. Five men, four girls dressed to the nines, and Mrs. Harden herself strutting around like she's excessively proud of us all. The men are older and look important. I am most curious about them, but I pause to take in the girls as well. I'm pleased that none of them is as beautiful or as well dressed as I am, yet pleased too that they seem neither plain nor unsophisticated. It would be depressing to be stuck in a brothel with some rubes. Once the silence gives in to voices, laughter, and the clinking of champagne glasses, I continue my descent, the dress caressing my body, a cloud of fragrance accompanying me, and the glow from all the attention coating me like gold dust. Mrs. Harden takes my hand as she ceremoniously introduces me first to the crowd, then to the man she had told me I would entertain this evening. His grip on my hand is firm. He is not an unpleasant man. Tall and dry, with an air about him that could be either confidence or haughtiness. I'm hoping for confidence.

A servant approaches and hands me a glass of champagne. I toast the man next to me, then let the bubbles dance in my mouth. I never allow myself more than a few sips, but I always thoroughly enjoy my first one, and tonight it tastes better than it has in a long time. Perhaps, I tell myself as I walk into the parlor on my new client's arm, as candles flicker, jewels shine, and the first notes of a piano permeate the atmosphere, perhaps I will enjoy my return to work more than I had thought possible. Perhaps it was a silly idea to have wanted to stay in a hotel and live a chaste and boring life of long walks and early breakfasts.

My companion's hand glides from my elbow to my waist, then a little farther down. I laugh and shimmy away from him, taking a seat on a single chair close to the piano. It's always best to keep them waiting. A servant passes with a tray of what appear to be olives, but only offers them to the men, which enrages me. I will complain to Mrs. Harden tomorrow. My companion, Mr. Williams, pulls up a chair for himself and sits very close to me, a little too close.

"Are you having a nice evening?" I ask.

"The best." His accent is one I can't place. Is he a Yankee? Mrs. Harden only told me he was new to Galveston and looking to buy a cotton warehouse, which is lucrative indeed. I smile and clap without much warmth as the girl on the piano finishes. She's skillful, no doubt, but displaying too much enthusiasm about her performance would make me seem too easy to impress. It would discourage Williams from thinking of me as a great prize, and trying hard to please me, and it would limit his self-admiration later when I would show myself very pleased indeed.

Clearly the other women in the room have not been schooled in such strategies, or have decided to ignore these lessons. For there is loud applause and calls of "Bravo, Victoria," followed by requests for a new song. Another girl, young and red haired, not bad-looking but perhaps too ebullient, joins Victoria at the piano and sings the lyrics to the next song. Some of the women in the room occasionally join in, and though there is a lot of laughter, I can't imagine the men are truly enjoying this sing-along. Williams rests his hand on my knee and I let him.

"Are you enjoying the music?" he asks.

"It's cheerful, but I've heard better. Do they do this every night?"

"I wouldn't know," he says frostily. I've committed a faux pas by suggesting he is a frequent client of this establishment. I could have bitten my tongue.

"Are you enjoying it?" I ask.

"Not particularly," he admits, and I laugh as if it's the wittiest thing I've heard.

"Then perhaps you might rescue me from it and accompany me for some fresh air on the porch?"

Disappointment flashes across his face. I know he was hoping I'd suggest retiring to our intimate dining room, but this man would have me undressed within a few seconds of closing the door, and my job is to prolong the desire. Outside the breeze is fresh, the air scented with the last nostalgic whiffs of jasmine of the season. I struggle to hear the crashing waves over the piano chords but I can't. Williams approaches and though it's not unheard of for a client to embrace a prostitute in a less than private setting, he hesitates, then resigns himself to standing next to me and looking into the garden.

"Tell me about yourself, Mr. Williams. What brings you to Galveston?" I bat my eyelashes and regale him with a look of curiosity men usually can't resist. But Williams's response is gruff. "I didn't come here to make conversation, for God's sake!" I've had impatient, petulant clients before. I make sure my smile doesn't falter.

"Would you care to proceed to supper then?"

"I didn't come here to eat either," he growls. My spirits sink, but I don't let it show.

"We can skip supper, then," I say brightly. I toy with the idea of suggesting we rejoin the party by the piano, because that would be humorous, but this man doesn't seem inclined to take a joke. Much as I dread being alone with him, I take his arm and lead him back inside, up the stairs, and down a narrow corridor, to a room where, just as I predicted, as soon as I close the door, which I only pretend to lock, he tugs at my clothes, then orders me to remove them.

I keep smiling. I step away from him, say a quick prayer — though recent developments have shown God doesn't look too kindly upon prayers from girls like me — and start swaying my body to the music coming from downstairs, singing the lyrics to the song they're playing in a low voice, almost a whisper. It's a joke between me and my favorite clients, also a joke between me and myself, that the very parlor songs I abhor are rendered charming if sung privately, while dancing and undressing, with only a subtle hint of irony — an irony only the more intelligent men can detect and appreciate. Williams is unlikely to be among them, but it's worth a try.

I undo my top buttons before he can complain. I lift my skirt, make eye contact, and smile. The change on his angry face is barely perceptible, but a glimmer in his eyes indicates I might have a chance at actually amusing him. I do have to move fast, though, in case the teasing irritates him. And so I dance and flirt but get out of my clothes faster than I would for a more good-humored man. I take his hand and lead him to the bed. What follows is fast and clumsy, painful, in fact, after my weeks of chastity. I realize I will have to fake enjoyment, something I'm loathe to do, as I prefer to truly deliver, but Mr. Williams collapses on top of me sweaty and exhausted before I have the chance to even start my performance. All I can pretend to enjoy now is him lying on top of me, though he is crushing me and I can barely breathe. I purr into his ear like a kitten. "That was really something."

"Yeah, like you've never done that before. I don't know why I'm paying a hundred dollars for this."

I summon my best, most lovely, most patient self. "If you relax, Mr. Williams," I say in a low voice, "I will give you your money's worth."

I wiggle myself free of him, take a moment to adjust my hair in the mirror, then ask if he'd like to enjoy a drink and cigar while I show him what a hundred dollars a night can buy. I pour less than a finger of bourbon, because a man like Williams is unlikely to perform again if he imbibes more, and that would be a disaster for his ego.

"You gonna do more of that singing and dancing?" he asks without enthusiasm as I light his cigar.

"I've got much better things in store," I say as I lower myself onto him, moving slowly, knowing full well it'll take a lot of doing before he's up to the task again. I let him take another drag of his cigar, then take it out of his hand, and let my breasts caress his face.

What seems like an eternity later, Williams is fast asleep with a satisfied look on his face. I'm exhausted, and my body is sore from all the moving and swaying. My mouth tastes like the filthy cigar. I wrap myself in a robe, grab my clothes, and leave the insufferable man to sleep away his night of passion. The fact that he will be back for sure is both a blessing and a curse. I walk down the corridor, listening for muffled sounds from behind closed doors. On the way to my room I knock on the servant's door, and open it to make sure she's awake and jumps to attention.

"I need a bath, and I need you to warm up and bring whatever meal the cook had prepared for Williams and me for supper," I say. And I do hope she will not drag her feet because I'm famished and tired and my patience has already been worn thin. While waiting for my bath, I gargle with cologne, trying to make the taste of the vile cigar and the vile client disappear. Luckily, Sarah, the servant girl, moves fast, and in no time at all I'm in the bath, pouring out a few drops of expensive scented oil into the water and taking a moment to admire my own body.

I am one of those women whose beauty resides first and foremost in the features of her face, with dark, mysterious eyes shadowed by long black lashes, a small but expressive mouth, a delicate nose, feminine cheekbones, and a slight widow's peak, now hidden behind my new bangs. But my body is not bad either. I'm of average height, slender, but with hips that are muscled from regular physical exertion. If I don't eat or rest enough, I occasionally fear becoming too sinewy, like a Greyhound. While my hips are not as curvy as I'd like, men love my generous bosom, which I like displaying in low-cut dresses, but some comment on my small but decidedly round and firm derrière. There was a client in new Orleans who liked to bite it, and I allowed it because he was a charming fellow and he never bit me hard. Now, as I look at my legs in the bathwater, I see, much to my satisfaction, that my curves have filled out a bit during my respite at the hotel.

"I will go bring your food now," Sarah says, as if she too is thinking that a certain level of voluptuousness is desirable and should therefore be maintained. "Mrs. Harden said you were with a difficult man." I make a face to show my exasperation with him, and Sarah laughs in a way that shows true complicity. I'm tempted to laugh with her, but I check myself. Too much familiarity can be dangerous, and laughing at the expense of a client is unwise.

Later, dressed in a clean chemise, I sit up in bed as Sarah brings me the serving tray. I'm pleased to find a small dish of the olives I was passed up for last night, as well as a portion of delicately sautéed fish with rice and vegetables, a dinner roll, a slice of cake, and a glass of lemonade.

"I can bring wine if you prefer," Sarah says.

"No. This is perfect. How did you know?"

"I noticed you don't drink much. And I myself love lemonade when I'm completely exhausted."

I take a moment to look at her, although I'm famished, and I need her to close the door so I can fall upon my food like an animal. She's not plain, and she's obviously not stupid. I wonder why she's a servant girl in this house, not something more. I wonder how many times in her life someone allows her the luxury of a cold glass of lemonade when she's exhausted and my guess is hardly ever. Why would a pretty girl choose to be a maid rather than a courtesan?

I remind myself that Sarah's problems are none of my concern and that being overly sentimental can only lead to undesirable outcomes. Instead, I allow myself one of the greatest pleasures I remember from my former life in New Orleans – to feast, exhausted yet thrilled to have dealt expertly with a difficult client. I relish in my victory. And then, having washed all traces of Williams off my body, having satiated my hunger, I set the empty tray outside my door, lock it, for this room is mine alone, and sink into my clean white sheets. I am too tired to reach for any of the books on my nightstand. Instead, I turn off the light and sink into a deep sleep. I dream of Marie, for no lock can keep out the ghost of a woman I have wronged.

CHAPTER 4
A NEW CLIENT

My next weeks at Mrs. Harden's are mostly uneventful. I settle into my new routine, balancing my loss of freedom with the occasional thrills and victories my profession affords me. Williams is by far the most difficult client. He remains unpleasant though he softens with time, and many of the others are gallant enough to make up for his rudeness. I even get to enjoy the occasional interesting confession. I learn more about Galveston, its cotton exchange, its warehouses, its marine traffic, and its commerce. One of my more amusing clients is the captain of a ship. But so far, there is nobody who captures my attention in such a way that I truly anticipate their return. I'm not talking about infatuation here, for a prostitute enamored of one of her clients is a most boring cliché, and an example of extreme foolishness at that. But without having unwise feelings, a girl can still be most curious about some of her clients and enjoy them above all the rest.

I almost give up hope of such delights, until the evening when Mrs. Harden presents me to Aristotle Fontenot. The man by the strange name is short and dark, but stocky in a most pleasant way. A solid man, attractive despite his low stature, attractive most of all, because he seems to be in the possession of the type of self-confidence that eludes most men. That, and a fine sense of humor. Aristotle is the owner of several stables and a shop, a most unsophisticated but profitable business. His hand, as he grasps mine is rough like a working man's and a contrast to his manners, which are refined in a most natural, unstudied way, and with the first smirk from beneath his black mustache I know that I like him.

Indeed, my evening with Aristotle is so delightful, I almost forget I'm being paid to keep him company, and handsomely at that. Like most men who lack neither money, nor intelligence, nor self-assurance, Aristotle is jovial and generous. Our meal together before we retire to the bedroom is prolonged and interesting. He delights me with tales of his humble upbringing in Louisiana and the ways in which he worked his way up from stable boy to stable owner, then amassed the rest of his fortune.

He rings for the servant and asks for more of the artichokes he noticed me enjoying, more of the fish. He convinces me to drink more than just a few sips of champagne, not through insistence, which I find tiresome, but through the ease with which our conversation and laughter flow throughout the evening. When I laugh away his questions about my own story, he notices my desire to deflect, raises his eyebrows, fixes me for a long moment in a scrutinizing but not unfriendly gaze, then is kind enough not to persist. This, I am mostly grateful for. Because the story of his own upbringing was something I had to steel myself to, the Maw Maw that raised him in the bayou so similar to my own Maw Maw, whom I cannot allow myself to miss. Neither can I allow a client to know that I am not in fact a French prostitute, but a Cajun girl, fleeing a murder scene in New Orleans.

Besides his generosity with the food and his kindness in not prying about my past, Aristotle seems more refined than his humble beginnings in countless other ways. In fact, he exhibits more kindness than etiquette, which I find genuine, refreshing, and a little disconcerting. Also, he's not beyond enjoying tawdry or even blasphemous jokes – which I abhor in the company of certain men, yet find amusing in the company of others. He's among the latter, so I allow my humor to be brash, and he responds in kind.

But he doesn't touch or grope me during our meal. He sits apart from me, studying me with curiosity and obvious desire, but seems to be a man who knows enough about the finer things in life to not want to rush. Even as we walk into the adjoining bedroom after our copious meal, Aristotle does not touch me. Part of me is fascinated, part of me fearful that maybe, for all his charm, there might be something wrong with him. But no, men who cannot perform never have this much confidence, this type of jovial spirit. As to men who don't really like women – and I've dealt with a few of those, even a sad young lad whose father thought I might be able to change his natural proclivities – well, men who prefer men are often more than delightful company, but they don't look at me the way Aristotle has all evening.

As we enter the room and I pretend to lock the door, I feel a frisson of anticipation and desire. I look at my companion and realize he might be beating me at my own game, keeping me waiting instead of the other way around. I laugh and let him kiss my hand, enjoying how his lips on my fingers feel more risqué than much bolder gestures from others. I take a few steps back. There's no more music coming from downstairs at this late hour, but I start humming a melody as I move my body in a slow seductive dance. Aristotle watches me, his arms crossed over his chest, a smile on his lips, a twinkle in his eyes. I undulate and sway, I tease with every motion, I drag each gesture out, waiting and gaging his reaction before undoing each and every button. He watches me and laughs, the subtle parody not lost on him, and, much to my delight, despite our shared knowledge that this dance is a joke, desire is aflame in his eyes, and I know I am winning.

He wants me, he's under my spell. But just when I think my victory is complete, he grabs my waist, and joins me in a dance so seductive I don't want it to ever stop. I don't remember the last time I felt this weak with anticipation. I find myself loving the dancing and laughter, yet hungering for more, hungering for every kiss, every caress of his roughened hands on my smooth skin, wanting this man more than I've wanted anyone in a very long time.

When I finally make my way upstairs, the sun is shining bright, grackles are whistling outside, and I have a huge smile on my face. I have to knock on Sarah's door repeatedly. The poor soul has fallen asleep. As she adjusts my bath water, dipping her fingers in it to make sure it's just right, I cannot help myself. I have to ask.

"How come you're just a servant, not a prostitute, Sarah? Have you ever thought what fun it would be?"

She blushes lobster red. "Oh no, Ma'am," she stammers. "No, no, not me. No offense. Ma'am."

I laugh as I drop my robe and see her avert her eyes from my nakedness. I let myself sink into the bathwater. As Sarah, still flustered, heads downstairs to bring me a glass of lemonade and a small bite to eat, I don't feel the need to scrub my body with the usual vigor. If traces of Aristotle still linger on my skin, it's a souvenir, not a blemish.

CHAPTER 5
THE CAROUSEL

The days and nights proceed in haste. I hardly get to catch my breath. There are moments of joy and excitement through it all, but never quite the leisurely luscious peace I'd experienced in what I now think of as my vacation at the downtown hotel. Even moments of delight, or simple sensory pleasures, like stretching my tired body in my clean bed, or stepping into the warm Gulf water, letting it soak my stockings and shoes, and inhaling the salty breath of the ocean, even such moments seem rushed, more fleeting than ever, as if I'm constantly one step behind my own ability to enjoy life. But there is a richness to my life too, I remind myself. Glitter and glamour, as if I'm perpetually riding on a carousel full of lights and mirrors, and as it goes faster and faster, the music louder and louder, I'm both exhilarated and dizzy. To steady myself I decide to start taking piano lessons in the early afternoons. I tell myself these lessons require discipline, concentration, a sense of rhythm too. The metronome gives me hope most of all. If I learn to follow its guidance, perhaps I will no longer feel like I'm perpetually a beat behind in my own ability to enjoy things?

I refuse Victoria's help, for I cannot stand her and also because after what happened with Marie I wish to maintain my distance from the other girls. The music teacher is a stern and skinny man, a man who comes reluctantly, who brings religious pamphlets and takes every opportunity to lecture me. At our third lesson I set him straight. I tell him that I shall cease to call upon his services if he keeps bringing his moralizing to the lessons. I tell him I enjoy my profession and am unrepentant. I require his help in learning the piano and nothing more. And if he wishes to continue to profit from my ill-gotten gains, for I do pay him handsomely indeed, he will have to keep his opinions and his religious views to himself. From then on, the insufferable man stops bringing pamphlets and keeps his conversation on the subject matter of our lessons. His lips often are bunched together to form an unattractive white line, but I resolve to keep my gaze on the ivory keys and the metronome, not on his self-righteous face.

My sense of rhythm improves, but only on the piano. In real life I'm still spinning on the carousel, still going way too fast. I try to increase the duration of my beach walks, but the afternoons are getting hotter, and mornings are taken up by much needed sleep. I awake dizzy. I wonder if I should perhaps consult a witch and ask to be released from whatever curse Marie burdened me with in her final moments, but what use is seeing a witch if I cannot tell her the truth? Besides, should I come across one who truly has the power of insight, she might see what I've done, and I'll be exposed in a way I can ill afford and am not willing to face.

And so I buy more dresses, buy more French perfume, and try different foods in the hope that I might experience some delight so profound it would feel tangible instead of fleeting. Aristotle, who obviously knows nothing of my dilemma, is helpful in this regard, for as a frequent client he occasionally sends gifts or flowers, or surprises me with fine wines and foods. His visits are a fine pleasure, filled with laughter, our physical encounters intense and glorious, yet even pleasure seems fleeting as if I'm chasing the waves on the beach, which crash and dissolve before I can behold their wonder. Nothing can transport me to a place of joy where I am not aware of the quicksand below my feet.

My mirth at Aristotle's jokes is authentic. The carnal pleasures I enjoy with him are authentic too. His working-man hands on my luxury-loving skin are so firm and yet so tender that I crave his touch long after I've retreated to my own room. Yet even these fine pleasures feel stilted, as if I'm watching from the outside as an observer instead of fully experiencing the moment. With other clients it's all even less satisfying. Which piques me, because in my former life in New Orleans I prided myself in achieving true pleasure even with the most insufferable men.

What I have not lost, ironically, is my capacity for grief and annoyance. While everything pleasant is dulled as if glimpsed from afar while in perpetual motion, negative experiences are still acute and piercing. My annoyance with Victoria and her vulgar ways — her too loud voice, her fits of laughter, her abundance of overly suggestive jokes — often transforms into a powerful headache that keeps me from getting much-needed sleep. Williams's unpleasantness, which I keep navigating with a grace and skill I am proud of, occasionally causes me stomach pain and even nausea. Mrs.

Harden has to order sparkling water for me, and the doctor is summoned on more than one occasion. She charges me more than these services cost out of my pay, and the chagrin burns like hot coals.

Perhaps the low point of it all is an evening when, due to a muddle or some idiotic calculation on Mrs. Harden's part, I'm not sure which exactly, I end up entertaining insufferable Williams, while a striking but rather unskilled girl named Ruby gets to dine with Aristotle. I feel the anger and jealousy like a punch in my gut, but I pull myself together enough to find a clever way to play this game, to make Aristotle want me even more. I lock eyes with him as I let clumsy Williams embrace me, and across the room, normally reserved Aristotle lets his hand wander up Ruby's thigh while looking straight at me as if to challenge me to a battle of wills. Shamelessly I climb onto Williams's lap, and soon enough we are engaged in a sort of perverted dance, where Aristotle and I tease each other using our companions' bodies as props. Willing myself to keep my mind on the game, I chase away all memories of a similar situation, all memories of Marie and everything that led up to that awful night in New Orleans. I brush my lips against Williams's. I let him bury his nose in my cleavage. I grind my body against his manliness that takes forever to harden, imagining the corresponding body parts in Aristotle and how different they might feel.

For a split second I have a vision of a voodoo doll, and I almost lose my composure, but my willpower is strong and so is my discipline. I pretend to enjoy Williams's hands grabbing my waist in a possessive gesture, pretend to enjoy unfastening another button for him, letting him fully admire my breasts now. I feel his member stirring as I reach inside his pants. But Williams unexpectedly stands up, throwing me off him in a fit of anger. "I didn't come here for this disgusting orgy!" he screams, adjusting his breeches as he storms out of the room. Ruby gasps in shock, but Aristotle and I roar with laughter.

"Are you quite all right?" he asks as he helps me up, but mirth and adrenaline erase the pain of my fall, as does Aristotle's attention. "Well, if you're sure that you're not injured, darling, I for once, would not one bit mind an orgy," Aristotle declares. Again, I have to push away memories of Marie – the little double act we had perfected, her hands and lips on my body, our success with clients – but Aristotle's desire exorcises her, as does my own hunger for him. Poor Ruby might as well not be in the room, though each time she inserts herself into our embrace I feel a sharp pang of anger and disgust. Once more chasing the specter of Marie out of my consciousness, I grab the silly girl by her fake red tresses, and use her as my prop as I did

Williams, touching her in the ways I wish for Aristotle to touch me. Another voodoo doll, my dark mind whispers, but Aristotle's uncontainable passion erases that thought.

For once I lose myself, but only briefly. Pleasure is sharp yet fleeting, and afterwards as we all lie in tangled sheets, and Ruby lays her head on Aristotle's chest, my annoyance is so strong it takes my last drop of self-composure to hide it. Our conversation in her presence is stilted, artificial, and doesn't go to the depths it normally does. I take great satisfaction in Aristotle making eye contact with me as if to warn me not to get too personal in front of Ruby. As I wash her off my body later and go to bed, still piqued and nauseated, I take comfort in the knowledge that as much as Aristotle must have enjoyed the thrill of being with two women, he'll probably still ask for me alone in the future because he enjoys the intimacy and complicity of our encounters. But what if I'm wrong?

CHAPTER 6
RETRIBUTION

Despite Aristotle being generous enough to pay double and thus compensate for Williams demanding his money back, Mrs. Harden is royally angry with me the next day and once again decides to help herself to part of my hard-earned compensation. As we had agreed when I joined her house, she normally takes fifty dollars of the hundred I earn each night, but on this occasion she only lets me have twenty-five and declares that I should consider myself lucky not to be cast out or otherwise punished. But punished I am, and in the most horrible fashion. For she coaxes Williams into not giving up on his weekly visits, and makes a special arrangement with him to meet me directly in one of the bedrooms when he comes, thus skipping the visit to the salon altogether. The first time I see him after our debacle, he slaps me hard across the face, so hard that tears stream out of my eyes against my will, and against my will too, a scream escapes me. Nobody storms through the unlocked door to make sure I'm unharmed. I struggle to regain my composure, to smile as if nothing has happened and to proceed with my seductive yet expedient dance. My jaw, however, trembles, and I still feel my face wet with tears, so I know this must be a grotesque performance.

Watching me, Williams laughs, and I fix a smile on my lips to spite him. When he approaches me, I'm afraid he's going to strike me again, and I shrink from him in fear before I can control my impulse. It's a half gesture, a small slip-up, but he seizes it and grows emboldened like never before. After all my work, and all my efforts, I've finally learned what Williams requires for his pleasure, but the knowledge doesn't bring comfort, only revulsion. He doesn't strike me again, but the glimmer of fear he saw is enough to keep him going all night. I will myself to smile and act like I'm enjoying myself, but I'm well aware that I'm nothing but a sad spectacle.

Later, much later, when I finally crawl back upstairs, when I see the horror on Sarah's face, and when I finally look at my own reflection in the mirror, I realize how ridiculous my pretense of enjoyment must have been. For my cheeks are not only wet from tears, but a steady stream of blood gushes out of my nose. The doctor is summoned, once more at my expense. The blood stops and I'm given a tranquilizer so I can sleep. When I awake, my nose is swollen, my face bruised, and Mrs. Harden declares me unfit to work for at least three nights. This is a loss she cannot stomach and so, to my relief, she declares that Williams will be barred from the premises from here on out.

Before she can think to charge me for more than the doctor's visit on account of my inability to work, I accuse her of not sending anyone to my rescue when I screamed. We exchange strong words, but I stand my ground. In the end, my three days of respite, Mrs. Harden decides, are to be treated like my monthly female trouble, a time when I take a break and am not paid but am housed and fed as if I were working. That is acceptable to me, though my anger at her lingers, as does my humiliation and a deeper sense of fear. I know Williams will not return, but part of me feels that his attack on me was more than him acting of his own free will. What if this is part of Marie's curse, part of her retribution? What if it was her slapping me in the face, just like in my nightmare, using Williams as her marionette? Can Marie have such powers?

By the evening of my first day of recuperation, I decide I cannot linger in my room, prey to my own unpleasant thoughts. I ask for Sarah's help in tightening my stays and find a rather understated dress, and a hat with a veil that covers my bruised face. I go out for a long walk. I take the streetcar on Bath down to the water. On the boardwalk by the Beach Pavilion, I stay away from people as if I'm an untouchable. Am I not? But I do take comfort in their presence around me. As I breathe in the salt air and listen to the waves crash, to the voices of people and the cries of seagulls, my tension eases, and the claustrophobic feeling of being alone with Williams in a room where no one came to my rescue, where I had to dance and entertain and pleasure with my face covered in blood eases its grip on me. I shall try to forget it, just like I shall try to forget Marie's lifeless body and the little mirror I held to her face to ascertain she was indeed not breathing. I have, among other talents, a great capacity for controlling my own mind. I can push away thoughts, feelings, and dreadful images, lock them up, banish them, and summon more pleasant ones in return.

I walk the beach and think of Aristotle. Not of our awful night with Ruby. I banish that from my mind as well. I think of Aristotle being entertaining and gallant. I think of the presents he's sent me, the flowers. I also think of books I like, of my favorite foods, of my favorite dresses. The thought of Sarah comes to mind, and I welcome it. She is the one presence in Mrs. Harden's house that I enjoy, the one soul I feel kinship with. Though of course Sarah didn't come when I screamed either. Was she afraid? Or did she not hear? I decide it's prudent not to get too attached, but I do enjoy her and her attentions. I also enjoy the sunset on the beach, something I rarely get to see because at this hour I'm usually getting ready for the evening's entertainment. Tonight, I tell myself, tonight I shall enjoy food and books while the other girls are working. But later, upstairs in my room, the music and voices from downstairs grate on my nerves as I try to read and eat, and the vilest headache torments me. It's as if a beast of some sort has seized my head in its claws and is slowly puncturing my skull.

The next night, I resolve to stay out a bit later, to walk around still even after dark. I'm hoping the exercise will make me tired enough to sleep, but I also wish to avoid the hours on end hearing music and voices while confined to my room. Perhaps it's not the wisest thing for a woman alone to do, for at one point a drunkard calls after me, and at another time I have the distinct feeling that a man is following me. I duck into an alley to avoid two boys who appear to be inebriated, and their laughter follows me as I hasten my pace hoping to reach a street that's well-lit and populated before they catch up. My heart is racing by the time I return to Mrs. Harden's and let myself in through the back door, but the adventure is not unwelcome.

Having escaped a real or imaginary menace makes me feel resilient, crafty, and spry. Perhaps it's the little boost my self-image needed after the debacle with Williams. That night I sleep better, and the next night I slip out again. I don't bother to cover my face, although the bruising is now a dark purple, and Mrs. Harden will have to contend with me being out of commission for longer than intended. Let the bruises put off anyone who might pursue me. For once, I think being unattractive could be an asset. My spirits are even high enough to think of this as a joke.

And so I wander. I wander the streets of Galveston at night. I walk all the way to the beach and delight in seeing the vast darkness, the lights of ships shining in the distance. I have never been aboard a ship, except, of course, the steamer that brought me here from New Orleans, and I resolve that once I retire I shall travel. That thought delights me. And the people averting their faces when they see my bruises amuse me in a way I never thought possible. The night air is balmy and salty and I'm alive and feeling free. I'm feeling the return of possibilities. The return of my own power. The return of my self-reliance, my humor, and my sense of adventure.

It's late when I walk back to Mrs. Harden's. I don't know how late. I do not carry a watch and have never been trained to tell the hour by the moon and stars. Sailors would know that. Once my face heals, when I next get to entertain a ship captain I shall ask. That would make for interesting conversation.

I'm unaware, as I wander down a well-lit sidewalk, of the shadows growing toward me, until I feel a grip on my elbow, and before I know it, three drunken men are upon me, pulling me into a dark alley. I struggle and hiss, I spit in their faces, but it's no use. They laugh their coarse laughs as two of them press me against the wall, and a third pulls at the front of my dress. I scream. I angle my face so whatever light there is can reveal my bruises. A knife shines in the moonlight, its cold metallic blade pressing against my throat. "Shut your trap if you don't want me to rough you up worse than whoever smashed in your face!" the man threatens as he undoes his pants. My guts churn and my mouth fills with vomit but I don't dare spit it out. I don't dare move or breathe or make a sound. My mind has forgotten all prayers. I'm unaware of anything but the blade against my throat. There's a shout from one of my attackers. "She's nothing but a prostitute, she won't mind that much." Next thing I know, the knife blade is gone, and I fall to my knees, retch into the weeds, wipe my face with my skirt.

When I look up, I see a man putting away his gun. A different man, one who doesn't seem like a threat. "They're gone," he says. "Did they hurt you?"

I can't find my voice. He reaches his hand to help me up. He's an attractive man, well dressed, and I'm suddenly aware that I'm kneeling in a dirty alley, that I have vomited in front of him, that my face is bruised and my dress torn. Quickly regaining my composure, I motion to cover my exposed breasts. He looks away, but not before I see a flash in his eye that tells me he's not oblivious to my ample bosom. He reaches in his pocket for a white handkerchief, and I'm not sure if he means for me to wipe my eyes or cover myself with it.

"Your face," he says. "By God, did those bastards do that?"

"No. No, you arrived just in time. Thank you. That was another accident." I can't bear the look in his eye. This man is sorry for me and I can't stand it. I cover my chest with his handkerchief as best I can and assume the most righteous posture I can summon under the circumstances. "Please don't think I'm a vagabond or a street girl. I come from Paris and work at Mrs. Harden's." I'm cautious to stress my French accent and bat my eyelashes seductively – a gesture which is hopefully not too ridiculous given the state of my face. "I am the best paid woman in Galveston. This all was a huge misunderstanding, and my face—"

"Let me look at your face." His voice is not unkind. "I am a doctor."

"I assure you I've had excellent medical care, but if you offer, I don't see the harm in a second opinion."

At this he laughs, again, not unkindly. "My carriage is in the street. I was visiting a patient. If you'll allow me," and he quite formally offers his arm, "I could look at your face at my practice. Then I shall drive you home. These Galveston streets are not safe for a woman alone at night." I wish I could argue, but I sense only minimal judgement for my profession. As to accompanying him, I'm too curious to resist, and my instincts tell me he did not rescue me from my attackers in order to harm me himself. So I smile, and instead of seizing his arm, offer my hand.

"I'm Aimée Bonnard. Pleased to meet you."

He brushes my fingers with his mustache. "Likewise, Miss Bonnard. What an honor. Doctor Claude Tarner, at your service." We step into the light, and walking next to him, I feel as strong a current of attraction as I do for Aristotle. Best be careful, I tell myself. Though I have never been attacked and brutalized before this most unfortunate week, I'm savvy enough to know that the shock of it all might make me susceptible to misplaced feelings. I tell myself that while Tarner is by all means an attractive male specimen, and a most chivalrous one at that, I must treat him with even more caution than I do my clients. Because after all, this is a man who has not paid a small fortune for my company, and that's a type of man I'm not sure how to treat.

CHAPTER 7
A NEW ACQUAINTANCE

D̶r. Tarner steers the carriage to a two-story Greek revival house nestled behind live oaks. It reminds me of New Orleans, a memory as unsettling as the events of the evening and my confusing attraction to my savior. I revert to calculations for comfort. How much is this house worth? How wealthy is the doctor? Is he even a man who could afford my services? We enter through a side door and proceed down a hallway to a room that appears to be his office or practice. I see a sizeable mahogany desk with papers scattered across, a glass cabinet full of vials and medical tools, a chair for patients to recline in, a scale, and various framed drawings of the human body on the wall. The room smells like some of the old pharmacies in New Orleans, and just like in those places, there's a carafe of water with two glasses set on an end table. The doctor invites me to sit in the patient's chair.

"Would you care for some water? Or perhaps something stronger?" He hands me a metal basin and a glass of water in which he releases a drop from a vial. "You will feel better if you rinse out your mouth," he says, and seeing me grow flustered at performing such an unladylike act in front of him, he directs me to a small washroom. I enjoy closing the door behind me and being alone. I take a moment to look at myself in the small mirror above the sink, and after gargling with the water that tastes like medicine, I wash my face and straighten out my hair as best I can. I take pains too with the handkerchief covering my bosom. I come out still disheveled and bruised, but with some of my dignity restored. I strive for good posture as I walk across the room. Despite my purple face, I must have regained some of my shine, because the doctor smiles.

He pours brandy from a decanter for the two of us. I toast him as if we were at a party. I don't drink much, and never the hard stuff, but a sip of the brandy burns my throat in a most strengthening fashion. I set the glass down, because even under the circumstances I do not wish to let myself fall prey to the danger of alcohol. In fact, it's vital that I keep my wits about me.

"What a lovely practice," I tell the doctor. "What sort of patients do you usually tend to?"

He smiles. "Relax, Miss Bonnard. I want to look at your bruises, and would like to disinfect the cut on your neck."

My fingers instinctively seek out the place where I still feel the impression of the knife. I shiver. There is indeed a small cut and it stings when I touch it, but there's no blood on my fingers.

"It's a small scrape," he says. "It will not leave a scar, we'll see to that. And I'll make sure it doesn't get infected."

Just then, I hear footsteps and a door opening. An older woman in a starched pinafore enters the room, her hair disheveled as if she'd been asleep.

"Why, Doctor Tarner, I'm so sorry. If you'll excuse me, I—" Her face turns red as she averts her eyes from me, and I know instantly the old biddy knows what I am and thinks I'm here for some dalliance with the doctor, as if girls as expensive as myself actually paid house calls to men like him.

"I'm sorry we woke you, Mrs. Bock. Miss Bonnard here had an unfortunate accident, and I'm tending to a small cut on her neck. Could you perhaps be so kind to fetch me some iodine?"

At this, the woman meets my impertinent gaze, for I will not lower my eyes in deference to a judgmental servant. Her face softens when she sees my bruises. "Oh, no! Dear child," she exclaims. "Why, right away, doctor."

Child? I'm anything but a child. But I don't bristle when her hand touches my forearm in a ridiculous protective gesture. In fact, I enjoy her touch, which makes me wonder if perhaps the one sip of brandy and the whole misadventure in the alley have turned me into a sentimental sap.

The doctor holds a compress against my neck. It doesn't hurt or sting. It smells like iodine. He then takes his time looking at my face, touching the bridge of my nose, asking where it hurts. I don't protest, don't remind him I've already been seen by an excellent and most expensive physician. While I do certainly hope he will not send me a bill for his services, I do wish to prolong this visit. And I do wish for him to touch me. In fact, when I think better of it, I feel that even a bill would perhaps be interesting. I'm curious how much he charges. And it would certainly create a precedent for our correspondence, would it not?

He asks if I've been getting headaches, if I am able to sleep. Then he asks Mrs. Bock to prepare a soothing chamomile tea for me. She leaves. The doctor's eyes meet mine.

"Since we're alone," he says. "If you don't mind, Miss Bonnard, please tell me about the accident to your face. And please don't say you opened a cupboard door or fell down the stairs. I've seen this sort of injury on women before."

"Well, it has never happened to me before and I assure you it won't happen again. Unlike the women who supposedly fall down the stairs and hit their own faces with cupboard doors, I have the freedom not to be pledged for life to my assailant, and I assure you the man will never be welcomed again at Mrs. Harden's."

"That certainly is good to know. I still would like to know how exactly this happened."

"He slapped me. And I promise you this is most unheard of. He was a most difficult client and I was always most gracious in entertaining him. I do take pride in helping the moodiest men have a lovely time. This was, as I say, unprecedented and it shall never reoccur."

The doctor smiles, a smile that reaches his eyes. I take that as a good sign. "What I wish to know, is was this one blow or several, and was it done with an open palm or a fist?"

"One," I say, "open palm." I'm somewhat disappointed he's not interested in me elaborating on my account of Williams. My pride would certainly like the opportunity to show this was an aberration.

The doctor looks carefully at my eyes. Asks me to open them wide, look in one direction, then the next.

"You shall be quite all right," he finally concludes.

"I assure you," I say, "I have a very lovely life."

Mrs. Bock returns with chamomile tea and cookies. I suppose she persists in viewing me as a child. As I drink my tea, at the doctor's suggestion, she retires. Before she leaves us, she bids me goodnight and invites me to come back. I want to roll my eyes at her charity, but something stops me. I hesitate between a thank you and a smile, and decide on the smile. When her worried eyes finally look away from me and she closes the door behind her, I am both relieved and slightly disappointed. I remind myself that it's my acquaintance with the doctor, not his servant, that I wish to prolong.

"I don't have my purse with me," I say. "Please be sure and send me your invoice at Mrs. Harden's."

"That won't be necessary."

"But I insist. A girl like me always pays her own way. And I take pride in being able to afford to do so."

"Yes," he says smiling. "You've already claimed to be the best paid woman in Galveston. Though I may wager Mrs. Harden herself might be paid even more?"

"We share our profits equally," I say, but his point is not lost on me, so out of pique I add, "besides, I'm skeptical of business lessons from someone who gives away his services for free."

"I take it you never do, Miss Bonnard. Well, what a shame!" His words pierce me. But I don't wish to follow that train of thought.

"Neither should you. Running a charity house has never benefited anyone. I insist you send me an invoice."

"And I insist on sending you something else," he says. "I will send you the name and address of a friend of mine. I think it would be wise to consult a specialist on some of the other risks of your profession."

"A specialist in prostitutes?"

"A specialist in women's health, venereal disease, and—"

I laugh. "I'm not a rube, doctor. I've worked in some of the finest houses in Paris and know all about condoms and use them all the time." This is a blatant lie. I do know a great deal about these inventions, but no man wants to use them, and no business-savvy woman should insist. Especially since unfortunate accidents can be averted with a diaphragm. If all else fails, there's always surgery, but that is neither painless nor devoid of risk.

The doctor laughs. "Most useful, and most unpleasant inventions, don't you think?" I cannot help but join in his mirth. "Though you will probably tell me that you can make not just morose men but also condoms enjoyable?"

"A girl can try, but some things can't be helped."

"So I assumed. Which is why I would suggest you do go see my friend. Syphilis, my lovely Miss Bonnard, is no trifling matter."

"You would imagine I don't entertain sailors!"

"Much to their loss, but syphilis doesn't only befall the poor."

"How charming! I generally prefer an invoice to a lecture. Unless I'm paid to listen, of course. Shall I tell Mrs. Harden to reserve you an evening?"

He offers me his arm. "Let me drive you home, Miss."

CHAPTER 8
DARKNESS

I sleep fitfully and awake past noon. When Sarah brings my coffee, she doesn't notice the scar on my neck. My face is still purple, and a slight yellowing has occurred. It's unattractive for sure, but I choose to take it as a sign of healing. I remember the doctor's fingers touching my face, remember the taste of the brandy and his physical presence next to me. Shreds of conversation come back to me from the night before. Have I conducted myself with too much pride? Or perhaps I was not prideful enough? Was I a sorry sight? Yet he was kind, for sure, and so even was that old judgmental servant of his. He was kind and warm. He laughed a lot, and found me surely amusing. But his comments about syphilis still sting. As does his lack of interest, though I don't know if it truly was lack of interest. After all, even while lecturing me about venereal disease, the doctor was laughing and flirting.

Yet as deliciously ambiguous as flirting tends to be, and I pride myself on being an unparalleled flirt, the terms of engagement are clear from the beginning when a man is a paying customer and murky at best when the man is not paying and the lady in question can act of her own free will. Not that I've ever been forced to anything. The closest it ever came to that was that dreadful encounter last night, and I'm determined to bury that as deep in my memories as Marie's death. No, I was never forced nor violated. I always acted completely, utterly, and unapologetically of my own free will, but always entered willfully into a bargain. Can sexual relations ever be something else?

I now regret stating so firmly that I never give away my services. Should I have left the door open to that? Should I have alluded and tried to entice? It would have been crass and unattractive to offer to repay the doctor in the flesh, but I could have used subtlety and subterfuge to intimate that maybe in the future… Would he even be interested in such a possibility? He laughed off the use of condoms, and rightly so. That makes me like him better, as he's not that innocent. But neither is he reckless. Does he view me as a potential carrier of syphilis and other diseases, and does that thought eradicate all desire?

Unable to bear this, I decide that I need a distraction. I eat and dress, put on a hat with a veil, and go shopping. At Garbade, Eiband & Co I have shopgirls show me new fabrics, new hat pins, new fragrances, new boots. I hear the whispers about my veiled face, but they are hushed and subdued, the shopgirls not wishing to upset a well-paying customer. I sign for my purchases with pride and order them delivered to Mrs. Harden's. I have a dinner of fried shrimp in a restaurant.

I take the streetcar back home where, in addition to my packages, a bouquet of yellow roses awaits me in my room, with a cream-colored card set next to them. Expensive flowers, exquisite, fresh and fragrant. Aristotle must have learned about my predicament. Or maybe not. Maybe he's just being attentive because he likes spoiling me. Or maybe it's another client. But when I open the card an unfamiliar script greets me. "I hope you're feeling better. Here is the address and telephone of the specialist we discussed. Your friend, CT." I feel a little faint, as if the room is suddenly wobbly, the way I imagine a cabin on a ship to be in stormy weather.

What kind of man sends a woman expensive flowers while at the same time reminding her that she might be diseased? I lie down on my bed without changing out of my dress, and when I finally call for Sarah to come help me loosen my stays and escape my corset, it's because I can't tolerate it any longer. I feel stifled, my room unpleasantly hot, and the scent of the roses overpowering. I ask Sarah to open the window. I ask her to brew chamomile tea like the doctor's servant did, and she suggests she might even prepare a chamomile compress for my face. *How well she feigns to care for me*, I think. Still, her attentions help and must be rewarded. After she serves my tea, after she goes to great lengths to prepare a compress and cool it, I give her a small tip and insist she take the yellow roses for herself. Yet as soon as she carries them off to her room I regret it.

The card is still on the table. I examine it at length. I look at the handwriting, examine each loop, imagine his fingers on the pen. There was a woman I knew in New Orleans who could tell things about a person's character by the way they shaped their letters. I never let her look at mine. But I sure wish I knew someone like that here, someone who could tell me things about this doctor.

I make myself take a short walk in the evening. I have to. I cannot let the attack break me, cannot let it change my ways. But I return to the brothel before dark, and I steer clear of alleys. As I walk back to my room, I consider knocking on Sarah's door and asking for my flowers back. But that would be unfair and overly sentimental. In fact, when I return to my room and see the doctor's card on my nightstand, I rip it to shreds and flush it down the commode. I won't allow myself an obsession. And I do not need a specialist to teach me about venereal disease. I have been schooled for years by Madame Rouge and by other girls on how to examine a man's member for suspicious signs, and if I've never come across anything they've warned me about it's because I've only worked with well-heeled clients who do not engage with the kinds of girls who entertain sailors.

But I remember, despite myself, some of the stories those men I wish to forever forget told Marie and me on that last awful night in New Orleans. Those men were as well-heeled as they come, but they bragged about looking for cheap thrills in all kinds of places. They even sought after forbidden pleasures with women of different races, in houses that allowed such things. I shudder at the thought of some of the acts they described, and their insolent laughs when they said that "girls who are truly desperate would do anything for a hot meal." But I cannot allow my mind to go there. I will not recall those men or their words, or what happened that night. Because in the end, even girls who are not desperate for a hot meal can be convinced to do unspeakable things, can they not?

Before I have a chance to compose myself and lock away the darkness invading my thoughts, I wonder if perhaps I too am desperate, but in a different way. Perhaps I am not different from the hungry, but my hunger is of a different nature, and it will devour me all the same. I sit upright in bed and open my eyes. I fix them on the wallpaper of my room, on the magnolia blooms I had so liked when I first saw this place. I concentrate on the white petals, on the thick luscious leaves. I walk to my open window, breathe in the salty night air, look over the rooftops to where I know the water is. I think of ships in the port, think of the waves and the fish beneath. I sit at my desk and open my ledger, write down today's purchases, subtract the sums and take comfort in all the money I have earned and saved. I open my favorite bottle of cologne and take a whiff. I let my hand caress my favorite dresses, then play with the glass baubles in my jewelry box.

When I feel myself calming down, I lie down on my bed and try to read. I force my mind to stay on the pages. When I finally tire enough to hope that I might sleep, my dreams are haunted by Marie. Her hands close around my neck. I cannot breathe. Somewhere between sleep and waking, I gasp for air and touch my skin as if to ascertain that nobody is in fact strangling me. The nightmare was so vivid it's hard to shake it off. Was it a nightmare or a hallucination? I read somewhere that people with syphilis experience hallucinations. Could it be that I have it? Could it be that Marie doesn't even need to haunt me in order to have her revenge?

I almost wish I hadn't flushed the doctor's card down the commode. Or perhaps that was indeed a brilliant thing to do, for it was that card that brought on this onslaught of nightmares and anguish. I remind myself that my unfortunate encounter with those men in New Orleans did not include the kind of act that would lead to diseases. They polluted my mind, my soul, but my body remained unscathed. Perhaps the damage done to my soul is irrevocable, but my mind is my own. I shall not allow them to infect it.

Even Marie, much as I wronged her, shall stay out. I shall forget her name. I shall forget her likeness. I shall forget I ever knew her, and when the day of reckoning shall come, God will have to remind me who she was and how I failed her. This I promise myself. I will purge her from my mind. Marie and the two men, like my attackers the other night in the alley, shall be forgotten, banned from my consciousness. As I finally drift back to sleep, I ask myself if perhaps the doctor should join them too? Should I also cover him in a shroud of oblivion?

CHAPTER 9
AN ORCHID AND AN OFFER

Each subsequent day of my recovery – which takes longer than Mrs. Harden and I had bargained for – my face makes progress toward returning to its normal color, and my mind makes progress toward forgetting what I need forgotten. Under the brim of a protective hat, I nurture my body and soul with sunshine. I decide that darkness is best avoided and that I need light, bird song, flowers, all the beautiful things. I resume my piano lessons, and as I grow steadier and more disciplined, my nerves settle. Hateful Victoria complains that I practice too early in the day, and Mrs. Harden requests I do not touch the keys until noon. I read late into the night, trying to keep myself on the schedule of a prostitute, because once I resume working I do not wish for dark circles under my eyes to take the place of the bruising on my face.

To my delight, I am asked to return from convalescence early. Aristotle requests my presence, and it is just the boost I needed. He sends me an orchid in anticipation of our *tête à tête*, and I am as delighted to receive it as I am to learn that he has requested to see me alone. I would not wish for another night sharing his attentions with Ruby, and while my intuition tells me that the *ménage à trois* is bound to reoccur, because even the most sophisticated men are pretty childish about such amusements, I'm glad to know it will not reoccur so soon. Part of me wonders if it's the double price rather than his desire for my superior conversation skills that prompts Aristotle to ask for me alone, but I admire the orchid long enough to banish such negative thoughts.

I delight in knowing, also, that Ruby has not received an orchid or any other offering. Then I chide myself for even wondering about that. It's one thing to accept the immature nature of men when it comes to their egos and desires. It's quite another to question Aristotle's clear preference for me. Ruby is nothing but a toy, like one of those devices Marie once described to me, which she told me one of her clients paid good money to watch her play with.

I was both repulsed and curious at her accounts, wondering if perhaps she had made some of it up. I was torn between wishing that particular client would never request my services, and a morbid sort of jealousy toward Marie, who was always steps ahead of me in her experience and sophistication, Marie who got to open doors I would have been afraid to walk through. Marie was aware that her excursions to the darker and more adventurous side of desire were not my cup of tea, and she loved to mock and tease me, making me out to be a prude – although by then I was a successful prostitute too, one who entertained every night, had extensive knowledge of pleasures of the flesh, and greatly enjoyed them. But the sinful acts I enjoyed seemed wholesome when compared to the adventures of Marie, which often included an undercurrent of danger, moments when she confessed she felt genuinely afraid, before succumbing to pleasure that was more overwhelming than anything she'd experienced with the sorts of safe and mostly polite clients I liked to entertain.

Of these encounters she bragged just enough to make me wonder and obsess. I didn't know, back then, that this was part of a strategy. That I could not recognize the game she was playing is surprising, considering how well I had learned my lessons about temptation, about planting desire, curiosity, and lust so firmly into someone's mind that they become beholden. Marie used my own weapons against me and I never was the wiser until it was too late. In an irony greater even than the one that allowed her to entice me using strategies I should have recognized, her own web of temptation closed around her, leading to her demise. I was too jealous, too covetous, too eager to win. My judgement was clouded by pride. My actions were supremely selfish. And my actions led to Marie's death, for which I am as much to blame as anyone. Even herself.

But why after being so good, so disciplined in my thoughts and emotions, am I thinking of this now, on the eve of my much-anticipated rendezvous with Aristotle? I do not wish to drag this darkness into my meeting with him. I wish to be my most wonderful, light, breezy, yet still insightful self. I wish to prepare body and soul for this most delightful companion. And prepare I must. My face not having healed completely is a problem, but a surmountable one. Mrs. Harden and I study different types of lighting in different rooms of the house. The bruising, faint now, can be disguised with the warm yet subdued glow of candles, as well as with the careful application of powder. I am to await Aristotle alone in a dining room set up just for the two of us, then escort him to an adjoining bedroom also only lit by candles.

I place the orchid he gave me on the nightstand. I dab some of my favorite fragrance onto the pillows, even into the heavy velvet drapes that keep out any trace of light. The cook prepares a special meal of shrimp in decadent butter. I wear a low-cut red velvet dress, and a faux diamond pendant that falls into my décolletage, calling his attention away from my slightly bruised features. Though frankly, between the powder and the candlelight, my face looks nothing short of lovely. But it is entertaining, seeing his eyes dart to the shiny object between my breasts even as we make dinner conversation, and I use seeming natural movements of my body to make the object catch the light. All of it is as enthralling as a cat playing with a ball of yarn.

There is one moment when, while looking at my face, something changes in his eyes and I wonder if perhaps he's noticed the bruising. "I love the shrimp," I say, meaning to distract him, and he immediately heaps more off of the serving platter onto my plate. He even spears one with his fork and feeds it to me. We laugh. He wipes the butter off my lip with his callused finger and a frisson of desire passes between us. Surely he hasn't noticed anything out of order. The precaution is probably redundant, but just in case, I rearrange my position so that the bruised side of my face catches less light, and the fake jewel between my breasts sparkles. I see it reflected in Aristotle's longing glance. I can feel the current between us intensify as he feeds me more shrimp, taking pleasure in my enjoyment of them, taking pleasure too in prolonging the tension until it becomes both delightful and unbearable.

After the shrimp, there is bread pudding with a luscious bourbon sauce. As Aristotle feeds me, I relish each delicious bite and the anticipation of what is to follow. I ask about his business and am amused by his inability to concentrate. I take my allowed sip of bubbly, and an extra one for victory and courage, for this is nothing short of a glorious comeback.

Finally, when we are both satiated from our indulgent meal and can no longer contain our hunger for each other, I lead Aristotle into the adjoining alcove. He asks that I keep the dangling jewel on as I straddle him, and I gladly oblige. He is hypnotized, and my own reflection in the mirror above the bed hypnotizes me in turn. The rapture in Aristotle's eyes, the glow of candles, the fragrance that permeates everything, the delicate orchid watching over us with its magical blooms opening up like the most sensitive part of my own body, all of it is intoxicating beyond anything I've experienced, a feast for the senses more decadent than I thought possible.

"You are a goddess," Aristotle whispers, his rough hands on my muscular thighs. "You are a goddess," he cries out louder, over and over again, and I can't have enough of this, I want to melt and die just so that time would stop and the essence of this moment would be imprinted on my consciousness forever. This, I tell myself, this is what I was created for, who I was meant to be. And in that moment, I am truly happy. The carousel stops. Or perhaps the horses are spinning faster than ever. I feel like I'm transcending the boundaries of my own self, melting into the vastness of the

Universe. I wonder if this is the type of overwhelming pleasure Marie was talking about, but I do not want to think of her now. I do not want to think of anything at all. I am not fully here. I'm losing myself, dissolving. All I can do is feel and melt into the vast unknown, into a sea of blissful, mind-numbing intensity.

Afterwards, I feel dazed by the temporary loss of control. My heart is beating fast but I can't stop smiling. Aristotle pulls me close, cradles my head to his chest, kisses my hair. His hand reaches between my breasts, touching the shiny crystal. What a miracle a piece of cut glass can be. "One day," he says, "one day I will buy you a real one. I will set you up in a house of your own, and you will never have to worry about nothing."

A sour taste invades my mouth, as if I've eaten too much bread pudding, too much butter, breathed in too much fragrance, moved on top of my lover too long. He squeezes my breast, and I contain the nausea and dizziness that has taken hold of me. Was it that second sip of champagne making me sick? Or was the feast overall too scrumptious? Must one always pay a high price for the most exquisite of pleasures? Aristotle talks about his business plans, the ways in which he seeks to expand, the properties he wishes to acquire, including a house not far from here, with a shady porch, a house he wishes to install me in as his personal mistress.

I try to listen with my usual skill, try to have the required enthusiastic reaction, but my mind is incapable of focusing. I feel dizzy and faint, and when Aristotle is finally done talking and moves on top of me for a second round of what is usually a most delectable experience, I stifle the kind of nausea I generally manage to keep at bay with even the most revolting clients. When he kisses me, something he does do on occasion, and which I tend to enjoy, I summon all my self-control not to be sick, and when he nuzzles my neck, then my breast, then clumsily in the throes of passion tries and fails to take the shiny jewel I'm wearing into his mouth, I find him so ridiculous I could scream.

Aristotle laughs, and I laugh with him, marveling at how unforced my acting sounds. When he finally succumbs to pleasure I act that part out too, and he collapses on top of me, satisfied and utterly fooled. When he finally rolls over, reaching for his cigar, I light it, then wrap myself in my robe and slip out to find a washroom. I run the water, retch as quietly as I can, then rinse my mouth out with cologne three times, tap my face with a wet washrag, reapply a fine coating of powder. I sashay back into the bedroom like the goddess Aristotle paid to be with, not the mortal that just crumbled. The fake jewel still dances between my breasts, and he is still too blinded to see the deceit on my face. "You know what I love about you?" I whisper, taking the cigar from his hand, vanquishing my revulsion as I take a deep, intoxicating drag. "I love that you can go all night. You're a stallion, my dear Aristotle. An absolute stallion."

CHAPTER 10
WHAT DO I WANT?

The next day I try to dissect my feelings. For it wasn't the champagne, the rich meal, or the excess of passion that made me sick the night before. Though there is always a chance that a man might say a thing like that just to strut his feathers, then never mention it again, Aristotle's offer changes things between us. And I am not prepared for this change, nor ready to adopt a strategy to deal with the implications of our new arrangement, should it really come to pass. I do not even know how a smart businesswoman responds to such an offer, and not being close to Mrs. Harden, I have no one to guide me. Even Madame Rouge, whose guidance and mentorship I presently miss, wouldn't be much help in this predicament, as a madam only stands to lose if one of her best girls leaves, thus I could not trust her to give impartial advice.

What bothers me supremely is that the offer of such an arrangement alters the balance of power between Aristotle and me. Should I show myself interested, he would no longer find me as elusive and worthy a prey as before. Nothing but ownership to spoil the charms of even the most exquisite goods. How many dresses have I coveted at the store then grown tired of once they were hanging in my closet? But outright refusing the offer could cause offense to my potential benefactor, so I must feign some interest. Perhaps the key is to show polite yet moderate enthusiasm but find rather obvious ways to change the topic, making him think I don't wish for the arrangement to come to pass. Would that not be rejection though? And while men are enticed by teasing, they are either enraged or completely disgusted by outright rejection. So I must be cautious, diplomatic, and charming, and this new level of pretense complicates my work.

Of course, another important matter to consider, the most important perhaps, is whether I want the arrangement to come to pass or not. What fool would not want a house of her own? For even if in time Aristotle would tire of me, if I were smart enough to get the deed in my name, between the house, whatever other generosity he might bestow on me before boredom sinks in, and my current savings, I'd be set for life. Wouldn't that be the life I dreamt of on my last days staying in the hotel? And yet, something about such a future – not that it's a sure thing by any means – strikes me as sad and stifling. To think of Aristotle, so far my favorite, as the only man I entertain, fills me with boredom and revulsion. To think of owing him and only him my favors makes me angry. I do not understand the rage nor the disgust. But it is there, in my heart, in my body, and I cannot ignore it. I am nothing if not mistress of my feelings. But for once, maybe, though my reaction is unexplainable and illogical, I decide that I must not reign myself in, but instead follow my intuition. Was that how Marie felt on that awful night? Did she have a sudden bad feeling about the situation, and did she try, at the last moment to avert tragedy? I am suddenly seized by a longing to talk to her so strong it shocks me more than my unexplained revulsion at Aristotle. Perhaps I have gone mad. Perhaps I do have syphilis and these are the symptoms.

I try to remember everything I know about the disease. Then I chastise myself for these unproductive thoughts. I do not have syphilis nor any other ailment. My face even has healed completely. I am a woman at the height of my health and beauty. And if my instincts tell me that I do not wish to be Aristotle's mistress instead of working as a luxury prostitute and splitting my gains with Mrs. Harden, perhaps my instincts are correct. Perhaps my subconscious is trying to tell me something that my calculating brain can't anticipate nor grasp. Again, I think about how a similar thing happened to Marie, and then I banish that thought, banish all thoughts that are unpleasant, in fact, and take myself for a much needed, invigorating walk on the beach.

That evening's client is amusing enough to take my mind off Aristotle, my fears, and my calculations. I don't experience rapture, but I tell myself perhaps this too is safer. Perhaps experiences too overwhelming are destabilizing, leaving me dizzy and confused. Balance is needed in all things, and I am above all an artist when it comes to creating the perfect balance. When I retain control of myself is when I reign supreme. And yet, the previous night's moments of pure ecstasy haunt me. They haunt me in a different way than Marie's specter or my unexpected disgust with Aristotle's offer. They haunt me because I am not sure if that type of nearly transcendent physical encounter is the best I can aspire to, or the most dangerous thing to be wary of. I am relieved to experience pleasure again, yet pleasure that doesn't shake me to my core. I am relieved yet part of me is disappointed. It's as if I have tasted the nectar of the gods and now am given mere wine. But then again, I remind myself of the abyss I sank into after my fleeting euphoria. Wouldn't I rather have the kind of pleasure that doesn't exact its toll? Wouldn't I rather remain mistress of myself?

The next few days are uneventful, and I manage to regain my composure. I buy fabric for new dresses, enjoy my piano lessons, take walks, and even manage to read a little, though it's not entirely tempting when my nights are long. Then Mrs. Harden tells me Aristotle has requested my company and my blue skies darken. Am I ready to see him again? Have I decided how to act? Of course, I will not show hesitation or doubt in front of the madam. I keep my composure and act pleased. I keep my composure even when she tells me Aristotle has not asked to see me alone. Aristotle has asked to see me and Ruby.

What I experience is not revulsion, but anger. Red-hot anger. As I prepare for the evening, I'm preparing for battle. I need to eclipse Ruby, to annihilate her charms. But the thought is pure poison, first of all because it calls into question my superiority, of which I'm certain, and second because it reminds me once more of my feelings toward Marie, and of how competing with her clouded my judgement. If given the chance again, would I act differently? Would I risk Ruby's life to win? Win what? Why does Aristotle now seem like such a prize, when only yesterday I bristled with defiance and disgust at the thought of becoming his mistress?

Of course, Ruby is no Marie. Marie was, despite my distaste for her, both a worthy rival and a superior being. Ruby is laughable in comparison. I despised Marie, loathed her and envied her all the same. I look down on Ruby and almost pity her, which does not imply compassion but rather disgust. Yet still, Ruby is a person. A person much beneath me is a person still. Would I want her to perish? Would I want her to suffer? I shudder. I cannot allow myself such thoughts, cannot allow myself to pull Marie out of oblivion and draw parallels between this situation and the one I faced with her. But although things are different now, and the dangers are not the same, a part of me I usually manage to silence tells me that if I allow myself to hate Ruby I am losing whatever shreds of my soul are still intact.

Unfortunately, not hating her proves impossible. For she descends upon Aristotle and me better turned out than I've ever seen her, in a new dress, her hair tastefully upswept, and the rouge on her cheeks applied with more mastery than usual. Her white bosom heaves alluringly with each breath, yet her movements have lost the vulgarity I've noticed in her before. Mrs. Harden must have worked extra hard on Ruby's education lately. And Ruby must not be as daft as I thought her, for the best teachings are lost on a girl of no talent and no intelligence.

A different pang of jealousy and alarm pierces my heart. Is Mrs. Harden now grooming Ruby to be her next prize horse because she saw her hopes in me dashed by my recent accident? Or has perhaps Aristotle committed the imprudence of hinting toward his intentions when discussing me with the madam? Though seeing Aristotle's eyes light up with desire for Ruby, I gather his plans of installing me in a house of my own are far from his mind now. In fact, he barely notices my presence. His gaze doesn't meet mine. I know there's only one way of capturing his attention, only one way of becoming the star of this show.

I inch closer, grab Ruby by the waist, and as distaste briefly flickers upon her face – for her schooling is yet incomplete, and her talent might after all have its limits – I smile at Aristotle and let my hands slowly explore her body. I remember every move of the performance I would engage in with Marie, and as much as it pains me to draw those memories out of the dark place where I wished to banish them, my body operates as if by instinct, as if these were the steps to a dance I know so well, I no longer need to think while executing them. I lock eyes with Aristotle, before I gaze deep into Ruby's goat-like pupils and brush her lips with mine, first softly, then with more ardor. I rip the front of her new dress open – a cruelty I despise myself for, but cannot help – and let my kisses trail from her neck to her collarbone, then farther down.

"Don't stop," Aristotle cries out in a strangled voice, and my hands, now sore from tearing at the lace and silk, continue ripping Ruby's dress, my lips keep exploring her body. As I do this, the silly girl finally starts coming to her senses, and with an embittered look in her eyes starts tearing at the seams of my bodice. Unlike her, I'm a natural at putting on a show of credible enjoyment. I shift ever so subtly from exploring her body to letting her explore mine, letting her hands and lips advertise me to Aristotle in all my glory. Soon, it is both Ruby and Aristotle kissing and touching me. I wrestle expertly into just the entanglement I desire until Ruby becomes superfluous to our arrangement, a mere decoy, just like she was in our previous encounter. My coup de grace is when, after an intense and mutually satisfying romp, as Aristotle and I both lie spent in each other's arms, I send Ruby out to bring us a carafe of cold water.

I have a sudden glimpse of myself as Marie, and it's both sickening and gratifying. I decide to examine these feelings later, or rather never. When Ruby returns, I meet her at the door, take the carafe from her, and before she can get her bearings, close the door in her face and lock it – something that goes against protocol, but I will worry about the consequences later. Alone with Aristotle, I pour us both glasses of cold water and make it my business to see that he is alternately refreshed and exhausted until all of his forces are spent and he falls into a deep sleep. He looks thoroughly contented, and I take pleasure in that, though much of the evening was not to my liking. And though my physical desires have been satiated as well, and though the breakfast Sarah brings me is delicious, and my bath scented with the finest oils, I have a feeling that something vital is missing. Neither Aristotle nor I mentioned the house he'd promised. And we did spend much of the evening alone. There was plenty of opportunity to bring it up. Just yesterday I was sure that I did not want the house nor all that such an arrangement would entail, but now, at the thought of it having been nothing but an empty promise, I feel a most shocking sense of despair. Was it an insubstantial offer issued without thinking in a moment of passion? And if so, why do I care?

CHAPTER 11
PLAYING GAMES

The next day the whole house overhears a fight between Mrs. Harden and Ruby. The silly girl is making a fuss over her torn dress, insisting that either I or the madam should pay for it. To my relief Mrs. Harden tells her in no uncertain terms that she is not too bright. Ruby screams too about the affront of sending her to fetch water and the door I had locked. "Who cares?" Mrs. Harden answers. "You stand to make a lot of money from doing nothing but having Aimée tear at your dress, do you not? If you're complaining for being paid without working, I shall see to it you don't get paid at all." There is more screaming, crying, protesting. Then I hear a sharp cry, then another and my heart stops because I realize Mrs. Harden has slapped her. Bile rises in my throat. I didn't think it possible, but the silence that follows is sinister enough to confirm my suspicions. I hear a door slam, hear Mrs. Harden's footsteps, and then again, that sinister silence.

Nausea doesn't leave me all afternoon. Nausea accompanied by guilt, because in some ways I was the start of that chain of events. It's as if I myself had slapped poor Ruby. And what for? For what reason did I tear her dress, for what prize did I cast her out and lock the door? I enter my pay in my ledger and try to take solace in it. But come evening, as Sarah arrives to help me get ready for another night of entertaining, it's clear to me what I have to do.

I find my purse and rummage through it. It's likely that I have enough cash to cover Ruby's dress. But once my fingers touch the coins inside my purse, I hesitate. I did not cause Ruby to be slapped, nor her pay to be withheld. It's as if Ruby slapped herself. I cannot be responsible for her acting rash and picking a fight with Mrs. Harden. I can also not take responsibility for Mrs. Harden being unfair or despotic. And surely, having worked in this house for a while, Ruby should have known that her outburst could have such consequences. I, for one, did not, and I am shocked.

My trust in the madam, limited from the start, for I am not naïve, was quite diminished after my misadventure with Williams. But did I think her capable of hitting a girl? Such punishment is both heinous and unwise. Surely Mrs. Harden is not as strong as Williams, though she is a large woman, so Ruby's face would not be as badly damaged as mine was, but bruising and swelling could still occur. Besides, what kind of inferior person resorts to violence to settle a dispute with a business associate? Perhaps I shall not stay long in this house. Perhaps I need to look for alternatives. Maybe becoming Aristotle's mistress would be advisable after all. But what if he wasn't serious about his offer? The fact that he didn't mention it again doesn't sit well with me.

I decide to put away my purse, but noticing Sarah's eyes on me, eager and full of hope, I change my mind. I place a few coins into her palm. "I need a few favors," I say. "Go to the florist in the morning and buy me the most beautiful Easter Lily you can find. Have them charge it to my account and bring it to me post haste. I mean to have it by the time I finish my dinner. Also, do, with your utmost discretion, inquire about Ruby's health, will you?"

The coins jingle in Sarah's pocket. I am as assured of her discretion as I am of Mrs. Harden's care for me and the other girls, but what am I to do? Servants will gossip, and the times when this serves me far outweigh the times when I wish they could keep their useless commentary to themselves. Best not to think of them and their loose lips. The lily is a much more pleasant thing to devote my attentions to. I visualize it, white and fragrant, its pot tied with a satin bow. The image of purity, which I myself certainly am not, but the contrast will not be lost on a man of intelligence and humor. Yes, yes, I tell myself. The best way to take my mind off Aristotle, and thus ensure that I can keep my power, is to open myself to a new and perhaps more interesting obsession.

The next day, by early afternoon, I am turned out spectacularly in a lace shirtwaist that buttons up my throat – delightfully different from my state of undress the night of my attack in the alley, yet provocative in its own way, for a man concerned with a tiny scratch near my collarbone is bound to look for it and not see it, which should lead his mind to thoughts of undressing me. I've paired the ruffled blouse with a powder pink skirt, and am wearing a parasol and dangly earrings with tiny gemstones, a nod to the fact that I am, even when dressed chastely, by no means chaste. I smile at my reflection in the mirror. He shall like that. And hopefully he'll find the Easter Lily delightful and amusing. For how often indeed does a respectable gentleman have the pleasure of receiving an Easter Lily from a whore?

My ride on the streetcar is full of sunshine. An old lady smiles at me, which confirms that nothing about my appearance betrays my profession. Even the dangling earrings can be seen as an eccentricity, perhaps a tad improper during daytime and on an ordinary day no less, but an act of vanity and bad taste that can easily be forgiven in a young person. I find myself hoping that even the doctor's old servant will approve of the Easter Lily and of my attire. Perhaps she'll stop feeling sorry for me now, seeing me in my expensive clothes, my face restored to its normal glory, a healthy glow in my cheeks, and my offering both whimsical and pricey enough not to have been bought by a woman in any state of desperation.

I pause in front of the Greek revival home, thankful for my memory and my sense of direction. Like everything else on the Island it looks more serene in daylight, nestled behind blooming oleanders, kept cool in the merciful shade of the live oaks out front. Specks of light dance on the white columns, caressing the shadows of branches and leaves. Birds sing and whistle, and if I still my beating heart, I can make out the sound of waves in the distance. I let it guide my breaths, taking a few moments to calm down. For a flushed face is charming, but I need my composure in order to complete this errand. I call to mind the serenity of my days staying in the hotel, the wholesome pleasures of early morning breakfasts in my room, of evening walks on the beach with the breeze on my face, of salt air coming in through my open window. Once I am calm enough to be both serene and well-spoken, I let myself through the wrought-iron gate, gather my skirts, go up the stairs to the front door, and knock. Soon I hear footsteps, and the lace curtains move, revealing a young maid's face, not that of the old servant. The door opens and the girl eyes me with curiosity.

"You come to see the doctor, Miss?"

"Yes."

"Appointments through the door on the side."

"This is not a medical appointment," I tell her, not losing my smile nor my friendly tone. Luckily I know how to talk to difficult people, even imbeciles. "I am a friend."

She reaches for the lily, but I don't offer it to her. "I can give this to him," she offers.

I keep my smile and my potted flower. "I wish to give it to him myself. I can wait."

Just then I hear a different set of footsteps, and the old servant from the previous night appears. I wish I could recall her name. Her face shows first confusion, then settles on a placid yet unreadable expression.

"Miss…" She has forgotten my name too. I smile brightly.

"Bonnard," I say. "Aimée Bonnard. It's good to see you again, Mrs. … I'm sorry, I seem to have trouble recalling your name too, though you were so very kind when I met you." I find myself talking too much. Why does this woman make me nervous?

"I'm Mrs. Bock. Why, how lovely to see you again," she says, and I see her eyes examining every inch of me. What is she looking for? More bruises? Evidence of depravity or abuse? Signs of dangerous vices? I square my jaw, smile and curtsey, a sign that her once-over has not been all that discreet, a gesture at which we both burst out laughing. "Go on, then," she says to the dumbfounded servant girl, "bring us some tea and cookies in the parlor, please. Do come in, Miss Bonnard. Oh, what a lovely lily!" It passes from my hands to hers, and as I follow her there's a tinge of sadness that darkens the sunshine of our encounter. When was it last I had a friend? But let me not get ahead of myself. A shared moment of mirth does not equal a friendship. And it's not for my lack of social graces that I have forever lacked in the friendship department, but rather for my prudent nature and common sense. For look what happened with me and Marie. Didn't that friendship start with complicity and laughter? Wasn't there pure and honest joy in us trading confidences and dresses and sharing adventures early on? Even the first few years at Madame Rouge were sweet with the delight of having a sister in this world. But no, I will not think of all that now. The specter of Marie is not welcome in this house. I am determined to enjoy my visit.

The lacquered floors squeak under my footsteps, and I take a moment to sway my hips so my petticoats rustle. In this lemon-polish-scented haven, I can imagine myself a fine lady, respectable as they come, enjoying all the trappings of a sedate bourgeois life.

"What a lovely home," I say as Mrs. Bock leads me into the parlor, a dark yet not unpleasant room, with wood paneling on the walls, and a most charming love seat opposite two narrow chairs surrounding a small table. I cannot for the life of me imagine the doctor in this room, nor sitting on this furniture that is entirely too delicate for his manly frame. No, the good doctor did not decorate this space, a woman did, and by all means a woman other than sturdy Mrs. Bock who is as likely to break these chairs as the man of the house. I shift uncomfortably and hesitate to sit, because I wish to allow her priority in choosing whichever seat might hold her, and I wish to do so without being too obvious. But once again, she laughs good-naturedly, and advances toward a bench I hadn't yet noticed, a wide and solid window seat in front of a tall end table. She sets the lily on said end table, and after resting her own heavy self on the bench, not without a groan that lets on how difficult it is to be so old and large, opens the heavy velvet drapes just a crack, letting a few rays of light fall on the white flower. The effect is a charming one, and it eclipses the awkwardness of the moment. We both smile, and I drag a chair across the room to sit near her.

"Is there a Mrs. Tarner?" I ask. I regret my directness immediately, as Mrs. Bock's demeanor changes. It is a shift imperceptible, perhaps, to someone less trained in reading other people's moods and righting whatever ails them. But I am less of an expert in pleasing women than I am in pleasing men, who are far easier to placate. So if my question is unsavory to Mrs. Bock, and it is understandable why, I do not know how to remedy my misstep and set her mind at ease.

"There was," she says curtly, and I am unsure what to understand. Did she pass? Did she leave? Further inquiries are only to make her more suspicious. Instead, I resort to flattery, something that women too enjoy almost as much as men do. "So the responsibility of this household falls entirely upon your shoulders. I wish to compliment you on how lovely this all is."

"Why, thank you," she says, but I can tell her good mood is not restored. By the time the servant enters with the tea and cookies, I wonder if Mrs. Bock regrets asking me to come in. One thing is clear, though, much as it's not to my liking. If I am to have any hope of regaining her good graces, I am to drink my iced tea quickly, come up with a few more neutral pleasantries, and take my leave without asking to see the doctor. There is no guarantee that she will even tell him I was here. No guarantee that he will notice the lily, or that the shrewd woman, protectress and in some ways mistress of this house, will not take it to her own room and never say a word about it.

But it's the gamble I must accept if I wish to ever come back. Not much of a gamble, I console myself, sipping on the strong sweet tea, enjoying its coldness in my mouth. The flower is fine as can be, but in the grand scheme of things, was a minor investment in my curiosity. If I shall come back, which I am presently unsure of, I shall try the side door which leads straight to the doctor's practice. Some female gatekeeper might wait for me there too, but hopefully not Mrs. Bock. In any case, perhaps seeing the doctor again is not important. After all, I came here only to distract myself from more real concerns involving a man who is of real interest to me, a man who might change my life if he truly wants to, and if I choose to let him.

"Thank you so much, Mrs. Bock," I say, setting my empty glass down on the silver tray the servant brought. "How very gracious of you to offer such refreshment. I must keep you from your activities no longer. I know you must have a very busy day." Her demeanor brightens visibly, and even more so once I turn down a second glass of tea.

"I hope you enjoy the lily," I say, standing up. Its scent trails me as I walk out of the room, and I dare hope that even a creature as oblivious to details as a man might notice this fragrance and inquire. But would the doctor even enter the parlor with the delicate chairs? I'm tempted to suggest Mrs. Bock take the flower to her own room — but that's too obvious a manipulation, and she seems intelligent enough to sniff out that kind of duplicity. So I bid my farewell and walk away. I carry with me a sense of loss, but am determined to churn it into something more productive. After all, I have succeeded in diminishing Aristotle's hold on me by feeding a different kind of longing and frustration. It is not lost on me that the types of games I play with clients I also play with myself, and that thought is both empowering and depressing.

CHAPTER 12
ENGLISH HUNTING DOGS

That evening I entertain a new client, a Mr. Ardoin, and the fact that he is from Louisiana gives me pause. Yet I quickly dismiss my apprehension. There's more to Louisiana than New Orleans, and not everyone in New Orleans knew Marie nor Madame Rouge. In fact, Mr. Ardoin is a cotton farmer, and I take comfort in the knowledge that his rural existence probably kept him far away from our glamorous house of ill repute. Then again, he is here, in Galveston, in a house not much different, and if he can afford my services now he could probably afford to be entertained by girls like myself and Marie in New Orleans too. He does not look nor sound familiar – but how sure can I be that I remember all of my past clients? And why would I remember the clients of the other girls? I tell myself I need to let go of these irrational fears. I smile at Ardoin and encourage him to talk about himself, about his business, about what brings him to Galveston.

"I like you," he says to me late into the night. We've had a most satisfying encounter, and he is now getting dressed. I help him by tying his cravat. "You remind me of someone, though I don't remember who."

"Another girl wearing the same perfume?" I ask flirtatiously, because my new scent is bound to lead his memories astray should he really have met me in my previous life.

"I'm not sure, but it'll come to me." His hand touches the knot of the cravat as if to ascertain I've done it properly. "It was a picture," he says, stopping in the doorway, and my smile freezes on my lips. "A picture of a girl in the Quarter. I'll bring it next time." He's jovial as if the news would please me.

"The Quarter?" I feign confusion even as my stomach tightens in a knot.

"In New Orleans."

"Oh, la Nouvelle Orleans," I say in my French accent, batting my eyelashes. "Is that nice? I've heard a lot about it."

"You would love it, my dear French girl. In fact, I'm surprised you came here to Galveston instead."

"Well, so did you!" I say, laughing. "More business here, just like you said."

At this he seems pleased. I hope he forgets all about the picture. Because unfortunately I know just what he is referring to and it's the stuff of nightmares. It was Marie and I, almost ten years back, who posed together for photographs. A luxury and an indulgence, but luxuries and indulgences were what Madame Rouge traded in, and among those luxuries and indulgences we were the choicest ones. The pictures were taken in the photographer's studio. We stood in glamorous low-cut dresses, holding flowers, as if we were society debutantes, not prostitutes. Madame too, fussed over us as if she were our doting mother, not the woman selling us to the highest bidder.

We had our hair done and our makeup. The studio was dark and somber, and the light from the photographer's contraption kept blinding us. We found it funny, because so many things were funny then, and we were young and spoiled and even our friendship had not yet turned sour. We had each brought several dresses and our best baubles, and traded accessories with relish, delighting in flashing the photographer's assistant glimpses of our silk stockings, then laughing about how flustered he grew. Here was a young man in dire need of a visit to some girls of the night, though obviously he would have to seek out some more suited to his meager budget. To him, we were unattainable, the way fancy hats and dresses had been unattainable to us before we started working at Madame Rouge. We were painfully young and the memories of a more impoverished life were recent and acute enough to coat our newfound wealth in an aura of magic. We still relished each luxury, each bottle of fragrance, each fine pastry, each silk ribbon and glimmering bauble.

Now we were having our picture taken at Madame's expense, decked out in the finest gowns and putting on makeup that cost more than our families' Sunday suppers. Madame had several pictures printed on fine cardstock. My only chagrin was that, while she offered them to our most important clients as keepsakes, Marie and I were allowed to each have one, but only if we ourselves paid for it out of our wages. We both gave in and probably paid more than our copies cost, but I loved displaying mine in a silver frame by my bed. And in a silver frame by my bed I left it when I left New Orleans. I shouldn't have.

I should have taken it with me and destroyed it, yet what good would that have done? The copies Madame had given to clients were still at large. Did Ardoin truly have one? Had he been Marie's client? Or had perhaps our pictures circulated to a larger circle of men? I can only pray he misplaced his copy, can only pray he was confused and maybe has a picture of some other

64

girl, not me. I can pray too he never comes back. Or that he forgets. And I can pray that I forget too because living in fear of something that shall never come to pass is exhausting and unnecessary. After all, even if the picture resurfaces, even if it truly is us, all I have to do is marvel at the likeness, then distract him from the matter and never mention it again. Having come up with this most excellent plan I am finally able to sleep.

The next day I awake refreshed, having slept way past noon. I enjoy my coffee and paper, and delight in the most unexpected correspondence: a note from Dr. Tarner. My heart vibrates. So Mrs. Bock did actually tell him about the lily? I have either underestimated or overestimated her. Either she's not wily enough for deceit, and guided by some moral compass that prevents her from lying when she knows a lie would be most useful, or she is smart enough to know that I might turn up again and that her losing the doctor's trust would keep her from beating me at my own game. I can't decide which of the two it is. But I'm too eager to read the doctor's note to devote much thought to his servant at this point.

"Dear Miss Bonnard,

Thank you so very much for your beautiful and thoughtful gift. I was quite sorry to miss the pleasure of seeing you. I would like to remedy that if possible. Would there be a time when you might do me the honor of accompanying me for a walk?"

I smile. How very charming! Also, how lovely that a walk would escape the old servant's scrutiny. Of course, there is the matter of my schedule, which is most inconvenient for walks. I'm asleep in the mornings, and getting ready to entertain in the evenings when the heat finally breaks. Would the doctor indulge me with a walk on Sunday, my one free day? There's only one way to find out, and prolonging the anticipation is good for me right now.

After all, my main goal is to distract myself from worrying too much about Aristotle and his intentions toward me. I write back to the doctor suggesting a sunset walk on Sunday. It's a test of sorts, as most respectable people have better things to do on a Sunday evening than walk around town in the company of a woman of ill repute. I even suggest he meet me in front of Mrs. Harden's house. A little payback for his irritating suggestion that I might see a specialist about syphilis. Should he find me and my occupation so objectionable, he will not be amenable to meeting me here. Would I be disappointed? Yes, very. But it's the risk of this suggestion that creates enough of a stir in me as to truly take my focus away from the whole matter of Aristotle and the house he promised.

The timing is excellent, for Aristotle does indeed request my presence. In fact, he does so on the same evening Ardoin already had, and at the last moment Mrs. Harden decides that Aristotle shall have precedence and that Ardoin is therefore to see Ruby. I am both angered and pleased when she informs me of this arrangement. For the idea that I am so easily replaceable, and by stupid Ruby, no less, is disturbing, but on the other hand, I would rather see Aristotle than Ardoin, and Ruby being otherwise engaged is most convenient. I gather Aristotle did not request to see both of us together, and that is reassuring and validating. And although part of me resents the thought of Ruby entertaining Ardoin, I remind myself I only care to have exclusivity with the most important clients. And in the grand scheme of things, winning Aristotle and all the opportunities he brings would be worth it even if I were to lose my other clients.

As I bathe, dry my hair, apply lotions, pomades, and fragrances, and carefully choose a dress, jewelry, and undergarments for my encounter with Aristotle, I make it a point to think of Dr. Tarner, and the response I'm hoping to receive from him about our walk. I slip into my silk stockings and wonder what it would be like to have the doctor touch me instead of the men I am so used to, men who pay a small fortune for the privilege. I dab a little bit of rouge onto my lips and imagine what the doctor's kisses might feel like, dab perfume between my breasts and imagine his hands cupping them. My heart beats faster, and a most becoming flush rises to my cheeks. I smile at my reflection in the mirror. I'm definitely in a playful mood.

Ready for some male companionship, I welcome the opportunity to engage in the most passionate acts with Aristotle while imagining being with the doctor instead. This thought gives me a lot of happiness for it is both thrilling and an excellent strategy. Men want a woman most when they can sense she's holding back. They have an instinct for it, sniff it out immediately, and it incenses them in the best way possible. Their hunters' instinct gets activated when the prey slips through their fingers even as she's caught, and there's no better way to be elusive than to bring an imaginary lover into the mix. It's ironic that Aristotle, who introduced Ruby into our *tête à têtes*, should now have to share me with a third of my choice, and a person who will be more of a presence between us than poor Ruby, even in the flesh, ever was.

That evening, emboldened by my secret fantasies, I outdo myself. I am glorious, divine. Aristotle can't have enough of me, and after he's exhausted himself thoroughly and given us both considerable pleasure, still sensing that he is unable to fully possess me, he holds me in his arms for longer than any client ever has and whispers to me anew about his plans to buy me a house. *Yes,* I think. *Yes, we shall live happily there, the three of us. You and me and my imaginary lover.* Emboldened by my deceit as well as by my newfound freedom – for I now tolerate the embrace better than I did before, imagining the doctor's arms around me instead of Aristotle's – I ask questions about the house and make demands. A sun room full of plants. A library. An English hunting dog, of the kind that has an elegant body. "A Pointer?" Aristotle asks, amused and surprised. "I shall get you two!" And at this my discomfort melts into delight. I laugh with him, and for a few fleeting moments I am fully there, the doctor forgotten. When Aristotle finally falls asleep, he releases his grip on me, and I slip out of his arms, out of his bed, out of his room. For a few delicious stolen moments, I stand in the doorway and watch him sleeping. I imagine the English hunting dogs and I smile.

CHAPTER 13
BEACH WALK AT SUNSET

When the doctor's response arrives, I feel a sense of elation I haven't experienced in a long time, not since my glory days in New Orleans, or perhaps those serene days I spent at the hotel upon arriving here in Galveston. The future, both near and distant, seems full of opportunities for play and wonder. I spend an inordinate amount of time wondering about what to wear on my walk with the doctor, yet I resolve that, just as I like to imagine him in my bed when I'm with Aristotle, I will imagine the two English dogs my client promised running free on the beach when I'm walking with Tarner. Free, I think. Free and playful. It's what I myself have always aspired to be.

On Saturday night, my last evening of work before my much-anticipated beach walk, I descend the stairs to find Ruby staring at me in a most peculiar fashion, while whispering with another girl. I pay them no mind. After all, it's no surprise that jealous women would subject me to scrutiny and gossip. I look past them as I walk toward my intended companion for the night, a banker who is surprisingly young and actually not bad looking. Unfortunately he is an arrogant young man, and therefore not much of a challenge, as his ego is easy to stroke and his conversation endless. I amuse myself as best I can by trying to discover what his most compelling qualities are as a conversationalist. The self-aggrandizing jokes are not amusing, the tales of his travels consist entirely of bragging about expensive amenities, and his taste in books or music is practically nonexistent. He fancies himself a connoisseur of wine but there's hardly an art to ordering the most expensive bottles without understanding the subtleties of taste. I find, however, that of all possible topics, it's somewhat interesting to hear him carry on about the cotton exchange. I pretend not to have a head for numbers, and he delights in explaining things I already understand. It's not exactly titillating conversation, but I find it rewarding to see my clients happy and animated, and explaining how the cotton exchange works to a poor guileless girl like me sure seems to bring him a lot of satisfaction.

The physical aspect of our encounter is rather dull, but I find ways to make it more pleasurable for both of us, without letting on that I know more about *ars amoris* than he does. I praise his every move and show great admiration, and use all my charms to distract him from the fact that it is my body, not his, that's doing most of the work. There are men who are positively lazy lovers, who are unwilling or unable to physically exert themselves, so that night I get double the exercise making up for the young banker's lack of ardor. Later, as I bathe, taking the utmost care to scrub off all traces of the week's last client, I delight in the fact that I'm so utterly tired. I will sleep well, I tell myself. I will imagine the English hunting dogs curled up next to me as I drift into a deep and peaceful slumber, and the next day I will awake refreshed so I can look beautiful for my meeting with the doctor.

Sunday surprises me with unexpected rain, and I panic. If this weather keeps up, I will have to postpone my walk with the doctor until the next week, and I don't think I could stand quite this much waiting. But Sarah, who notices me being put off with rain on my one free day tells me that quick showers are common this time of year on the Island, and that the Weather Bureau has forecasted no major downpour. Sure enough, no note arrives from the doctor asking to reschedule our outing, and by the time I finish my dinner the sun is peeking through the clouds and the rain has ceased. I opt for wearing the same skirt and lacy shirtwaist I wore the day I delivered the lily. I'm determined for the doctor to see another side of me than he did the night he rescued me from my attackers, and also, after having had a full view of my bosom, I think it's more provocative to have to use his imagination to recall it as it lies hidden under all that lace. My face is aglow with excitement, so I skip rouge and other artifices. I look just like a well-to-do fully respectable girl, mind you one vain and silly enough to wear dangly earrings on a beach walk. I'm fully pleased with myself, and fully confident as I step out into a glorious island evening to meet my new friend. His carriage is already there. I had ascertained that before descending, as it would not befit a lady to wait.

His face lights up when he sees me, and I relish in the knowledge that not being under the impression of a most shocking attack, I can now observe this man better. I am composed and able to think and analyze. I am also better equipped to exercise my charms, and no longer feel at such a disadvantage because I am not used to dealing with men who have not chosen to be clients. After all, a man is still a man and I do know how to talk to them. They all crave flattery and admiration, and striking the right balance between offering and withholding it will make them crave it more. Perhaps this conversational dance is even more alluring if not paid for. After all, freely bestowed praise should be more credible, as should my curiosity seem about a man I choose to spend time with of my own volition.

The doctor offers me his arm and helps me into his carriage, and this small gallant gesture jolts my earlier composure. The proximity of his body, the glimmer in his dark eyes, it all is more intoxicating than encounters with men I know for sure I will be intimate with. It's as if with my clients I'm drinking the drinks mixed with colored water Madame's bartenders would offer us girls "for our own protection," and with the doctor the real thing. Is desire more rampant in the world outside a brothel's walls, a world where people are expected to be chaste and proper?

"How lovely to see you again, Miss Bonnard," the doctor says, not a trace of irony in his voice. "You are a sight for sore eyes indeed."

I smile and take my time with my answer. "Surely you say that to all the girls."

He laughs, taken off guard, but is smart and quick enough not to point out that he doesn't interact with other girls like me. Or does he? I remember his joke about the condom, and the thought that a respectable man is not necessarily an innocent one brings me both pique and comfort. If only the world were as forgiving of the trespasses of women!

"All the girls are lovely," he points out, "but you, my dear Miss Bonnard, are especially so."

I smile, displaying my perfect white teeth. I don't say any more, as if the compliment is natural.

"And how was your week, doctor?" I ask, as he signals the horses to go.

"Can't complain."

"Please tell me about your practice."

"It's a small practice," he says. "I mostly make house calls, but not everyone can afford those. So I have days when I see patients in my own practice for minor ailments."

"You mean you see them for free?"

"Mostly, yes. Though not many come. It's surprising that poor people are likely to avoid free treatment from a professional, but are quite amenable to spending whatever little money they have on tonics and snake oil."

I laugh. I knew girls in New Orleans who thought their *gris-gris* could prevent pregnancy. "So what kind of people come to you?"

"A few old ladies whose rheumatism is beyond the power of medicine, a newspaper boy who broke his leg, a girl scratched by a cat."

I laugh at this last one. "Do the girls come who entertain sailors?"

"Sometimes," he says.

"And do you send them all to your friend who specializes in syphilis?"

He laughs. "You must forgive me, dear lady. I believe I've offended you."

"I am not easily offended."

"That's a good quality. I believe you are quite the diplomat. There is certainly an art to what you do."

"It's not like medicine. Not nearly as complicated nor as useful as resetting a broken leg."

"Actually," he says, "a broken spirit is a much more delicate and dangerous thing. The work you do is very useful."

"That's me," I say, "an angel," and at this we both laugh so heartily I'm afraid we might frighten the horses.

When we reach the beach, we find that it is covered in white mist and smells delightfully salty. In front of the Pavilion, whose roofs are barely visible through the fog, the doctor entrusts the carriage to an attendant and helps me down. He offers me his hand again. We walk into the mist together. I want to ask more about his business as well as his charity work, about his background, his education, about his patients, his friends, and his pastimes. But a companionable silence has descended upon us and as the mist envelops us in its aura of salt, I am mesmerized by the beauty of simply walking, listening to the waves crash and the cries of gulls, the pleasure of being with someone but not needing to talk. For once, I do not have the obligation to entertain or delight. I am not paid to fill this silence, and my vain desire for the doctor's admiration, for his devotion even, is trumped by my delight at simply being. It's a moment more restful than sleep or than a soothing bath after a difficult night, a moment I can enjoy without strategizing, without wondering what's next.

When I'm tempted to open my mouth to make further inquiries, to seek out opportunities to flatter the doctor, I remind myself of the two English dogs Aristotle promised. I imagine their joy at running free on the beach, imagine their slender bodies darting in and out of the mist, their long legs plunging into the waves.

"Have you ever had dogs?" I ask my silent companion. The question is as lighthearted as it is unexpected.

"Only as a boy. I've always wanted one since, but I've been too busy. How about you?"

"Could you not have one now?"

"I suppose. Though Mrs. Bock is hardly fond of them, nor is she young and spry enough to take care of one."

"Perhaps someone else in your household could?" I'm thinking of the servant girl I saw, though she didn't strike me as intelligent or compassionate enough to be entrusted with the care of a living being. But the doctor's thoughts take him elsewhere for I sense his demeanor change. The look in his eyes grows remote.

"When my wife was alive," he says, "we talked about dogs and children. But those things were not meant for us."

"What happened?" I am used to men opening up about painful things from their past, though it takes some doing, and as much as they love talking about themselves, if they allow themselves to get emotional they end up resenting me for witnessing it.

"She was rather delicate." He stops, looks into the distance. It's obvious he doesn't want to say any more. His face is closed, betraying no emotion, as if he's practiced not letting himself show whatever feelings this revelation brings up in him. Is he hiding pain? Anger? All I can tell is that the doctor does not like talking about this topic. I know how to avoid such closed doors, know how dangerous they can be. The doctor does not seem like the kind of man who would lash out at me for asking, but respecting his privacy seems both kind and wise.

We walk a few steps in silence.

"I would like a dog or a cat," I say. "But can you imagine a dog or a cat in a brothel?"

He laughs. "I would not exactly call the house you live in a brothel."

"Whatever one may call it, high- or low-end, it's what it is and I don't find it shameful. After all, we've already established I'm practically a saint."

We both laugh, and I'm glad the conversation has taken a lighter tone. It's important, though, to not always step away from quicksand.

"So," I say, pausing and looking at his face. "Do you frequent such establishments, doctor?"

His eyes meet mine. His lips curl into a smile. His pupils dilate, and I smile back, for it is clear as day in this moment that the doctor wants me. It is clear too, that I want him, and this is uncharted territory, an exchange of energy not governed by the protocols of a business transaction. There is a frightening kind of freedom here, but perhaps it's impossibility that makes it most alluring. I do not have a bed to call my own to which to invite a man of my own choosing. As for him, his house is guarded by Mrs. Bock.

"Yes," he says. "There is a girl on Postoffice I enjoy seeing. She's in one of the finer houses, though not one as sophisticated as yours."

I smile. "How often do you see her?"

"Perhaps once a week, sometimes more, sometimes less. Our interactions are, how shall I say? Brief."

I laugh. "That seems economical. You are not fond of conversation, then?"

"No. Though I'm sure that for many of your, ahem, patrons it's what's most needed."

"Among other things. And are you then not afraid of the diseases you were so keen to warn me about?"

He laughs heartily. "Knowing the risks, I am not one of the patrons who resist protection. Besides, ironically, some of the girls who charge less are the most insistent."

"They see more men," I say. "It's natural that they are more exposed. I only entertain one client each evening, and they are the most upstanding members of society."

"We all know the very rich are immune to diseases," he says and the irony is not lost on me.

"It is a most interesting life," I say, deflecting.

"You are a most interesting person, Miss Bonnard. I give you that."

"Interesting because wealthy men pay lots of money to spend time with me?"

"Interesting because you are curious about people. You would make a fine scientist."

"I will consider that when I retire."

The mist is clearing now, giving way to the blushing light of sunset. A flock of seagulls flies by, screaming loudly, yet their cries amplify rather than disturb the peace of the marine landscape.

"I have an idea," the doctor says. "If you would meet me again, and perhaps be so generous as to volunteer an hour of your precious time?"

I know he is not asking what I almost wish he would ask. "An hour doing what exactly?"

"What you do best, Miss Bonnard."

I squint my eyes into the dying sun, a hesitant smile on my lips. He laughs.

"By that," he says, "I mean your purely angelic side, the healer in you. I want to try something."

"Try what?"

"I need you to sit at an old man's bedside and be your charming self."

"You want me to seduce one of your patients?"

"I want you to talk to him. I believe you might cheer him up. He is terminally unhappy."

"Is that the nature of his illness?"

"Not entirely. But it's possibly the most dangerous part. Would you accompany me to see him? Perhaps sometime this week?"

I draw circles in the sand with my parasol. "You saved my life," I say. "It would be wrong to begrudge you a small favor."

"Also, you're curious, admit it. You'll find this to be a most interesting old man."

"I'll trust you on that. Though, frankly, most people are interesting, don't you find?"

He smiles at me in the golden light of a glorious sunset. "You are fortunate to think so," he says. "And so am I."

He escorts me off the beach, back to the carriage, and we commence the journey back to town. I cannot help but ask, "Is this why you wanted to meet me? You were hoping I would agree to comfort your patient?"

He looks at me and I hope that my face is beyond lovely in the glow of the dying sun. His eyes gaze into mine, teasing. "What were you hoping for, Miss Bonnard?"

I look away, not merely out of coquettishness, but because his question makes me melt. I hide behind my eyelashes, then meet his eyes again, a question, an invitation between us. "I really do not know," I whisper. "I find that I often do not know exactly what I want. It's much more interesting not to know, in fact."

This seems to satisfy him as well as myself. Sometimes it's best to say a whole lot of nothing, but say it in the most feminine and alluring voice. As the sun dies and we navigate the city streets back to Mrs. Harden's, we settle upon an early afternoon when I can accompany him to the house of his patient. It's true that I'm looking forward to that particular outing, both as an opportunity to see the doctor again and because I am indeed curious about the man he wants me to meet.

In front of the brothel he pauses, takes my hand in his, and brings it to his lips. I shiver.

"Will you think of me," I ask, "when you are with your girl?"

He laughs, biting his lower lip, and I am assured that now that I've said it, it will be impossible for him to do otherwise.

CHAPTER 14
A PROMISING YOUNG ARCHITECT

The next week is slow. Aristotle doesn't visit Mrs. Harden's, though he does send a gift of flowers and chocolates. The clients are unremarkable, except for one. He is new to the brothel, new to Galveston even. Mr. Brighton is an accomplished architect, young to be so successful, and most good-looking, an Adonis with chiseled features and curly blond hair, dressed in an exceptionally well-cut suit. He comes in as the guest of another client, a portly cotton trader for whom Brighton is designing a grand new home. The visit to Mrs. Harden's, and a night with the most expensive woman in Galveston, is a thank you gift to express appreciation for the project.

I like Brighton, and over dinner I enjoy talking to him. We have retreated to a private dining room, while the cotton trader, more brash than his architect, has taken two other girls into a suite for his own amusement. I am thankful we could excuse ourselves from that raucous party, as the man I'm to entertain seems intelligent and refined, and I welcome the opportunity to dine with him alone. We talk about the Island and he tells me about the different styles of houses being built, about a need to raise most constructions as a precaution against storms, which some ignore, believing the Island is unlikely to be hit. It's informative and pleasant, but the conversation gets trickier once he brings up Paris. He wants to know my opinion on Hausmann, wants to know which *arrondissement* I lived in. Not finding a suitable opportunity to suggest yet not completely admit that my Paris story is a joke of sorts, I change topics and start talking about the Eiffel Tower, which I have read about and even seen pictures of in the papers. I find that he likes the construction, and we both agree that it is striking, modern, and a pleasant addition to the city. I redirect our exchange back to Galveston, and we talk about the Beach Pavilion. I then ask his opinion about various other buildings, ask what he thinks of the hotel I stayed in, ask what he thinks makes a fine hotel.

Our supper goes by pleasantly enough, and when we make our way to one of the rooms, I find myself both relieved and regretful that it is over.

This is definitely a most interesting man to talk to, but our conversation is dangerous. I resolve to read up on Parisian architecture before our next meeting.

In the room, Mr. Brighton stretches out on the bed and reaches for a cigar, which he does not want me to light. I stand before him smiling, wondering for a second if I should commence my languorous dance. This seems to be a man who would appreciate the irony. But a sudden inspiration directs me to lie down next to him instead. He looks at me like someone assessing a precious artifact, but does not touch me. My instincts tell me to wait. Finally, his fingers caress my cheek ever so lightly. Again, it's as if he were touching a work of art, not a flesh and blood woman.

"Let me save both of us some embarrassment, my dear," he says. "You sure are pretty, and I love a pretty girl, especially one who dresses well and makes good conversation. For a few minutes there, during dinner, I thought this might be worth a try. But it's not going to work."

It finally dawns on me, what I should have sensed from the beginning, except in his case it is not obvious at all, even to me, with my experience and my gift for being observant. I look at him, searching for clues I've missed before. *No,* I think. There is nothing that gives him away.

"You don't like women?" I ask. "I would have never guessed."

"Good."

"Your client obviously doesn't know," I say. He lifts his eyebrows. "You came because you didn't want him to suspect?"

"I also thought I might try. An experiment. But no, it's not worth embarrassing us both."

"You would know," I say, for in the past I've attempted to help men like him overcome their attraction to their own gender, and the attempts were most awkward indeed. "In fact, I venture to say, you will be happier accepting certain things than trying to change them."

"How very wise," he says in a cutting tone. "I suppose that verdict is worth my client's money?"

"I meant no offense. Your secret will be safe with me."

"I would hope so. Not only do you have a pretty penny to gain from your discretion, but, darling Aimée, we all have secrets, don't we?"

His eyes on me are amused, not unkind, yet I feel as if a beloved pet had unexpectedly bit me.

"Now, now," he says. "Don't look so disappointed, my love. I've absolutely no intention of telling anyone you've never been to Paris. In fact, I shall show you some magazines, some architectural gazettes, and some maps, and help you do a better job faking familiarity with the city. We shall secretly study together during our *rendezvous* and become friends. It will be marvelous! You can come to my office and we can pour over your study materials at leisure!"

"I... Everyone else knows it's a joke!" I protest. "I hardly need any expertise, it's not like men come here to discuss my life and travels."

"Yes," he says. "Everyone else is taken by your charm and too dazzled to look beyond the surface. What I see is a bit deeper, though. You, my dear, have a secret. It's not the lie about Paris, which is transparent enough, and in its own way so stupid it is clever. It's like you're hiding something in plain sight. But it's the necessity of the lie in the first place that I find intriguing."

"A jealous lover in Atlanta," I say hastily. "Not a charming thing to bring up."

He smirks. "And not the truth either. Not that I have any interest in uncovering what you wish to hide. All I ask for is absolute discretion."

"You already have that. My services include discretion. No need to threaten me."

"I mean absolute discretion. You won't discuss me even with your madam. And when I make arrangements for you to come see me in my home, you will pretend I want what all the other men want."

"I don't visit men in their homes."

"You'll visit me. You'll find it pleasant. You'll have to be doubly discreet, of course. I don't want it known around town that I had a... professional in my home. But a few vague rumors about an elusive veiled lady coming to see me would be a good investment."

"Why even do that? I'm sure nobody questions you, and—"

"There's a lovely young lady in one of the social groups I frequent who has a notion that I might propose matrimony."

"It's not unheard of," I say.

"I have considered it. It's part of why tonight's experiment was useful. I would think it most cruel to marry a young woman not knowing if I could possibly change my ways. And no. If I'm not tempted to try with you, I've not a chance with her."

"Her loss, and mine too," I say. "I'm sure she will be disappointed, but it's kind of you to want to spare her a lifetime of suffering."

"She'll find someone more suitable. Now, will you visit me?"

I nod. The glimpse he just offered of himself as a conflicted young man trying to do the right thing is more convincing than his subtle threats.

"I sense you're warming to me, but you're still ill at ease, darling," he says, caressing my hair. I'm starting to get used to being petted as if I were a doll or an Angora cat. "What can I do to help you trust me? Because, really, I have evolved to be most intuitive – someone in my position has to be. And I can sense it with certainty, that you and I could have some fun together. Just not of an intimate nature."

I cannot help it, my fear only deepens, and I hate to suspect that he might be able to sniff it out, like a highly trained hunting dog.

"I mean you no harm, dear girl. Perhaps I was mistaken to mention Paris, but I do feel that you are overall practical and direct and I truly can help you. We can help each other. You'll be an expert in Hausmann boulevards before you know it." He looks at me and smiles, now examining a strand of my hair as if it were a fine fabric he's considering for one of his projects. "Whatever your secret, it cannot be as dark as you think it is. I can sense that, just as I can sense you're hiding something. Would it put you at ease if perhaps we started by trading lesser secrets? Tell me if you're in love with any of your clients!"

I laugh. He sits up in bed, Turkish style, and offers me the cigar. I shake my head. After all, this man is not interested in me faking enjoyment in things I don't truly enjoy. I can shed at least one layer of pretense with him, and it's interesting to see that having revealed his own secret, his demeanor has changed too, his mannerisms, his voice even. They now let me see what I would have never guessed about him before. I wonder how hard it must be to spend so much of one's life watching one's every move, one's every inflection, pretending all the time, never letting one's guard down.

"Of course, you are too smart to fall for your clients, aren't you? But surely you might have at least a little infatuation?"

"I do have a favorite client."

"Is it me?" We both laugh. "Come on, lovely girl, tell me all about him."

"I won't," I say smiling. "You're not the only one who benefits from my discretion. I don't discuss my clients."

"Good girl! But you did look away, and so I know there's more. Is it perhaps someone who's not a client whom you fancy?"

"Perhaps," I admit.

"Oh, excellent! Excellent, darling! Now that is a man you could freely discuss, don't you think? And don't you wish they would bring us more cake? I see you don't drink much, and neither do I, it absolutely ruins one's complexion. But a little more cake wouldn't hurt us, would it?"

"I don't know about cake," I say. "And I don't know about the type of confession you're interested in. What I do think would be most recommendable in our situation is a pillow fight."

"A pillow fight?" He seems both appalled and delighted.

"Well," I say. "It's customary for people to make a bit of noise from behind these doors. And also, to emerge a bit disheveled. Lastly, too, I think it would be supremely satisfying to smack your smug face with a pillow!" I do indeed take one of the lovely down-filled cushions and throw it at his head. He retaliates without missing a beat, and soon enough we're struggling and laughing, properly mussing up the sheets and working up a sweat.

By the end of the night, I feel torn between being charmed and utterly apprehensive. This could indeed be an amusing new acquaintance. I am fascinated by his worldliness and his chameleon ways, the art of transformation he's perfected. But even if I do know his secret, how safe is mine with him? I do enjoy his company, and it could all be a marvelous diversion, but I feel pressured into it, and I don't like the subtle threat that runs through our budding camaraderie like a crack through a precious porcelain vase.

CHAPTER 15
THE PATIENT

By Wednesday I have forgotten all about Mr. Brighton. I've made myself forget. After all, he's not that important. He might not even return. And if he wishes for me to visit him in his office or in his house, Mrs. Harden might not agree to the arrangement, and if she does, I might as well tell him I find Hausmann boring, am not interested in learning about Parisian boulevards, and would rather he tell me interesting things about his work here in Galveston. I think the point he was trying to make is that he has as little interest in destroying me as I do in destroying him. And don't people already suspect that I made up my life story? Have I not already ascertained that they do not care? For if I'm not from Paris I could be from a million other places, and the mere knowledge that I've embellished my personal mythology, as any clever girl would do, does not mean they can link me to my sordid past in New Orleans. The only one who might be able to do so is probably Ardoin, but since he hasn't seen me as of late, would he too not have forgotten?

In any case, come Wednesday I do not wish to trouble myself thinking about these most unpleasant matters, because I have a meeting with the doctor in the early afternoon, and I am most curious to meet his mysterious patient. Of course, going anywhere in the early afternoon for me is akin to having an early morning appointment for others. I have more coffee than usual, and rush through my dinner so I can still devote enough time to my toilette. The doctor awaits me in front of the brothel.

"You look lovely," he says. "I only wish my patient could actually see you!"

"We are not going there?" I ask, confused.

"We are, my dear lady. But the problem, one among many, in fact, is that my patient is blind."

I have never before entertained a blind man. What I've heard is that in the case of such an infirmity all other senses are heightened. Touch and scent contribute more to passion than eyesight does, but I am not to entertain this man in my usual fashion. I am merely to talk to him. Will my voice alone be compelling enough if he can't see how pretty I'm turned out?

We stop in front of a large clapboard house, ring the doorbell, and are shown in by a young Irish servant.

"Miss Bonnard is here to read to Mr. Cohen," Tarner says. "She is the actress I was telling you about. I think it might help improve his mood."

The girl gives me a humorless nod. She's a thin Irish girl, hair as red as Ruby's, or perhaps even lovelier. After all, hers is natural, and I'd bet one week's wages that Ruby's is not. This girl here would be pretty if one could overlook the lack of substance to her figure, and a certain look in her eyes that gives her an air of utmost gravity mixed with a tinge of panic, a bit like a hunted animal. I am reminded that many come to Galveston from foreign shores, and that among them there are certainly those with a story they wish to bury. The thought emboldens me. Surely it's more productive to put us all to good use in our respective industries than it is to dig up our pasts.

"I want to show you something before you meet Mr. Cohen," the doctor says to me, and leads me into a vast salon succumbed in darkness. As he turns on the lights and my eyes adjust, I see that the room is full, floor to ceiling, of large oil paintings, some framed in sumptuous golden frames, some unframed, leaning against the walls. I don't fancy myself a connoisseur of art, but these paintings are most striking. Landscapes open in front of my eyes, marshes and swamps and beaches inundated by the most beautiful light, egrets rising majestic from among lush Gulf Coast greenery, their white feathers a striking contrast to the darkness of bayous and marshes, waves crashing to shore, sea foam shining in the sunlight. I can feel the hot sand, feel the cool respite of each bluish shadow, the motion of each wave, the awe of encountering each bird and basking under each open sky. A few portraits look down upon me too, women's eyes truly alive, questioning, hoping, their smiles suggesting half-uttered promises, their hair waiting to be unfastened from tight buns, their jewelry sparkling as if real. Island buildings shine in the bright Galveston sun and take respite in shade. They look real and yet they look painted, for the colors are rich and vibrant and I can see the brushstrokes. So luscious is the texture that I actually want to touch it. I am transfixed, enchanted, something that rarely happens to me in the presence of art, for I am more interested in earthly pleasures and would choose a scrumptious meal over a painting any day. But these are different. They do something I didn't think a mere object could do.

Tarner watches me, and he looks pleased. "You seem to like them," he says.

"Yes. These are remarkable. Your patient... He is a collector?"

"He was an artist. A most prolific artist. He painted all of these and more."

"And he is blind?" I am horrified, aware of a huge loss, a huge sadness. No wonder Tarner's patient is morose. Tarner takes in the understanding dawning on my face.

"Now you know why he needs comforting. I think you will be good for him."

But I am speechless. "I need a moment," I say.

"Take your time."

I wander through the room as if lost. I look at the paintings – a collection of enchantment but also a map of a loss so great I'm not sure the vast ocean could contain it. Finally, I nod to Tarner. "Thank you," he says, but as he leads me up the stairs and into the sickroom, I am more nervous than I was even before my very first intimate encounter with a man, when I was a silly inexperienced girl of fifteen making her debut at Madame Rouge's.

The doctor pauses before a door. He knocks, and I find myself dreading what we'll find inside. A man's voice answers, and the doctor pushes the door open. The room is dark and smells like an old person – medicine and urine, dust, and boredom. I hesitate, but step inside. The old man sitting up in bed is grey and disheveled, his eyes vacant.

"I have brought my friend, Miss Bonnard," the doctor says. "She is a talented actress and she's come to talk to you and cheer you up. Aimée, this is Mr. Cohen."

"Hello, Mr. Cohen," I say in a voice that doesn't betray my apprehension at being here. Perhaps the doctor is right, and I am an actress after all.

"An actress," Mr. Cohen says, his cracking voice containing no enthusiasm. "What kind of acting do you do and where?"

I look at the doctor, but obviously he cannot whisper my lines. At a loss as to what to invent, I decide to take a gamble. If I make the old man laugh it's half a battle won. "At a very fine house on Postoffice," I say. "I do some quite remarkable acting for one hundred dollars a night." It is only the doctor who laughs.

"I have no use for that," Cohen says. "No, no, that all is long gone like everything else. Claude, you did not pay the lass that ungodly sum, did you?"

"I'm here as a friend, Mr. Cohen."

"Well," he says. "I can't make any use of you, so what's the point?"

"I actually was hoping to talk to you. Do you mind if I sit by your bedside?"

Tarner brings me a chair. "May we have some privacy, doctor?" I say, although I don't know that being alone with the old man will help matters. Still, I try. I ask him if perhaps he'd like me to read to him. "Deirdre, my servant, does that," he says gruffly.

"That's a good thing," I say, picturing the redhead downstairs working her way methodically through a book, reading in a voice that lacks inflection.

Or perhaps I'm being unkind. If she puts her sadness into the reading, it might be touching indeed.

"Yes," he says. "Marvelous. What else you got?"

"Well," I say, hedging my bets and deciding if I should attempt this or not. "I was hoping you might want to tell me about your paintings?"

"What about them?"

"The nature scenes," I say, thinking quickly. "They are so luminous. Did you actually paint them outside?"

"Do you know anything about art, miss?"

"Nothing at all, honestly. And I've never much cared to pay attention to it. Which is why it's remarkable that they made such an impression on me."

"And what impression is that?"

"I could feel them. It's as if I could feel myself there, in the marshes, with the herons and egrets, the air salty, the sun too hot in my face. I could hear the waves. And then again in other paintings I was in the shade and there was a light breeze. I could feel everything as if I was in nature, and yet I also could feel the paint in a way, never lost the awareness that I'm looking at paint, that I can trace the brushstrokes, and the thickness of it. It made me want to touch them."

"That so?" he asks. I can't tell yet if he's warming to me or not.

"Do you ever touch your paintings?"

"No."

"Would you like to try?"

He laughs. "You got some funny notions, girlie."

"Yes, sir. Lots. But I think it might help. I mean, part of the pleasure is the texture, is it not?"

"I suppose. I never thought of it that way."

"But you must have been aware of the texture when painting, were you not?"

"It's not all planned and calculated. It's art."

"I can relate to that with my acting," I say.

At this he finally laughs. "Where did Claude find you?"

"In an alley," I say. "I got attacked one night as I stayed out too late on my evening walk, and he saved me. And where did he find you?"

"In this bed, where else?"

"Have you been bedridden for long?"

"I am not bedridden. I've no reason to get up."

"Have you been blind long?"

"Now you don't mince words, do you?"

"What's the point? It seems that I'm unlikely to get you more upset than you already are, and if I'm to be of any assistance, I need to learn a bit about you."

86

"And of what assistance could you possibly be? I sure can't paint you. As for other things, I'm afraid I'm no longer interested."

"I'm mostly good at keeping people company. And helping them feel better. It's not just the physical aspect of the encounters that helps with that, you know? Some men are in need of good conversation, perhaps a new perspective?"

"So you have come to tell me stories of your wild and crazy nights?"

"It's my nature to be discreet and the services I offer require it. Besides, I bet you have better stories to tell than I do."

"Nobody's ever paid me a hundred dollars a night," he says.

"I doubt it. How much did you charge for your paintings?" At this, again, he laughs, and his laughter is easier, less stale. "Also, did you go with girls like me, or not so much?"

"I didn't have to, back in my heyday," he says. "I had more women throwing themselves at me than I knew what to do with. But I would sometimes pay girls like you to sit for me as models."

"Naked?"

"Sometimes, though that was not always the challenge. I could get my lovers to pose nude, but it was harder to get a woman to sit still for long enough if I didn't pay her."

"I've never sat for an artist."

"Well, you're a good decade too late if you wanted to sit for me."

"That, sir, is entirely my loss."

CHAPTER 16
A PARTNERSHIP OF SORTS

I wouldn't say the meeting is a great success. The old man is neither charmed nor amused. This will take some doing. But it's the sort of challenge I cannot resist. As I descend the stairs to find Tarner waiting for me, I am determined to return to this house and find a way to reach Cohen, to pull him out of his loneliness and loss, and get him to have a good time. Some sparks of joy must still be hidden somewhere inside him. I'm determined to find them and pull them out.

"Thank you," Tarner says, before I even had a chance to tell him how the visit went. "That was kind and generous of you. I know he isn't easy to talk to."

"I've encountered worse," I say, though as many difficult clients as I've had, I can't think of one who is quite so justifiably closed off as Cohen. "I'd like to come talk to him again, if possible."

Tarner smiles. "Ambitious lady."

"I also wonder, does he ever sit outside?"

"He doesn't want to. I've suggested it repeatedly."

"I'll work on that."

And thus a new partnership is formed. I wonder if this is part of the appeal for me. Part of why I want to help Cohen. A partnership of sorts with the doctor is something I can't resist. And I do like to imagine, given the smile in his eyes, that he welcomes a partnership of sorts with me as well.

"I wish it weren't too hot for a walk," he says, as we leave Cohen's home. The sun is blinding and its heat has fangs. The tender moisture in the salty air seems gone.

"I wish so too. But perhaps there might be somewhere for us to take a coffee in a cool place instead? I quite like a coffee at this time of day, before getting ready for my evening."

He takes me to the lobby of one of the hotels. Being there with him is surreal. I think of the rooms upstairs, of the possibility of us being alone. I sip my cup of temptation and relish in the fantasy.

"You are not afraid of being seen with me?" I ask.

He laughs. "People tend to be very forgiving when it comes to a man's virtue as opposed to a woman's. Besides, a little blemish might rid me of all the society ladies insisting to introduce me to their daughters."

"Happy to serve," I say. I briefly think of Brighton. Empathy finally finds me, and I'm determined to cast my own fears aside next time I see him and reassure my client that he is beyond suspicion.

Coffee with Dr. Tarner ends too soon. We talk mostly of Cohen, and of things he could possibly still enjoy. We discuss our feelings of guilt, too, for we both feel presumptuous for imagining that certain experiences might still appeal to him when what he loves best and is so good at is forever lost.

"I wonder if this is how I'll feel when my looks are gone, and I shall have to retire," I say, and then feel silly. Comparing my work to Cohen's is blasphemy.

Tarner studies me carefully. "You, my lady, will always be beautiful. Besides, surely you are aware that your talent doesn't lie in your looks. After all, you are about to work your magic on a man who can't see you."

"Perhaps I shall reprofile as a nurse," I say lightly, but my words sound shallow. "Surely, doctor, you are not one of those do-gooders trying to save my soul."

"That would be tedious. I find the self-righteous quite boring. No, I was first and foremost curious what would happen if you met Cohen. And I am most definitely invested in his improvement."

"What ails him beside blindness?"

The doctor takes a sip of his own coffee. He seems lost in thought for a moment. "Not much, actually. For a man his age he appears to be very healthy. But melancholy can be as dangerous as any illness. In fact, it can be more dangerous."

"So you are treating him for that?"

"Yes and no. Modern medicine is ill equipped to deal with ailments of the soul, I'm afraid. I was first called to see him for a passing stomach problem, nothing a little baking soda couldn't cure. But I took a personal interest in him, and luckily he doesn't decline my visits. It's what gives me hope that perhaps he has not given up entirely."

"He has been blind for a whole decade?"

"The loss was gradual, but from what I understand it started then."

"And that's when he took to his room?"

"Not immediately, but in time."

"I will try to get him out of there," I say, though I have no guarantee that being outside will bring Cohen much happiness.

CHAPTER 17
MR. BRIGHTON'S OFFICE

I return to Mrs. Harden's with a heavy heart. Being in the hotel reminded me of my days of freedom before I entered this house. As I get ready for the evening ahead, I try to remind myself that my life holds much adventure and enchantment, and that during my coffee with the doctor, I have compared not being able to work with blindness. Why then do I feel resentful over having the evening taken away from me? I remind myself that the doctor too had to return to patient visits and other mundane concerns. Nobody besides the independently wealthy gets to while away their days doing as they please, do they? And among people who have to work, I am lucky to have a most interesting and profitable occupation.

A few days later, my assignment for the evening consists of visiting Mr. Brighton at his office after hours, sneaking in through a back entrance when everyone in the building is gone. Having talked myself out of my apprehension about him, I end up looking forward to the outing. After all, my evenings don't usually contain excursions away from the brothel, so this is a new kind of adventure. Also, his request to see me in his office strikes me as peculiar in the most interesting kind of way. I get the impression that he's not ready yet to let the wagging tongues suspect that he has a secret love interest. I wonder if he's still hoping he might succumb to my womanly charms, but my instincts tell me not to press him for answers.

Brighton's office is in a four-story building downtown. Being close to the port and all its commerce energizes me. He meets me at the back door, where I have presented myself wearing a hat with a veil, and leads me up three flights of stairs, then into a room with high ceilings, wood paneling, and wide windows overlooking rooftops and palm trees, the water beckoning like a promise in the distance. Inside this ample room, several large tables offer up a vast landscape of maps and plans.

Brighton gives me a tour of his offices. I stand transfixed in front of a window overlooking the port. He asks me to position myself in such a way that my silhouette is obscured by the thick velvet drapes. Wondering if my suppositions about the purpose of my visit are correct, I hide as instructed and enjoy the beautiful view. I see the masts of sailboats, the roofs of warehouses, the steam rising from ships. It all looks fascinating. Brighton points out some of the buildings we see. At a window facing in the other direction, he shows me the rooftops of the Beach Pavilion visible in the distance, explains some of the other landmarks. The Trueheart-Adriance Building, he says, is among his favorites. I can barely see it from here, but I know the building he's referring to, its elegant windows and intricate façade making it quite remarkable, more suited, in my mind for a shop selling hats or jewelry than the real estate offices it houses. Brighton explains with great admiration that it was designed by Nicholas Clayton, just like the Beach Pavilion and some other of the more notable island edifices.

After this interesting exposition on our most remarkable view, he guides me into a smaller room that must be his private office. There he unrolls maps of Paris, and traces my fingers over the grand boulevards. His guidance seems protective, indulgent. Being so close to him, and relaxing into his easy friendly presence, I don't know why I was ever afraid of him. I can only hope that he too is feeling more comfortable around me, hopefully comfortable enough to try the thing I still suspect he might want to accomplish. If I'm correct in my suppositions, I must say I admire his plan to bring me here where he feels most at ease, and create a feeling of complicity between us by studying the maps together.

There are a few moments when we stand so close, our pose would invite intimacy if this were a man susceptible to the charms of women. But no current of electricity passes between us, no touch lingers longer than necessary, no leaning in is prolonged and teased out into desire. I sense a few opportunities to initiate amorous contact, but given the situation, I decide to wait and see first if nature might take the lead. Nature, however, seems to have different plans for handsome Mr. Brighton. Perhaps more time together might serve us well. If he's still nurturing the feeble hope that his experiment with a woman selling her body might be successful, I find it best to allow him to fully relax around me, then let him take the lead.

After the architecture lesson, which is about as unnecessary as my presence here, but more pleasant than I'd thought possible, we sit on a leather divan meant for clients, and he offers me an assortment of bonbons presented in a pretty metal box. I allow myself to have several, and as I enjoy them, I tease Brighton, asking about his romantic exploits. He's not ready to share, so I regale him with the only tale I myself feel free to disclose.

The only story I have of a man not my client is the one of my acquaintance with Dr. Tarner. It's also the only story I have where there is a little bit of romantic tension. Aristotle briefly crosses my mind – Aristotle with whom my dealings are like a complex dance. But I need to keep my relationship with him confidential. So I tell Brighton about the doctor instead. I even tell him about my visit to the blind artist and my desire to find ways to cheer him up.

"You met Cohen?" Brighton is awestruck. "My darling, you do realize the man is a genius, a giant!"

"I saw his paintings," I say. "They are amazing."

"Indeed. You are lucky to have seen them. I have only had the fortune of seeing a handful in person. But of course, you do realize that for every painting still in that house, there are many others in private collections all around the country – the world, in fact."

I allow myself yet another bonbon, because Brighton's enthusiasm about Cohen, his familiarity with his work, strikes me as something that needs to be celebrated. I think of all the paintings Cohen must have sold. There's something there, something for me to grasp, but I don't know yet what it is.

"Where did you see his work?" I ask.

"The most striking painting of his I saw," he says, slowly unwrapping a bonbon of his own, "was in Paris, in a private residence. It is a portrait of a dear friend of mine. A lady. In fact, now that I think of it, you, my darling, remind me of her."

"How did she come to have it?"

"He used to spend summers in Europe before he went blind. It was quite difficult for her to get a commission while he was in Paris, but she persisted. She's a beautiful lady with great connections and a lot of money, so she arranged to be introduced to him, and while she paid a handsome sum for the painting, her charm helped in convincing him too. She loves to tell the story."

"Is she..." I ask. "Is she, like me, a..."

My companion actually blushes.

"There's no need to be embarrassed," I say, feeling a sudden fondness for him. "I'm not ashamed of what I do, and sometimes I feel that I'm really helping. And you have nothing to be ashamed of either, Mr. Brighton. You have a right to be who you are and if the world were more understanding you wouldn't need the help of women such as myself and your friend in Paris. Though, frankly, if we were all free to be, don't you think we might seek out each other's company anyway, just because we enjoy spending time together?"

He smiles at this. "So you're saying that it's not so strange that some of my dearest friends are women whose company I pay for?"

"I don't much mind the money," I say, laughing. "I'm sure your other friends enjoy it as well."

"She was a showgirl," he tells me, ever so tactfully shifting the conversation away from the money matter. "My friend in Paris. But she also entertained men privately on the side. Kind of like you do. I used to love going with her to the popular cafés. And I used to love going to occasional dinners in her private residence. It's where I saw the painting. In any case, she's older than I am by a few decades, but she's one of those rare ageless people, still ravishing, still the great seductress."

My whole being lights up at his words. I love to believe that there are women who don't lose their appeal with age, for among all my demons, losing my beauty is almost as scary as the specter of Marie.

"Is her home nice?" I ask, looking for a distraction from my sudden glimpse into the abyss.

"Lovely. And mind you, it's very expensive to have a decent apartment in Paris. Hers is a three-room apartment overlooking the Boulevard Saint Michel. It was left to her by a former lover."

"Lucky," I say, and the thought of the house Aristotle promised crosses my mind. I can't decide if thinking of it fills me with hope or dread.

That evening, we sit and talk, and eat bonbons. There are no attempts at physical intimacy, but I know that what is won, at great expense to Brighton, and with no sacrifice on my part, is a feeling of camaraderie and even warmth between the two of us. Perhaps this will help advance matters during our next encounter. For while I am amazed at the amount of money he's willing to invest in a project that might very well fail, I welcome the opportunity of seeing him again. He tells me he has a room for me in his home, and that our next encounter will involve me spending the night there. He has photographs of the Paris showgirl to show me. Her name is Odette. Which strikes me as a charming name indeed. I am most curious about her, yet a bit apprehensive. Odette is the name of a young girl, a slip of a girl in fact, sweet, and perhaps a little mischievous. But the lady in question is older. Will looking at her face be a reminder of what I might become?

CHAPTER 18
STRANGE BEHAVIOR

As I return to Mrs. Harden's, I decide not to disturb Sarah before going to bed. I am not hungry, and I can manage a perfunctory toilette on my own. I'm looking forward to having time to read for once. It's still early compared to my other nights, and having engaged intellectually but not physically, I am not tired. I climb up the stairs with a smile on my lips, looking forward to solitude and reading, when Ruby descends upon me like a dark cloud. She's coming out of her room, the room she both sleeps and entertains in, because I am the only girl at Mrs. Harden's who enjoys the luxury of not seeing clients in my own bed. She's carrying an empty decanter, which means her client is probably still there, waiting for more drink. She stops and looks at me in a most peculiar way, a tiny smirk forming at the corner of her lips. Her green eyes glimmer like a cat's in the semi-dark hallway. I feel the tiny hairs on the back of my neck rising. Is there a ghost in the room with us? Determined to continue walking, I nod as a perfunctory greeting, then pry my eyes away from hers. I stumble, almost falling down the stairs, and Ruby lets out a laugh that sounds like the cry of a bird. I grab the banister and hurry on to my room, and there I cannot shake the disquiet that seized me.

Calm down, I tell myself, as I wash up and slip into a light chemise. *She hates you, that's all. She's jealous. And probably still spiteful over her torn dress and Mrs. Harden slapping her.* But those eyes on me, they were so knowing. Am I imagining things? Or has the silly girl cursed me? Can Ruby possibly have such powers?

Marie once told me that it was green-eyed women who were best suited to the occult. But no, I cannot invite Marie into my room tonight. Not if I am to enjoy what's left of my evening. Not if I am to sleep. Was Marie the ghost I felt during my strange encounter with Ruby? Has Ruby summoned her? Can she do that? Why would I even entertain such a possibility? Ruby is not intelligent enough to communicate with the dearly departed. Her green eyes might be beautiful, but they hide no secret powers, only jealousy and spite.

There was something in her sharp laugh, though, as I stumbled on the stairs, something in the way I lost my footing under her gaze, that reminded me of that last night in New Orleans, of Marie mocking me in front of those two dreadful clients, of the ice chips in my dress, her cruel smirk as she spoke out loud what was meant to be a secret between us, a secret meant to protect us. I lost my composure that night too, lost my power, failed to take the right course of action. I allowed Marie's mockery to rattle me, and in a much smaller, much less significant way, I allowed Ruby to do the same tonight. I am determined not to give either of these women that much power.

I try to let my mind be absorbed by my book. I find it hard to concentrate at first, but eventually the story grips me and I forget about my torment. In my sleep, though, Marie returns. In my dreams she is there, looking at me with her own green eyes. "You cannot hide from me, Yvonne. I am part of you, I will always find you. How do you like that, little butterfly?"

I awake with a start. It's early still, the house asleep, morning birds I never get to hear whistling outside. I open the window, let the breeze and sunshine reassure me that I am in a beautiful place, that I have a most beautiful life. I will not let Marie spoil this for me. And I will most certainly not allow a dim-witted girl like Ruby to steal even a shred of my peace. I wrap myself in my favorite silk wrap and descend to the kitchen. There I help myself to fresh coffee from a percolator on the stove, hot milk too, and a bun. I take these up to my room to enjoy while getting dressed. I don't wish to call for Sarah this early, so I lace my corset as best I can, then, my breakfast completed, and the strong coffee dancing through my veins, I go outside and enjoy the rare luxury of a walk on the beach before it gets too hot. I delight in the crashing of waves, the salty air, the happy energy of sandpipers digging in the wet sand. When I return to Mrs. Harden's, I do ring for Sarah and ask her to bring a proper breakfast.

In the afternoon, Mrs. Harden calls me into her quarters to ask how my evening with Brighton went. She seems most pleased when I tell her it was most successful, and I myself am pleased with myself for being able to keep his secret without outwardly lying. She doesn't need to know our mutual enjoyment went only as far as studying maps of a city I've never been to, eating bonbons, and talking. Luckily, she's not eager for details. Instead, she does not hesitate to express her concern over the circles she notices under my eyes – my early morning beginning to take its toll. "You are seeing Aristotle tonight. You cannot afford to look tired. And to think that for once you've had an early evening." She rummages through her cupboard to look for a healing mix of herbs. She advises that I ask Sarah to boil these, then cool the resulting brew and prepare a compress I am to keep over my closed eyes for at least an hour.

As her back is turned, and her attention elsewhere, I take the opportunity to steal a glance at her ledger. I look at Ruby's name, carefully written several lines under mine, as her price is lower. I look at the name of Ruby's last client. Ardoin. Should I be afraid? Did her laughter last night indicate that she knows things I don't want anyone to know? Is the world truly closing in on me and my secrets?

"Here," Mrs. Harden says, handing me a jar in which I see, among other dried things, the round buds of chamomile flowers. I open the lid and take a whiff. The mixture smells sweet and mysterious. "Don't let the compress get too cold, though obviously it must cool and be pleasant to the touch. And if this doesn't help, you might try a silver spoon you hold first to a block of ice. We're having some delivered shortly for tonight. And I'll make sure your dining room has special lighting."

The compress helps and it doesn't. I know this from previous experience, but I don't say it to Mrs. Harden. By early afternoon the puffiness under my eyes looks better, but a most bothersome headache, the result of not sleeping enough and compensating with too much coffee, won't leave me alone. I try to doze with the stupid compress over my eyes. Instead, I'm trapped, fully conscious behind my closed eyelids. I will not allow Marie near me, nor Ruby, nor Ardoin. Instead, I make myself think of Cohen, of his work, of the show girl in Paris. I wonder if perhaps it would help if I talked to him about her. If recalling the story would be entertaining to the blind artist.

How many similar stories does Cohen have? How many people's lives has his work touched? Would it amuse or encourage him to think of the other paintings, the ones not present in his home? I wonder if he's kept in touch with their owners, if learning how the paintings' stories have progressed could possibly help his state of mind. Surely, there would be correspondence. I wonder who kept up with his letter writing after he went blind. The sad skinny Irish servant? I doubt it. Does Cohen have a secretary? Does he need one?

I sit up, and the vile compress falls off my face, staining my dress. I watch the yellow liquid seep into the white fabric. Perhaps I could offer to write some letters and find out more about how Cohen's favorite paintings are faring. Why read him novels when I could read him correspondence about his work and the people enjoying it? Emboldened by this thought, I resolve to ignore my headache and have a lovely time with Aristotle. I wear the necklace he likes, the crystal dangling between my breasts. But I won't let him see it until after dinner.

Sadly for me, Aristotle is not hungry, nor is he his jovial self. He seems distracted, and he rushes me through the meal, something that's not in line with his usual habits. We pass quickly to the other room, me stifling hunger pangs as I leave most of my shrimp uneaten on my plate. There, he doesn't take the time to undress or admire me. He completes the act quickly and somewhat brusquely, with us both standing up against the wall, almost fully dressed. I feign pleasure, but Aristotle seems too far away to notice.

"Good," he says afterwards. "That helped. Thank you, my dear." He adjusts his clothes and is out the door before I even have time to wonder why, if he needed such a quick fix, he would spend an outrageous sum of money on a full night with me, when there are many girls in this town renting by the quarter hour. Instead of being happy I get to once again enjoy an early night, I have a sudden impulse to cry like an abandoned lover. Obviously, I do no such thing. It's likely lack of sleep that makes me feel misty-eyed. It's not something that happens often. I didn't even cry in New Orleans when Marie died and I had to flee. The last time I did cry that I can remember, real tears, real sobs, real heartache, was when we buried Maw Maw, then later when they wouldn't let me keep her cat. But I can't think of Maw Maw now, or tears will start, and my eyes will be even puffier tomorrow.

Determined to banish my irrational malaise, I slip back into the dining room, pick up my neatly folded dinner napkin, and eat every bite of the shrimp left on my plate. I am still hungry so I decide to finish Aristotle's portion too. His vegetables also, his rice. The man barely touched his food.

There's something naughty about finishing a client's meal after he's gone, but it's as if the compartment of my soul that would normally delight in such behavior is now closed. I cannot be amused, and the food barely satisfies my hunger. I look at myself in the mirror above the table, and though, true to Mrs. Harden's promise, dim lights were arranged in the room to flatter my complexion, what I see is a woman who is not beautiful, but sad, sad in a most profound and ridiculous way. I look away from the ghastly sight, banish my most negative thoughts, and continue eating.

Once the plates are properly cleaned, I push away my chair and make my way upstairs. I knock on Sarah's door and ask her to come prepare my bath, then bring me every dessert in the house. I see a flicker in her eye. Is it mockery? Is it because I'm growing fat? I hide my body from her as best I can with a towel. Tomorrow I resolve to eat less and walk more. But tonight I must have all the sweets.

CHAPTER 19
CORRESPONDENCE

I awake nauseated and with my body twisted by cramps. It dawns on me why I was suddenly seized by melancholy and doubt the night before. Why I was so hungry. The curse is here, the bloody monthly curse. Mrs. Harden will be angry for I forgot and failed to give her proper warning. Though she herself keeps notes on these things. At least she'll leave me alone, I think. At least I'll have four free days, which I can hopefully stretch into six.

Days without pay, but free days no less. What a wonderful time to start working on Cohen's correspondence! I only wish I could summon more sunshine into my soul before going to see him. Then again, misery loves company, so perhaps a girl who's overcome by inexplicable sadness will be able to offer more empathy to the old man? Perhaps my sadness will dance well with his. Perhaps my current mindset is more suitable for understanding him. For I feel like the world has ended, and surely he does too. I can't imagine a decade of this. A few days is enough to drive an otherwise sensible woman to the darkest and most self-destructive thoughts.

Cohen agrees to see me. I find him as ill-humored as on our last visit. Undeterred, I jump right into my new subject matter, tell him a friend of mine was quite impressed with the painting of the showgirl in Paris, ask him if he could tell me more about her.

"Odette," he says. "Yes, I remember that one. I did a portrait of her, though I wouldn't say it's among my favorites."

"Which were your favorites?" I ask, hoping to seize this opportunity even if it means letting go of my curiosity about Odette.

"Doesn't matter," he grumbles. "I can't see them, can I?"

"But others can," I say brightly. "Many of your paintings are not even here. Do you no longer care about them if they go into someone else's home?"

He doesn't reply to this, so I press on. "Do you not care about any of the people who acquired them? The people living with them? Do you keep in touch with them?"

"I used to, but it got to be too much trouble. You see, even before I went blind, I preferred to have someone else write letters for me. Then it became too complicated."

"I can write letters for you."

"That so?"

"Perhaps your servant could show me some of your correspondence. I could—"

"You think people who haven't heard from me in years will want letters from an old blind man?"

"People who live with your art on their walls? I would imagine they'd be thrilled. And wouldn't you want to know how they are?"

"They're probably dead or decrepit like me."

"But your paintings survive and some might have been passed on. It would be interesting to see who gets to enjoy them now."

"Can you please ring Deirdre for some water?" he asks, with little interest in this line of conversation I had such high hopes for. I can certainly take a cue. After our refreshment is served, I ask Cohen to choose a book. For two days straight, I visit him and do nothing but read to him. At the end of the second day, as I descend the stairs, the servant stops me.

"Miss," she says, "he asked to let you in here before you leave."

I follow her down the corridor, to a room where, behind a locked door she opens for me, sits a large desk covered in papers in disarray. The walls are full of both bookshelves and paintings, but these paintings are different from the ones in the parlor. These paintings are not finished, white canvas glaring behind thin layers of oil. An easel in the corner holds a work in progress so fragmented I almost wish to cover up its exposed nakedness. The energy in this room is heavy, oppressive, more so than in the sick room. The air has a viscous quality to it, the smell of oil paint, turpentine, and dust overpowering. Without asking permission, I open a window. I pull the drapes open and push the shutters to let in some much-needed sunshine. I am rewarded with a gust of island air so strong, I must rush to catch the papers scattering about. As best I can, I secure them with paperweights then survey the mess.

I've lost track of time when the doctor finds me trying to organize the notes and correspondence I came across. The sky outside has bloomed a delicate pink. I'm dizzy from my hours of concentration, as well as from my monthly predicament, which always renders me listless and off-balance.

"My dear lady, what a wonderful surprise! But you look mighty pale! How long have you been breathing the musty air in this room?"

I tell him about my plans to cheer up Cohen by taking over some of his correspondence.

"That's quite ambitious and admirable. I'd hate for you to go to so much trouble."

"No trouble. It'll probably be interesting."

"I'm pleased you think so, but I insist you must leave this stifling room and get some fresh air. Are you not working tonight?"

"I have a few days off," I say, and hope that, although he is a doctor, he will not guess the reason. "It's a good time to start acquainting myself with this correspondence."

"That's brilliant," he says. "So maybe you will do me the honor of accompanying me for an evening walk and some supper? Perhaps while I check on Mr. Cohen, you can gather a stack of letters you wish to take with you, to study later, in a less unpleasant environment?"

"Would he not mind me taking them?"

"I doubt he'd care, especially if you later return them."

And so that evening, a stack of Cohen's letters tucked into my purse, I accompany Dr. Tarner on a delightful evening walk. We have supper in one of the downtown restaurants, and I order a steak. Though still faint from my condition, I feel myself fortified by the fresh air, the exercise, and the meat. The doctor regales me with stories of his patients, and I push away my listlessness and try to do my share to keep the conversation going. It's always hard when the curse is upon me. I feel like I only have a fraction of my usual spirit. It's normally so easy for me to be good company, and with the doctor it would be the most natural thing of all. But tonight I am not myself.

"You seem mighty tired, my dear lady," he says. "You must promise me to stay out of that stuffy room where Cohen keeps his papers. I hope you'll take your time reading the letters you got, and when you do return, you can always take stacks of correspondence and sit with them in the parlor. Now, may I tempt you with dessert before taking you home?"

CHAPTER 20
A DOLLAR EARNED WRITING

The next morning I awake feeling unsure of myself. It's what the Curse does – plunges me into a dark abyss where my light can't shine. Was I terrible company for the doctor at supper? Have I wasted the wonderful chance of enjoying his company?

I tell myself it's the curse dulling all excitement, making me feel as if I'm constantly amiss. Under normal circumstances I would not doubt myself, for on my worst day I am more charming company than just about anyone. I have a decade of training and discipline to fall back on.

Determined to return to a healthier regard for myself and my vocation, I ring Sarah and ask for a larger carafe of coffee than on a normal day, also fresh biscuits, bacon, and a little bit of fruit. At the last moment I reconsider and ask also for a buttermilk pancake with thick syrup.

"Are you in the family way?" the impertinent girl dares ask me.

"Quite the opposite," I say tartly.

"Oh, I see. It makes me mighty hungry too. I understand."

"Then hurry, will you?"

My appetite gives in to nausea as soon as I smell the bacon. I push it aside and force down a few bites of the buttermilk pancake. I drink the coffee greedily, waiting for it to clear my head. I lock my door, as I do not wish to be disturbed, and take the stack of letters out of my purse. Throughout a whole day of lying in bed and suffering through lethargy and a most vile mood, I arrange them into piles, then decide which of their authors would be the most amenable to hearing from Cohen after all this time. I decide that letters sent to him purely out of thanks and admiration, way after whatever outstanding invoice must have been settled, are the ones I should focus on. Of course, I can only guess at some of the context of the letters. I choose to prioritize the ones that mention a painting by name. I make a note of some of the others, so I can ask Cohen for more detail later.

I unlock the door and hide the letters under my pillow when Sarah comes to inquire what I'd like for dinner. She brings chicken and green beans as well as a fresh glass of cold lemonade, which I'm most thankful for. But the dark clouds of my mood will not be dispersed. My mind wanders from the letters to my bizarre encounter with Aristotle the other night. That man is as changeable as the sea. Of course, men in general are capricious, their attention and desire fleeting. I know that full well. But I did not expect Aristotle to treat me alternately as a goddess and as a disposable object. There is also the matter of our friendship, which I had believed in, although his penchant for adding Ruby to our *tête à têtes* should have warned me that he did not appreciate me as a confidante as much as I had hoped.

No matter, in the end, mildly bruised feelings are not important. What is important is my strategic position in this game. I need to make sure I maintain Aristotle's interest if he is to make good on the promise of a house for me.

What's tricky is that I will need to elicit Mrs. Harden's help without her knowing what exactly she is helping me accomplish. She will definitely want me to keep Aristotle enthralled, but can obviously not know I'm hoping to become his mistress and leave her establishment, taking with me not just my earning potential but also one of her most valuable clients. I wonder, more than ever, if being Aristotle's mistress would be a precarious position indeed. Once he has unrestricted access to my favors, he'll probably tire of me. But that too could give me much desired freedom as long as I got him to put the house in my name and give me a few other generous gifts before his passion cooled. If I had a house of my own, a house that was paid for, my savings could guarantee me an early retirement and a rather leisurely life. I picture myself walking the beach in the company of the doctor. Then I remind myself not to be ridiculous. A fallen woman, even one that retires while she is still pretty, must keep her hopes and expectations in check.

Depressed and anxious about my prospects, I return to Cohen's correspondence, and even start penning a draft of a letter to one of his collectors. I can read this draft to him tomorrow, and maybe it will meet his approval. But I can't concentrate. Now that the topic of Aristotle has been filed away, a new source of worry finds me, one more profound and darker. Has Ardoin shown Ruby that picture of Marie and me in New Orleans? And if he did, and if she recognized me, what exactly would a girl like her know to do with her suspicions? Would she discuss them with Mrs. Harden? I foresee a dead end there, as Mrs. Harden would not want anyone bringing trouble to her prize horse. But in my current state it's harder for me to believe this. Also, what if Ruby has connections in New Orleans? Someone to write to and inquire? What if Ardoin himself decides to find out how I came to be here, looking exactly like the girl in that long-ago picture?

My heart racing, it's difficult to get myself to calm down. I tell myself that nobody has the spare time or excess of imagination to pursue such a loose end. Not even vengeful Ruby. I will myself to concentrate on the letter I'm writing. I make myself pay attention to every word. By the time the sky starts blushing and Sarah returns with supper, I have written a draft I'm pleased with and I've hidden it safely in my purse together with the other letters. The thought of calling on Cohen the next day almost disperses my dark mood.

The artist seems surprised that I've returned, even more surprised that I've drafted a letter. I read it to him, and at first he's silent.

"Not terrible," he finally says.

"Tell me what you'd like me to change."

He groans, asks for me to read it again. He interrupts where he doesn't like the phrasing or wants something added. It takes some doing, but I finally have a draft he approves of. He helps me, too, to select former clients I should send the letter to. He doesn't, much to my chagrin, share stories of their paintings, but he does tell me the names of the works they purchased, and for now this is enough. Before I get ready to leave, he rings for the servant.

"Deirdre, give Miss Bonnard $2, please."

"There's no need," I protest.

"For postage."

"It won't be that much."

"I want you to keep the change as compensation for writing the letters."

"Again, there's no need…"

He laughs. "How much did you say you make a night, Miss Bonnard?"

I'm glad the servant has left the room, possibly in search of the money. "A hundred dollars," I say, not disguising the pride in my voice.

"That's a small fortune. And I'm sure you're well worth it, but you see, dear girl, writing is an art where you have to be exceptional to earn even a measly penny. They say that if anybody has ever given you any money in exchange for your writing, you must be very talented indeed. I'm only trying to pay you a compliment."

"I shall be most flattered then, and shall invest my writing honorarium in a new book."

"You love to read, don't you?"

"More than anything." As soon as I say it I wonder if it's true. It can't be. There are so many exquisite pleasures I enjoy, not least the thrill of charming and seducing the most difficult men. And in this I feel like I am finally making progress with Cohen. Too bad my week of respite is drawing to a close. But this is a good time to mail the letters, and perhaps by the time I get to return there will be some answers. A few of the collectors live as close as Houston which makes me hope there will be some responses soon.

As I leave Cohen's and head back to the brothel, I feel my good spirits start to return. This is the part of the curse I actually enjoy – life starting anew. Tomorrow I shall still rest, go to the beach, read, and the day after I will be myself again, ready to get back to work. By the time I find myself in this predicament again next month and have another full week to devote to Cohen and his story, I hope there might even be a response from Paris. Because among the clients Cohen told me to contact, I take the liberty to include a letter to the showgirl, Odette, Brighton's friend. I cannot help myself. Her address on the Boulevard Saint Michel was scribbled in the back of a leather-bound notebook, and I could not resist copying it. I need to know more about her. Unlike the other letters, where I indicated Mr. Cohen's as the return address, though I do identify myself as his secretary who would be conducting the correspondence, I put down my own address at Mrs. Harden's as the return address on the letter to Odette. It is a trespass, but a small one.

Besides, letters arriving for me from Paris should lend a note of credibility to my made-up life story, should Ruby be spreading rumors about the New Orleans picture among the other girls. Which I'm hoping is not the case. I wonder about mentioning my connection to Brighton in the letter to Odette, but I decide against it. It would come close to being a betrayal of his confidence, and it could only confuse the recipient. If I strike up a correspondence with her, and if I obtain Brighton's consent, I can always bring him up in a letter later.

The next day I go into the beautiful Customs Building, which is also a post office, and mail the letters. Afterwards, I have a whole dollar left from the money Cohen gave me. I close my fist around it and try to feel its imprint. A dollar. It's not much, especially to a girl like me, but what Cohen said about getting paid for writing struck a chord. I decide that I will fully enjoy this dollar and be proud of myself for the way I earned it. It is the only dollar I've earned in over a decade doing something different from my vocation, and though I most definitely don't plan on changing careers, it's interesting to think of many other girls for whom this would be a part of their wages to spend with economy and discernment. There are girls who sew or take in washing, girls who work as maids or shopgirls, girls who would know how to stretch a dollar buying sewing patterns and flour and milk and eggs or any number of the grim necessities of life.

Me, I spend it on a new book, a glass of Coca Cola at a soda fountain, and some penny candy. I find a bench to sit in the shade enjoying my new book. The sound of a steamer in the distance jolts me out of imagining life in New York as described in the story I'm reading, and returns me to the Island. I'm not a romantic, not by far, but thinking of a ship departing Galveston, taking my letter to the Parisian showgirl overseas holds undeniable appeal. I think of the other letters riding on a train toward

Houston. I smile. The book I bought is about some letters too, love letters misplaced, that could alter someone's life. Everything seems connected right now and for a brief moment, sitting outside enjoying the thrill of a brand-new book, thinking about the letters I wrote and the letters I'm reading about, I am perfectly happy. Can one truly be happy enjoying such trifles? Can one precious dollar occasionally buy more joy than a whole hundred?

CHAPTER 21
SOMETHING IS AMISS

A few days after my return to work, Mrs. Harden informs me that Aristotle requested my presence.

"I'd like to talk to you about him," I say. We are in her office, a small but chic room dominated by a feminine rosewood desk. It would be a lovely setup had Mrs. Harden's body not increased in proportion over the years, dwarfing the delicate piece of furniture. I suppose this is something I need to be wary of myself. After retirement, even the loveliest girl, not getting as much exercise as before, can turn into a heavyset matron if she doesn't watch her diet. Mrs. Harden, I know, is particularly fond of sweets.

She lifts her eyebrows in surprise. "Anything the matter?" she asks, fanning herself with a beautiful Chinese fan.

"Yes and no. It's just that the last time he saw me, Aristotle was uncharacteristically brusque."

"Did he hurt you?"

"No. It's not that. It's just that he was in a great hurry, and—"

"And what?" Her voice now is impatient.

"Well, I'm afraid his desire for me might have waned. I'm concerned about that. I wonder if perhaps we should put him off, give him a less experienced girl so he can want me more."

"He wants you to the tune of a hundred dollars a night, which is good enough for me. I'm not interested in giving him a cheaper treat when he asked for the most expensive. And if you wish to play games and cultivate romances, let me remind you this is a house of business, not a matchmaking service."

"I do think it would be good for business if his interest didn't wane," I say pointedly.

"So see to it that it doesn't. Make sure you entertain him properly. Why don't you worry about pleasing the men and leave the business side to me?"

She's angry now, and perhaps it'd be wise to retreat.

"It's like a dance with Aristotle and me," I say. "He wants me, then tires of me, then wants me again."

"How fascinating," she says with disdain. "Be that as it may, I run this house and I say you must see him tonight. Now go."

I dare bring up no further objections. I turn to leave, keeping my back straight, but when my hand is on the doorknob she calls me back in a sweet voice so different from the one she used before: "Aimée."

I face her.

"That's not even your name, is it? It doesn't matter, my dove. But I do think you should remember that a girl with secrets needs a certain kind of protection, doesn't she?"

My stomach turns, but I make myself smile. "I don't have secrets, but your protection is appreciated."

"Oh, but you do, my dove, and I've protected you, and I continue to do so. You better keep in mind there's nobody out there who would protect you like I do. You better not be plotting anything, Aimée, because should you attempt to leave this house before your thirtieth birthday, you would lose my protection and I don't want to imagine what trouble would befall you without it."

"I would not leave here, Mrs. Harden. I am happy here."

"How lovely to hear that. Now go get ready for Aristotle. And don't set your expectations on him. Men like him come and go and while they're here, they're good for their money. Surely a smart girl like you understands what's good for her?"

"Absolutely," I say. "I will wear my red satin dress."

"Good girl."

Alone in my room in front of my vanity, waiting for Sarah to come do my hair, I can't still my beating heart. What does Mrs. Harden know? Does she know about New Orleans, about Marie? And what does she know about my plans with Aristotle? Did he talk to her about his intentions? He surely wouldn't do a thing like that! Are there spies in this house, someone who overheard my conversations with him? We didn't talk about our planned arrangement in front of Ruby, but a servant clearing the table while Aristotle and I were in bed in the adjoining room could have overheard us. Still, the possibility that is most plausible, and in many ways most terrifying, is that it was nothing but her instincts that led Mrs. Harden to suspect I had plans to move out and become Aristotle's mistress. I only wish I could know if she truly has information to use against me or if she's bluffing. What use would it be to her to reveal my past once I've moved out? Would that not be a stain on her own house?

I feel threatened and cannot calm down. I snap at Sarah as she pulls a knot out of my hair. I take no pleasure in putting on my glorious red satin dress. Will I even be able to concentrate enough to entertain Aristotle? I try to think of the best strategy to use with him, then it occurs to me that my current state might actually be ideal. I can disguise my distraction as remoteness, I can incense him and stir his passion by once again being with him but not fully present. I recall the tremendous success of the night I thought of the doctor while entertaining Aristotle, and I instantly regret having requested Mrs. Harden's help when I don't need her at all.

Still, I have learned something. I have learned that she's watching me and that she'd stoop to blackmail to stop me from leaving. As unsettling as this is, it's useful information both about her character and my value. Will it stop me from leaving? I don't know yet. I only wish I had a way out that took me away from Galveston and this woman's sphere of influence, just in case she would really harm me. I only wish Aristotle would buy me a house somewhere else, somewhere far from here. Or maybe I could go myself, leave unexpectedly like I left New Orleans, start over once again in a new town. Maybe San Francisco? Would that be far enough? But what would I find there other than the whims of a new madam?

An hour later, sitting across from Aristotle in the dining room, I let my mind wander just as planned. I play with the food on my plate, poking little holes with the tines of my fork into the translucent flesh of the fish. I do exactly the opposite of what I normally do. Instead of hanging onto Aristotle's every word, I let him talk and wait a beat too long to have a reaction. He doesn't notice at first. This is not the courteous Aristotle I'm accustomed to. Like last time, there's something off, something almost manic about him. I almost wish to switch strategies and ask him what's wrong, but I decide to stick to my guns.

"You seem distracted," he finally says, putting down his napkin.

I wait a beat. This is entertaining. I wipe my upper lip with my napkin, place it back in my lap. "Sorry?"

"You seem far off."

"Oh," I say, taking another bite of fish, chewing it methodically before answering. "I'm sorry, I've been…" I trail off. I cast my gaze down to my lap, let my lashes tremble as if I'm about to cry.

"What is it?" he asks.

I look him in the eye, then look away. This is not a man who is indifferent to me. There is concern in his gaze, warmth too.

It jolts me like a bucket of ice thrown in my face.

When was the last time someone cared about me? Not the fake, manipulative warmth and coddling Madame Rouge used to win me over in New Orleans when I was just a girl, but real concern? Pain and fear wash over me. Because if this is real, it's worrisome and savage. Perhaps I have in Aristotle a true friend, and the games we've been playing are a superficial distraction. Perhaps underneath it all lies a deeper reservoir of affection, which in my vanity and greed I've chosen to ignore.

"It's nothing," I whisper, my bottom lip trembling.

"Something is amiss," he says. "And whatever it is, you can tell me." A piercing sadness overcomes me. I've been too shallow and scheming to be honest with him. Or with myself.

"I'm sorry," I say, giving him a crooked smile. "I don't want to spoil our evening. Let's just have a nice time."

"Aimée," he says, his voice serious. "Something is wrong and I want you to tell me."

I look away. I bite my lip.

"You are not telling me what is going on with you, so how can I tell you what is going on with me?" I finally say, looking into his eyes. There's a flicker there, something I can't read. The same savage thing I fear yet crave. "Last time you came to see me," I say slowly, "something was different. You were not yourself."

"I'm sorry," he says. "I behaved rudely, I know. I meant to send flowers."

I reach for his hand, clasp my fingers around his callused palm, take comfort in the warmth and roughness of it.

"I don't want flowers. I want you to tell me what's going on."

A smile spreads on his lips that reveals all his white teeth. "You're rather manipulative, aren't you, darling?"

I laugh. "Aristotle went to a whorehouse and found the women manipulative."

The heavy atmosphere is gone, but so is the moment when I could have confessed and asked him to return the favor. He lifts me into his arms, carries me to the bedroom, and I don't protest. Our lovemaking is playful and satisfying. Afterwards, we lie in crumpled sheets and I hope he will not hurry off like last time. When I notice he's relaxed, I offer to bring him a drink.

I tiptoe into the other room. The table has not been cleared, which means a servant might come in at any time. I have a fleeting thought of locking the door toward the hallway, but that could get back to Mrs. Harden. Instead, I do the opposite. I bring in the decanter of bourbon and two glasses, and I leave the door between the sitting room and the bedroom wide open. Any servant who might come in to clear, would retreat in embarrassment and come back much later.

I pour bourbon for us both, even a sip for me, because I love the smell of it. I crawl back into bed with my glass and let my fingers play with the black curls on Aristotle's chest.

"You know," I say, letting the melancholy scent of bourbon soften my voice, "just because I'm a manipulative whore doesn't mean I am not your friend."

He smiles. He takes my hand and brings it to his lips. "You're a great friend, Aimée. I'm lucky to have you."

"But you're not ready to tell me what's going on," I say with a smile. I feel him drifting away from me, not through a will of his own, but through the power of the walls people build around themselves for protection, walls that sometimes keep out well-meaning souls in addition to the malevolent ones. I cannot climb these walls, neither can I escape the ones I've built around myself. It's all so near, and yet so unattainable: Aristotle, the house, the two English Pointers...

"You won't tell me either, will you?" he says, his finger now caressing my face.

I smile a sad smile. "I can't."

"I might be able to help you," he says. "How bad is it?"

"Real bad, the worst kind of bad," I say. "And yours?"

He laughs and nods, shrugs. I laugh too, but it's the most honest conversation I've had with anyone in a long time, and it cuts deep. So I do the only thing I know to do in a situation such as this. I take the glass out of his hand, take a sip of bourbon, and give him a long intoxicating kiss. As I move my body on top of his, I smile and whisper, "It will all be all right." Though in my case I know that's not true, and I suspect that in his it isn't either. Still, there are moments when I believe my own empty reassurance, glimpses of peace as the rhythm of our bodies slows, not by my own design, but because Aristotle's callused hands grab hold of my hips and guide me in a gentle rocking motion that feels like calm ocean water on a sunny day, soft yet deceptively deep. The sensation is shocking, like falling into an abyss, falling down a long plush tunnel of dark mysterious moss, gliding towards the molten center of the earth. I don't know how long the moment is in which I forget myself. It stretches eternally, yet is too short. Aristotle, I realize, holds in his command the power to stop the carousel, but only briefly. When I become aware of biting my lower lip, of our bodies ceasing their gentle motion, of the room we're in, and Aristotle's eyes upon me, he has the biggest grin on his face and looks supremely contented, like he achieved something he was hoping for, something important, crucial even. A parting gift? Why am I thinking that?

I nestle close to him. Exhausted and satiated, I allow myself to doze off for a few stolen moments. It's the sound of the door in the other room that wakes me. I sit up, letting the sheet fall, exposing my breasts. The servant who entered, an older woman, gasps, then excuses herself and retreats.

"What happened?" Aristotle asks. He too was asleep.

"Nothing, a servant," I say. I smile at him as I slip into my dress and gather my things. Now that we're both awake, it's best to return to my room.

"Stay a while longer," he says. I lie down on the bed fully dressed. He does nothing but look at me and I look at him too, my eyes trying to memorize his features. I kiss him on the lips before I go, and as I walk through the long hallway, I carry with me the image of his tousled hair. I have the strangest premonition that I won't see him again. But perhaps I'm just tired.

CHAPTER 22
THE BATTLE OF GALVESTON

Melancholy sits with me the next day. I didn't know that Aristotle had the power to make me sad. Lust, that I knew was between us. Attraction, ambition, covetousness, a possessive urge to control the other. But somewhere in this garden of dangerous yet alluring monsters, some gentler feelings must have sprouted. I don't usually allow myself such sentimentality, such tenderness. Not since Maw Maw. Or perhaps, if I'm fully honest with myself for once, not since Madame Rouge charmed me on an unforgettable cold night in New Orleans, when I chose her to be my protectress and the person whose approval and affection I craved most. What a misguided emotional investment that turned out to be I wouldn't fully learn until a decade later, though the knowledge seeped in gradually throughout the years, helping me harden myself to the shock to come.

But now, at the thought of Aristotle's troubles, hot tears flood my cheeks. The outburst is unexpected, foreign to me. Am I really crying for Aristotle, for whatever trouble he might be in? Or am I crying for myself, for my shattered dream of an escape from this house? I tell myself that perhaps my nerves are still rattled from my confrontation with Mrs. Harden yesterday. What I need is a distraction, and the perfect one presents itself when Mrs. Harden sends word through Sarah that I am to visit Brighton in his office this evening, then spend the night at his house.

Perhaps a night away from the brothel is just what I need. I instantly cheer up. I wonder what the room is like Brighton told me he'd set up for me. I wonder what he'll serve for supper, if the food will be to my liking. I toy with the idea of maybe telling him about Aristotle, but I immediately dismiss the thought. It would be unwise for many reasons. In the end I decide to concentrate on what I'll wear and on packing my toothbrush, a jar of dental powder, a chemise, and a book into my bag. I bring my diaphragm, too, just in case, though I'm not sure it's necessary.

I also decide to call on Cohen before heading to Brighton's. I find him in a better mood than usual, and he shows a most promising glimmer of interest in my telling him what I bought with the dollar he gave me, and telling him about the new book.

"It's a new author," I say, "but I think one that shows real promise."

"A writer would know," he says. "Deirdre told me that a letter arrived from Houston yesterday. I didn't let her open it. I figured you might like doing so yourself."

I feel like a child being handed a Christmas present. I relish in cutting open the envelope, extracting the white creamy paper, and unfolding it to reveal what can only be a woman's handwriting.

"Dear Mr. Cohen, and Dear Miss Bonnard,

Your letter was very welcome in our household, and it arrived, in its own way, at a most opportune moment. My father, Dr. Rosen, passed away this spring at the ripe old age of ninety-five. I could not have wished for him to have lived longer, nor for your letter to arrive before his demise as he was no longer himself. What seems miraculous to me is that your letter arrived hours before the sale of my father's house was finalized, and that I found it in his mailbox on my last thorough inspection of the property before turning over the keys to the new owners. It is a letter that made me most happy, even on a day of complicated emotions, as it provides me with the opportunity of deepening my connection to an object I am already deeply connected to, and through it to my deceased father, and the long ago days of my happy childhood in my parents' home.

I never knew much about *The Battle of Galveston*, and by that I mean your painting, Mr. Cohen, not the historical event itself, for about the event I learned in school and heard more than I wanted to know from my father. Or perhaps I should say I know the painting better than the historical event itself, for I often tuned out my father's stories, which bored me – though now I regret it. The painting, on the other hand, has fascinated me for as long as I can remember. I've always loved looking at it. I don't remember the day my father brought it home – perhaps it's older than I am, though you can surely clear that up for me, but I do remember always loving it, especially the horses! I have looked upon your painting so many hours of my life, Mr. Cohen, that I have memorized every brushstroke. Though I still cannot tire of it and never will.

I moved the painting into my own home once my father's health declined to the point that he no longer left his room and needed permanent care. The painting, which I am too selfish to hang in the parlor where it belongs, hangs in my own personal study, where I get to look at it often, as it's the room where I write out my correspondence. Funny that I should be staring at it right now, as I take small breaks and think about the next line in my letter to you.

You see, Mr. Cohen, before you wrote to me, I never knew who painted this battle scene I've loved all my life. My father must have told me, but I

116

never paid much attention. I never had the painting appraised, or seen by an authenticity specialist the way I did with my father's other paintings, as I never had the intention of selling it. Now that I know you painted it, I am ashamed, for I have heard of you and your work and I am humbled to know that I possess such a treasure without knowing it. Though, to my credit, I can say that I've always recognized the painting as something valuable and meaningful.

I would be most grateful if you told me more about the painting and how it came to be in possession of my father. It is a cruel twist of fate that I did not appreciate his stories when he could share them with me, but long for them now that he no longer can.

Yours sincerely,

Mrs. Lucretia Zweig"

This was not the letter I had most anticipated, but it has the desired effect on Cohen.

"The Battle of Galveston," he says. "Dr. Rosen… Those are memories from what seems like another life." His lip curls into a smile. "Someone like you, born after the war, wouldn't understand. And you're better off for it."

"Did you fight in the battle?" I ask, ashamed of my lack of knowledge of history, my lack of ability to gage if such a thing is possible.

He laughs. "No, no. I was thirty-six years old in 1862, too old for the Confederate Army. My friend, Dr. Rosen, was too old too. We were condemned to watch from the sidelines as young men killed each other senselessly. But Rosen was a doctor, and he tended to the wounded here in Galveston, those poor young boys caught in the crossfire of history. It made an impression on him, on all of us."

He's quiet for a moment, and I wonder how I can prod him to tell me more, but to my surprise, after a sip of water, he continues. This is a good sign. Perhaps the correspondence about the paintings will indeed help draw him out.

"He left after the war and I lost track of him. He remarried, and I got swept up in my career. Years later, he came back to Galveston and by then I had achieved a small measure of fame, mostly as an artist of the South, which pleased me fine. Rosen came to see me and asked if I would paint the Battle of Galveston for him.

It was a strange request, for I didn't think a man such as him would romanticize the battle. Many did, perhaps out of spite or misplaced nostalgia. It wasn't easy being a Southerner after the war. What history chooses to remember is always filtered through the perspective of the winners. Nobody is truly right in a war, and the people who suffer the most are the ones who have no say in the matter at all.

I'm well aware of the horrors of slavery, so please don't think for a second I'm among the hypocrites who would defend it. Its evil was in our midst since before I was born. Its evil was unacceptable, but whoever sees the North as a champion of the rights of the Negro is sorely mistaken. Have you ever been up North, Miss Bonnard?"

"No," I admit. "The only place in the United States I've been to is Galveston. I came here directly from France."

He laughs out loud at this. "The hell you did. Where'd you really come from? Let me guess… Some small town in Louisiana where you learned a smidgen of Cajun French?"

"The Fourteenth Arrondissement," I say with as much conviction as I can muster.

"It don't matter, sugar! I'm not one of the men you must charm. I'm a poor Jewish boy from Louisiana myself."

"You were telling me about the North," I say. "I've always wanted to visit New York."

"Yes," he says. "New York is worth a visit, that's for sure. But don't expect to go there to find that they treat the Negroes they so wanted freed equitably. No, Ma'am. The wealthiest woman in New York caused a scandal by having a colored ladies' maid. Did you know? It was unheard of, and people within her own circle protested. How was one to employ a colored girl when there were good white immigrant girls looking for work? Such is the thinking in the Northern states, and don't you forget it. They treat the Negroes as foreigners, and many an abolitionist has expressed the view that they should be shipped back to Africa."

"What do you think of brothels," I ask him, "that offer girls of both races?"

He laughs. "I've been to such places in Paris and in New Orleans," he says. "Am I shocking you?"

He is not shocking me, for I have heard of more outrageous things, including a Cajun girl I knew at Madame Rouge who bragged about having once entertained a colored man of property. But the mention of New Orleans unsettles me, and I desperately need to take this conversation elsewhere.

"Let's get back to the painting," I say. "Because I don't think we should mention brothels or interracial copulating in our response to Mrs. Zweig."

"It was you who brought up the brothels, Miss Bonnard."

"I suppose out of interest in my profession, but also… I don't know. This talk of the races mixing or staying apart. I'm not sure how to articulate my feelings, but… There is malevolence in people who wish for the races to be apart, but there is something wicked too in the sort of people who look upon other races as a special sort of entertainment. I don't know how to say it, because in my line of work we all wish to provide something different, but I've learned there is a dangerous side to those who seek out the exotic, those who treat people as playthings, and I'm afraid…"

118

I stop abruptly. I'm getting too close to talking, even tangentially, about what happened that night with Marie.

"You're an intelligent woman," he says. "There can be a lot of darkness in seeking out the forbidden and the thrilling. And there is a long history of abuse of Negro women at the hands of white men. But no, we will certainly not write about such things to Mrs. Zweig.

In fact, when I painted the battle, I was seeking light in the darkness. I chose to focus on the soldiers as humans, not as heroes. I took a lot of poetic license and painted something that did not happen. What I captured was not the naval battle, but a scene of respite in the Confederate camp. In truth, the cavalrymen on shore would not have sat in camp so close to the fighting. For in the painting you can see the fighting in the background, a black cloud. But soldiers in the camp are cooking and trading stories of their homes and families. I tried to capture their youthful glow, their mirth at the stories shared. They look as innocent as kids around a campfire and I meant for this to be shocking. For what was tragic, to me, was not that the young men were monsters but rather that they were not. They were simple boys, most of them innocent and idealistic, but easily swayed into fighting for a monstrous cause. So the boys I painted show their youth and naiveté. Horses are grazing in the foreground. This I invented. There were no horses there in real life, only dismounted cavalrymen. But I added horses because I love them. I focused on them, because, of course, the animals were totally innocent."

His face changes as he talks. His blind eyes, even, seem less vacant. I'm lucky that the letter I read to him elicited such a response, that it contained a memory that would awaken his emotions. And although I still feel unsettled by my clumsy and strange mention of mixed-race brothels and peculiar clients, I find hope, too, in the realization that I like talking to him, that his conversation is insightful enough to draw me to speak my mind in ways I usually avoid.

"I did not explain my artistic choices to Rosen," he continues. I had my apprehension about whether he'd enjoy the painting with its glaring historical inaccuracies or not. If he expected a classic battle scene, or a painting true to actual events, he did not say so. He looked at my creation for a long time, tears glimmering in his eyes which neither of us wanted to acknowledge. We did not need to speak of the significance of that scene. In fact, nobody spoke of it, and a group of young boys cooking over a campfire, their horses grazing in the foreground, was forever referred to as *The Battle of Galveston*. Throughout the whole unveiling party everyone acted like I had truly painted the fierce naval battle, and it's funny to see that even Mrs. Zweig, who knew little of the origin of the painting, referred to it as such. Yes, we shall write back to her. Let me tell you a little more about Rosen. Let me tell you more about the party, Miss Bonnard, and you'll know how to spin these words into a story that will bring her comfort."

CHAPTER 23
CAKE AND SUFFRAGETTES

Later, I make my way to Brighton's office. There, I delight in surveying Galveston from above, both the port side with its activity, as well as the rooftops of the city itself, the glimmer of the Gulf of Mexico shining in the distance like a crown of diamonds. I'm in a good mood at the prospect of my paid vacation, curious to see Brighton's house, excited about our dinner ahead. We start our evening like last time, in his office, his finger guiding mine over a map of Paris, telling me about restaurants, cafés, hotels, and art galleries. My curiosity about the city and the stories he's telling me takes precedence over my expectation that, perhaps our physical closeness will create an opportunity for intimate contact. Bent over the maps, I forget to speculate about the purpose of my visit and my chances of success. Instead, I want to know where Odette performed, and his finger guides mine to Montmartre. I want to know where she lives too. His finger guides mine into a neighborhood he describes as very exclusive, the Boulevard Saint Michel stretching gloriously toward the Seine. He describes the trees lining it, the cafés, the many enchantments one can find by meandering down the side streets.

"I wrote to her," I say.

"You did what?"

"I decided to write to Cohen's collectors on his behalf and ask about the fate of his paintings."

"Interesting idea."

"Do you think I'll hear back?"

"I wouldn't know. Let's proceed to my home, shall we?"

There is a sudden shift in tone. There is something Brighton doesn't want to tell me about the Odette. Cohen too, did not want to talk about her, did not encourage me to write to her, dismissed her portrait as something he wasn't too fond of, though Brighton had described it as remarkable. Her address was in Cohen's notebook, but there were no letters from her. And my instincts told me not to use his address for the answer I'm hoping to receive. Why? What am I sensing?

Whatever it is, it will not enhance the enjoyment of my evening with Brighton, nor my ability to be of service to him if I bring it up. And he is, after all, a paying customer. Also, I myself am looking forward to a good time. And I wish to respect my client's secrets, which so far I thought extended only to his own preferences, but apparently might encompass information he can't reveal about his friends.

With my face hidden behind my veil, I slip into Brighton's Landau. There, I turn my face from the open window, and whenever we pass someone who might recognize the carriage, he pulls me deeper inside so I remain completely unseen.

The evening is fragrant with magnolia blossoms and jasmine, the breeze moist and salty. I ask questions about the houses we pass, and Brighton shares his knowledge about the various elements of style. His own house he describes as Italianate. A somewhat square two-story clapboard structure with a generous porch, it appeals to me instantly through its harmonious silhouette. Gas lights beckon on either side of the front door, and the inside, too, is lit up as if awaiting a special guest. The servants have retired, and Brighton assures me they will not return until the next afternoon, long after I'm gone.

Across polished floors, through tastefully and minimally furnished rooms with tall ceilings, he gives me the grand tour. There is a pleasant contrast between the dark mahogany furnishings and their white upholstery, quite refreshing and modern. The sketches on the wall, in thick golden frames, offer up black and white silhouettes of plants. "My sketches," he says. "You can always tell when an architect draws that he's an architect and not an artist. But I found that if I avoid drawing buildings and stick to plants, I lose some of the pesky precision that gives me away."

"I love them," I say honestly. "They fit very well in here. This house is so airy and modern."

"It's what I was going for." He seems pleased with my reaction. I survey the organized, almost staged clutter of books and magazines in the parlor, the Chinese pots containing white orchids, the crystal chandelier, the thick, green leaves of rubber plants.

"Are we alone?" I ask, because in the tasteful yet eclectic universe that is his home, the absence of servants, of which I've been assured, strikes me as magical. I feel like we are children left unsupervised.

"We are alone," he says, obviously sharing my delight. "And there is cake."

In a vast kitchen full of orderly cupboards, he prepares tea in a white porcelain tea pot. The cake, a glazed confection decorated with lemon icing and strawberries sits under a glass dome on the counter. He cuts two generous slices, then leads me upstairs, up a narrow staircase with a polished banister. There, he shows me to a room containing a four-poster bed full of white pillows, two nightstands showcasing orchids similar to the ones I saw downstairs, and a vanity table piled high with fashion magazines. He tells me to put on white silk pajamas – an unexpected gift – and join him for cake and tea in his own room. It feels like something children would do, or girls at one of those expensive schools where they are taught how to behave in society. Except maybe those girls would not be encouraged to wear silk pajamas. They make me think of women wearing trousers – something I myself have never tried. I survey myself from all sides in front of a mirror. I join Brighton, dressed in his own silk pajamas, and he invites me to sit next to him on the bed. We discuss the merits of trousers for women. I have certainly heard of ladies who wear them in public and the scandal it causes – similar to smoking. The controversy reminds me of the hateful person operating my bathing machine back when I was new to Galveston, who warned me not to take off my shoes and stockings.

"Oh, but you should, darling, you should!" he says. "It would undoubtedly cause quite a stir, but what's the point of already being scandalous if you are not to make the most of your freedom?"

"But I already enjoy my freedom more than society thinks I should," I say.

"So you do like what you do?"

"I love it."

He inches closer, smiles at me. His hand reaches for my knee, moves up my thigh. I smile, leaning toward him, offering him the chance to look at my breasts through the opening of the silk shirt, but he looks away instead. His hand is still on my thigh, warm through the thin silk fabric. Perhaps there's hope. Overcome by a sudden tenderness for him, I bring my lips to his and kiss him in the gentlest way I'm capable of. He closes his eyes, but his lips do not part. I trace my hand from his beautiful jaw to his neck, his collarbone, then let it slip inside the shirt of his silk pajamas. It's like caressing a statue. His body tenses at my touch. Undeterred, I let my lips follow the same path, let them trail farther down, follow the faint line of hair that leads from his well-formed chest to his lower abdomen.

"Darling, no," he says, when my hand reaches to undo the knot of the silk string. "It will not do. I cannot, will not. I'm so sorry."

"There's nothing to be sorry for. I'm paid to do as you wish." But I actually feel a bit like crying.

"I'm afraid I've hurt your feelings," he says.

"Bosh," I protest, chasing the tears out of my voice. "I'm not paid to have feelings. Besides, better to cause me a little disappointment, which I'm generously compensated for, than to cause heartbreak to your young lady."

"Yes," he says. "Heartbreak all around. She wouldn't be the only one disillusioned if I choose to marry her." I blink away my unexpected chagrin, steady my breathing, and choose to concentrate on what he's alluding to, which is most interesting and perhaps something he needs to talk about. Perhaps he's not as much in need of a lover as of a confidante.

"Are there other interested parties?" I ask.

His face closes up. "I'm sorry, dear. These are matters I can't discuss. Do you detest me?"

"Not one bit," I say, my voice infused with just a hint of teasing. I must restore the light, breezy, joking atmosphere of earlier in the evening. If I am to be any help at all, I must tread gentler in the realm of his confessions, than in that of physical intimacy.

"Can I at least offer a slice of cake as a sweet bribe?"

"So you wish to deny a girl pleasure and validation, and then you wish to also deny her supper and skip straight to dessert? Surely there must be something to eat here in addition to cake!"

Despite the best he can offer being a tin of sardines, the evening passes pleasantly with talk of fashion and even politics. Brighton believes women should be allowed to vote. Frankly, I have never given the topic much thought. I've always found the women who espoused the idea to be a tiresome and unattractive bunch of matrons and spinsters who oppose alcohol and other diversions and would probably cross to the other side of the street if they saw me pass.

"All women?" I ask. Although the topic is not one of my favorites, I know enough to be aware that some of the proponents of women's suffrage believe only white women should be given the vote.

"Only the pretty ones," he says, and we both laugh.

"Good luck with that, considering that the ladies advocating for such rights are not very attractive," I say.

Brighton studies me as if pondering an interesting thought. I stuff a bite of cake into my mouth to distract myself from the uncomfortable silence.

"The problem of the fair sex," he says, "is that women are so eager to criticize one another and tear each other apart. If they were actually able to stand united, there's no telling what they might accomplish."

At this rate, I think, I might eat the entire cake. What else is there to do?

"All right," I finally say, "that was a catty comment. I don't care what these ladies look like, and overall I might agree with some of what they're saying, but I don't like them advocating temperance."

"With a capital T," Brighton says, pouring us both more tea, which instantly restores the levity of the mood. "You don't even drink, though."

"My clients do."

"As do the husbands of many American women who then either see their children starve or end up having to endure violence at the hands of a drunken man."

"Maybe instead of temperance they should be advocating the abolition of marriage?" I suggest. "It always struck me as an oppressive institution."

"You might be right about that. But what would the unmarried ladies do for money? Especially since we've already established not all of them are blessed with good looks like you."

At this I laugh and swat him playfully with one of the pillows.

"If only casting votes could somehow line their pockets they would be set for life, don't you think?" I take another bite of cake, then add pensively, "You know, considering the misery of most marriages, perhaps you wouldn't be doing your young lady such a disservice—"

"Oh, enough about that for tonight!" he protests. "Let's agree to try once more another time, and for now let's talk of more pleasant things. I did promise to show you pictures of Odette, did I not?"

"That will indeed make up for your other shortcomings, even the supper of canned sardines."

The woman in the picture he shows me is a plump yet most attractive lady posing for the camera in her corset and pantaloons, yet displaying a large exotic feather in a headdress decorated with sparkly crystals. She is quite obviously older. One can note a few lines in her face, and her thick upper arms and legs seem to have lost their firmness. But the defiant, self-assured look in her eyes and the mocking curve of her smile render her most alluring. This is, perhaps, a woman who has not been beautiful even in her youth, yet her presence of spirit, even on this tiny rectangle of paper is so commanding I doubt anyone could resist her.

"Did you try with her?" I ask Brighton, instantly convinced that Odette must have succeeded where I failed, my jealousy mixed with admiration.

"I've tried a number of times. With her, and with a handful of others. It was easier to try in Paris, more anonymity, more acceptance of extravagance."

"Have you been to le Chabanais?" I ask.

"Yes," he says. "That is one very fine establishment where my money was wasted. And to put your mind at ease, dear, I've never gotten any further with any of the women than I have with you. None of them can hold a candle to you. You are for sure the loveliest of lovely creatures. I'm simply incapable of intimacy with the fair sex."

"Even with Odette?"

He gives a long sigh, looks at me sideways. "Especially with her, in fact. With her things were... different. But not in the way you suspect. I did seek her out initially hoping to succumb to her charms and prove to myself I could be like all other young men. But she helped me in other ways instead. Odette introduced me to other men much like myself."

"Men who sell their bodies to men?"

He laughs. "There is that, of course, as you'd imagine. But no, she introduced me to men who prefer men who discreetly form secret love connections and manage to be happy."

"And can't you do that yourself?"

"I can. Of course, it excludes certain things. Things like children, but…" A hint of sadness crosses over his flawless features, then passes.

"I prefer dogs myself," I say. "One day I will have dogs."

He wrinkles his nose. "The hair!"

I don't point out that children, too are messy. Our conversation flitters on, becomes more irreverent, and we finally exhaust ourselves laughing. I retire to my room, where nestled into my own mountain of white pillows I endeavor to read, but soon abandon my new novel in order to turn off the light and go to sleep. I dream of Marie chasing me up the stairs, the hardwood creaking under her feet. I jolt awake, my heart racing. The room is dark and I'm confused about where I am. I cannot pry the dream away from reality. I can still hear the stairs creaking, and it takes me a few heartbeats to realize I am in Brighton's guest room in my four-poster bed, and the sound of the stairs is real.

I get out of bed as quietly as I can, tiptoe to the door, and gently push it open. Whatever is out there, I'd rather face it full on. If Marie has come to get me, I will at least look her in the eye and tell her I made a colossal mistake. But it is not a ghost I see out in the hallway. It is the shadow of a man, a man who slips into Brighton's room and closes the door so carefully I think for a second I must have imagined him.

The next morning, I awake to sunshine and birdsong. There is a tray on my dressing table containing a cup of coffee, now cold, a slice of last night's cake, the morning paper, and one red hibiscus bloom. Sweet Brighton. I step out of bed and open the window. The house is near enough to the gulf where I can hear the waves.

As I enjoy my coffee, for even cold it's still delicious, I wonder about the man who snuck into Brighton's room last night. I smile. The man must be long gone, and Brighton, too must already be at his office. My presence here alone is a luxury, the traces of last night's disappointment gone in the light of day. For ultimately, it's more gratifying to have Brighton's confidence than his desire, is it not?

Part of me wonders, in fact, if I could move here permanently, offering Brighton a prolonged chance at overcoming his aversion to intimacy with women, and escape Mrs. Harden's clutches. But this type of arrangement still exposes me to her threat — and she could, in fact, ruin Brighton as well as myself. And it would not provide me with a house of my own.

My sadness over Aristotle, and his promise that will not come to pass invades me again. I think of the two English dogs with their thin athletic bodies and playful dispositions. Why is my heart so set on those dogs? What inside that promise has led me to hope for a better, brighter future? And what has it revealed about Aristotle that I cannot let go of? It was like cracking open his shell and finding an oasis of sunshine. Or maybe it was sensing my own inner light that enchanted me. Perhaps it was a promise that I would somehow transcend the darkness that Marie's death has cast upon my soul.

I fold the unread paper and put it back on my breakfast tray next to the empty coffee cup and half-eaten biscuits. I chide myself for choosing Aristotle, or anyone for that matter, to be my savior. There are no saviors out there. We must all save ourselves. That much I know, and the thought is both disheartening and empowering. It also requires more coffee. I put on my dress and descend to the kitchen, where I find a whole carafe of the dark brew I relish. A more enterprising girl would warm it up, but I tell myself it's not worth the risk of setting Brighton's house on fire.

I take my lukewarm coffee to the back porch, to the lush peace of plumerias and oleanders, where dark-winged butterflies glide in slow motion and shadows dance with sunlight. I am blissfully alone, the coffee strong, the sound of the gulf soothing, the breeze still refreshing. Brighton's yard is a long narrow path of greenery with a coach house in the back. I wonder if some of his servants live above it. Just in case, I hide behind tall hibiscus bushes as I drink my coffee. I wonder where the man slipped in who came to Brighton's room last night.

That the serenity of this place must coexist with secrecy both saddens and reassures me. For I have my own secrets, and they are darker. Still, here I stand in a patch of sunshine seeing pelicans glide above me in a perfect V. Am I worthy of any of these miracles? Will my conscience ever be at peace? Is there a way to make amends?

I think of my own act of kindness toward Cohen and take comfort in how unforced it is, how natural it comes. But my kindness toward him is enmeshed with my own curiosity, my own desire to escape the confines of my life, which, being more adventurous than most does at times still prove not to be as expansive as I'd like. There are many people whose existence and freedom are much more limited than mine and yet I've always wanted more. Am I too greedy? Is it what ultimately caused me to betray Marie in a way that proved fatal? But why think of such dark things on this sunny morning?

I drink my coffee sitting in a wicker chair on Brighton's back porch. I look at the pelicans and butterflies, enjoy the motion of trees swaying in the light breeze, the faint hint of salt in the air. I tell myself that if I knew then what I know now I would have acted differently. If I could turn back time and change my actions, I would. Perhaps a merciful God would take stock of the depth of my regrets. Perhaps my torment shows I am, after all, a human with a conscience.

I might have detested Marie, been jealous of her, but I would not have purposefully caused her harm. Perhaps I'm like the young boys Cohen painted in his battle scene, not a monster, but simply someone who got caught in a swirl of emotions that led to a terrible outcome I would not have wished for had I acted rationally. There is a shred of peace in that thought, and I decide to hang on to it – my life raft in the storm of guilt that occasionally threatens to drown me. Maybe I'm making progress in forgiving myself. I say a quick prayer that the spirit of Marie forgives me too. Maybe eventually she will find peace and so will I.

CHAPTER 24
A MAN IN TROUBLE

That evening I entertain the dull banker again. I am in such a good mood after my little paid vacation that I manage to make our encounter mutually enjoyable. I really am a talented courtesan, and maybe this is my own way of spreading a little goodness in the world. For aren't happy people more inclined to be generous and kind?

The next day, still in good spirits, I enjoy my coffee and skip reading the paper in favor of finishing the novel I'd bought with Cohen's money. I then go on a short walk, which is invigorating despite the heat. When I return to Mrs. Harden's, I go into the kitchen for a refreshing glass of tea. I've just poured the amber liquid into a tall glass and am contemplating the delight of enjoying it in my room before freshening up, when Ruby enters the kitchen.

"My, my," she says. "If it isn't the very extraordinary Aimée! Have you heard yet that your lover with the hands like sandpaper is in deep trouble? Apparently he's a fraud like you!" She laughs an insolent laugh, then sets an empty cup near the sink and leaves in a flurry of lacy skirts. I take a moment to regain my composure.

I force myself to keep my steps measured and my breath calm as I ascend the stairs to my room. Carrying the glass of tea helps. I concentrate on not spilling it, on not making the ice rattle. I don't know what Ruby is talking about, but whatever it is, feigned calm is my best protection.

In my room, I look for the morning's paper, which Sarah brought but I had cast aside in favor of the novel. Why had I done that when I always read the paper? Was it some sort of premonition? I remember with a start that I skipped the paper yesterday too, at Brighton's. How could I have allowed myself to do so two days in a row?

I cannot find the paper anywhere. Sarah must have taken it with the morning's dishes. But why? I do not dare call for her and ask. For if she's been instructed by Mrs. Harden—But surely, that thought is preposterous. I can't let suspicion drive me insane.

Is there still time to go to the Strand and buy another paper? I must be ready to entertain in two hours, and skipping my rest in order to go out again would look suspicious. I wish I trusted Sarah. I wish I trusted someone in this house. But my only ally is looking back at me in the mirror, telling me that I must drink my tea, allow myself a rest, then call for Sarah to help me dress, and act throughout the afternoon and evening as if vile Ruby had never found me in the kitchen, had never said anything to me at all. Tomorrow I shall ask Cohen's servant for a day-old paper and I shall try to talk to her about the goings-on in town. I shall try to talk to the doctor too if I have the fortune of running into him. One way or another tomorrow I shall learn what's going on, and until then I will not let anyone in this house know that I'm worried.

My self-control is exemplary, but tonight, in the company of a jovial ship captain, I'm tempted to let it go. I'm tempted to drink a whole julep, then another and let sweet oblivion wash over me. The captain would be the ideal client to get drunk with, but aside from the occasional glass of champagne, the drinks given to us girls by Mrs. Harden's bartender are sugar water, a mere decoy that gets the clients to spend more while keeping us from the dangers of inebriation.

Sometimes I feel like my whole life is sugar water. I could, of course, top off my drink from the bottle of bourbon in the room I retire to with the captain, but I resist the urge. I don't want to wake up parched and with a vile headache tomorrow. I also don't want to have my face disfigured by a night of restless alcohol-induced sleep. Above all, I don't want to lack the energy to go to town and find out what exactly Ruby meant.

That some serious trouble has befallen Aristotle is obvious, and much as I find it shocking, I had a premonition, or maybe just the foresight to anticipate that something of a malignant nature had seized him in its claws. He himself confessed as much, though he would not tell me what it was. But much as darkness and dread accompany my every breath right now, I need to keep my mind from worrying and speculating. I need to concentrate on my client, the captain, listen to his stories, and show him a good time.

The night creeps by slowly. The captain's stories are full of technical explanations of steamships and the various issues they might encounter, of dangers that loom at sea, of most tedious meteorological science. It's hard to stay focused and present, hard to keep my mind from the type of speculation I do not wish to entertain. When I finally return to my room, bathe, eat, and go to bed, the rest of the night stretches before me like an endless patch of darkness in which I stumble trying to concoct scenarios for what I might learn the next day. What kind of trouble might Aristotle be in, and could he possibly escape it? If I could help him, would I? Why even entertain that notion? There was, perhaps a bond forming between us, one that went beyond the alluring powers of jealousy and lust, but is this fledgling bond worth risking something – anything? Is it worth risking even torment or sadness or the agony of a sleepless night?

The next day I do set out to see Cohen, and once there I do ask the servant if she has saved the papers from the past two days. In the pantry, she shows me a stack of papers. "I save them for potato peelings," she says. I pick the two on top and take them into the parlor. She has a letter for me too, which I will open in Cohen's room and read to him, but the papers I wish to read alone.

I scan the first few pages and find nothing. Then I see it, black on white. "Illegal gambling operation taking place after hours in local store." Upon a tip-off from one of his employees, then an investigation, Aristotle is awaiting trial. It's unclear if a guilty verdict will result only in fines and the loss of his business, or if he'll have to serve a jail sentence. It's unclear too if he is currently under arrest or free.

I have an impulse to go to his store and ask questions, but surely that's unwise for many reasons. Association with me would not help his reputation, and the store might be closed while Aristotle's awaiting trial. There's much I don't know or understand about the legal system. I wish the article weren't short and cryptic, but it is. I read it three times over and in the end I have more questions than answers.

I wish I had someone to discuss this with. Can I trust Brighton or the doctor? And what information would they have, what way to read between the lines of the article that I've no access to? I am less educated but no less intelligent. Of course, what these two men have access to that I don't are additional sources of information in the form of other people. Perhaps I do need to confide in one of them and solicit their help. For now, though, I need to put this matter aside and go talk to the blind man waiting for me upstairs.

I take the letter and proceed to Cohen's room. I tell him the name of the sender, a Mrs. Ernestine Fox, and he smiles a wry little smile. "I didn't think she would write back," he says. As perceptive as I am, I must have missed something vital in our earlier conversations.

"Who was she to you?" I ask.

"A model." But I sense there's more to the story.

I rip open the envelope, and extract a sheet full of feminine writing.

"Dear Julian,

To think that after all these years I'd hear from you. My resolve to not write back has been eroded by time and waiting. The letter I fantasized about throwing into the fire unopened has taken so long that when it finally found me, I had to read it. I was not going to respond. But I don't feel like I used to, my friend, and now, two days after reading your words, I realize that the anger I thought I still held for you has long been extinguished, that even the sadness left in its place is long gone.

The portrait still hangs in my boudoir. I am coming to the realization that, unbeknownst to me, my feelings about it have changed as well. For years I looked upon it as irrefutable proof that you loved me and I was angry at your inability to risk your situation for the sake of that love.

In time, I've come to look upon it as a memento of my own youth and beauty. Now I know it's a memento, too, of your ability to see and to transpose what you saw onto a canvas. We are both changed, and I suppose what happened decades ago no longer matters. Someday the painting will hang in a museum. Whoever sees it will probably think "Cohen was talented," and not "the artist must have been in love with her." Perhaps I have come to peace with that. Am I being dramatic? You always hated me for it. But you should appreciate that I never took a match or a knife to your work of art. Your art has survived both my love and my anger. I hope that makes you smile.

Yours truly,

Ernestine."

One thing I've learned is how to let a silence linger. I sit with the letter on my lap. Sunshine peeks in through the open window, lighting up stray particles of dust. I have gotten into a habit of airing out the room when I visit with Cohen. I don't look at him, just in case he can feel my expectant gaze on his face. I allow for a silent breath. Two. Three.

"She never forgave me," he says.

"What happened between the two of you?"

"The usual," he says. "She was one of my models. We spent a lot of time together. We both got curious, but she thought it was more than that. She thought it was love, and she could never accept it wasn't."

"Was she..." I hesitate, not because I'm embarrassed, but because I do wish to find the right words. "Was she like me?"

"You mean intelligent and a good writer? Dear girl, I wouldn't know."

"I meant was she one of your models for hire? Did she work in one of the brothels?"

"She was a girl for hire," he says. "But she was transitioning from the house she worked in into the house of her lover, who adored her. She was fond of him too, but when she grew infatuated with me, she started questioning her feelings for him. She threatened to reveal our liaison to him, which was something that could only hurt her, but she presented the idea to me as if it were a threat, some kind of bizarre ultimatum.

"Seeing me completely unmoved, she decided to create additional tension by asking her lover to buy her the painting for which she had served as the model. This, I must say, was not an unintelligent plan. The man came to see me, and it was obvious that he didn't know I was involved with his mistress, only that she had posed for me in her days of economic distress. He was a pleasant man, well-off and well-bred, and I found myself wishing to have him among my collectors. The idea of him knowing about my involvement with Ernestine became more distasteful to me once I had met him.

"He decided to purchase the painting as a wedding gift for her. He told me he had been a widower for quite some time, and was determined to marry her and move her into his house in Houston. I believe Ernestine threatened suicide when she learned I would do nothing to interfere with her lover's plan. A little dramatic, I would say. But she didn't go through with it, and she never made good on her threat to tell him about us. The last time I saw her was when I went to Houston to hang the painting in her boudoir and wish her well in her new life."

"You didn't regret letting her go?"

"Never. In fact, I don't think about her often."

"Is there another woman that you do think about?"

He smiles. "Maybe I'll tell you some day, but one secret at a time, don't you think?"

"Sounds fair." The idea that he might be looking forward to drawing out his story for me gives me hope for his recovery.

"Not completely fair," he says. "Today I told you one of my secrets, and yet you've told me none of yours."

"My secrets interest you?"

"They're starting to, dear girl. Perhaps you really are succeeding in getting me to have a spark of curiosity again."

"That's a good sign." I decide to give in to an impulse I had during his story about Ernestine. "In that case I shall tell you one of my secrets. I shall even seek your advice if you're inclined to give it."

"That's more irresistible even than a secret. What blind old man doesn't want to be called on for advice?"

"I have a client," I say, "or perhaps the correct phrasing is I had a client who offered me a similar arrangement as the gentleman in your story offered Ernestine. Not the marriage part, I suppose, but he offered to buy me a house so I could live there and be his mistress."

"Sounds like a good opportunity. Just be careful to make sure he puts it in your name."

I laugh. "I thought of that myself, but you see, things were not that simple. The first time he mentioned it, although I must say I liked this client very much, I panicked as if it were a menace. But when he didn't mention it again I wanted it, and then just as I started to warm to the idea…" I trail off, wondering if I should tell him about Mrs. Harden's threats, but decide against it. "Well, I found out from the paper that he was charged with running an illegal gambling saloon and he's awaiting trial."

"Oh, my! There goes your house, I'm afraid."

"There goes my house. But I'm not even sure that's the problem. After all, I'm fickle enough to not even know if I want the arrangement or not. My problem is determining if I truly care about the fate of this man, and if I do care then what should I do about it?"

"You obviously care, or you wouldn't mention it. The trick is knowing if you care for him only when you can't have him or if you care in a deeper more meaningful way. A lover in jail is something an imaginative mind can turn into quite a romantic figure."

"I don't even know if he is presently in jail or free while awaiting trial. The article is most unclear and I don't know how to find out."

"We can find out," he says. "That's the easy part. We'll send Deirdre to inquire, or perhaps her husband. They'll tell us if the man is still free, they'll tell us about the magnitude of the charges, and all the gossip surrounding the matter. What they can't tell us, dear lady, is whether or not you yourself have a dog in this fight. And I'm not sure you yourself even know that. If he's in jail and you find yourself wanting to go to him, it might well be because you truly care for him, or it might be that his predicament appeals to your penchant for adventure and drama. I'm afraid the only help I can offer you in that regard is to plant a seed in your mind about writing back to Ernestine. You seem to like to poke a fire with a stick, so come back in a day or two with whatever letter you come up with, and I will have my servants report back on the talk that's going around town about our man."

"Seems like we both like poking fires with sticks."

He smiles. "The difference is that back when I could keep all the drama on a canvas I could actually enjoy a healthy measure of inner peace."

As I walk into the sunshine, now scorching hot, I think about this notion of inner peace. I've had my tastes of it, moments that are serene and infused with a wholesome glow, yet at the other pole of my eternal quest for bliss waits excitement with its dizzying aura of danger and confusion. Am I constantly swinging between the two like a restless pendulum? And which of these do I want? Which do I treasure more? Is there a magic formula, a ratio that works for balancing peace and excitement in one's life? Can they coexist?

I think of peaceful mornings followed by sizzling evenings – my fantasy of what life could be for me here in Galveston at Mrs. Harden's. What keeps me from this other than myself? I can still have that life. Can I not walk away from the Aristotle debacle and from the temptation of moving into my own house? Yes, I would have to turn a blind eye to the madam's despotic tendencies, to her potential knowledge of my secret, but our relationship is built on mutual profit and cut-throat negotiation, not friendship and affection. I have a good situation. Can I not put thoughts of changing it out of my mind and enjoy the luxuries, privileges, and thrills it affords me?

CHAPTER 25
A MARE CALLED LUNA

I take special care with my toilette that evening. I wear a low-cut emerald green dress and dangly earrings. I ask Sarah to put my hair up, and insist she redo it twice until I'm satisfied. I dab the faintest hint of rouge onto my cheeks and droplets of musk perfume between my breasts and behind my knees. Conversation stops as I descend the staircase, as it usually does, but this evening I take special pleasure in pausing to soak in the admiration. Mrs. Harden too seems to take special pleasure in introducing me to my new client. I wonder if the news about Aristotle bolsters her. Is losing a good client worth it if it means your top earning girl will not leave? I file away the thought for later, to call upon in moments of fear when the possibility of her knowing my secret makes me lose sleep at night. Surely she values me too much to lose me. For now, I concentrate on the new man, a portly construction magnate who's looking at me as if I were a sizzling steak.

"Enchantée," I whisper as he kisses my hand.

"Enjoy the evening," Mrs. Harden tells us as if she were the hostess at an upscale restaurant. I lead my companion into the parlor where he buys me a julep – pure sugar water. I sit next to him and press my hip against his as one of the girls performs a song on the piano. I see the color rise in his cheeks, and my amusement would be very much at his expense if I didn't catch a small smile under his mustache and a look in his eye that shows he knows what I'm doing. I smile back gamely, and move my leg an inch away. He does not follow my motion, but instead winks. He's not a man to devour a good steak without taking his time to appreciate it, and I'm glad for the diversion.

He's jovial and endearing in his own way. There is complicity between us, and once we are alone in the dining room, we enjoy a good meal and a lot of laughter. I'm having a good time, but it's nothing compared to the thrill of being with a man like Aristotle. What was it about Aristotle that I found so compelling? His admiration was more flattering to me than that of other clients, his conversation more engaging, and there was always that seductive dance between us, the push-pull of luring and dismissing. Perhaps a fickle man is simply best suited to my fickle heart. If there is more there, that strange feeling I had the last time I saw him, I prefer not to examine it too closely. For I do not like how thinking about him robs me of peace and joy. I do not like it at all.

The next day, I'm determined to seek a distraction. I pen a quick note to the doctor saying I'd like to update him on my progress with Cohen. A note arrives back by that evening asking if I'd like to accompany him for another beach walk on Sunday. My heart responds by beating faster, and I am satisfied. Apparently my heart has other forbidden places to visit besides Aristotle's jail cell. I purposefully recall the way the doctor looked at me on our first walk together. We were talking about something intimate and there was real tension between us, real desire. Then that dissipated once our common interest in Cohen intervened. But I could bring the desire back, if I were so inclined, could I not?

The next day, before setting off for Cohen's house to find out more about Aristotle's fate, I make a point of fantasizing about the doctor, and it helps. I even allow my mind to wander into a hotel room similar to the one I occupied when I first came to Galveston. I imagine the room darkened and cool, the bed white and inviting, and me being there with Tarner on a whim and of my own free will, our encounter prompted by mutual desire, not a business transaction. The thought is laced with the kind of indulgence that only forbidden treats have, as if imagining desire outside the boundaries of a brothel were a new form of pushing past taboos and limitations.

Though there is nothing revolutionary about it. Prostitutes, too, have lovers, men who woo them and bed them not as clients but as chosen companions, men they see in their free time. It's not something I've considered before, as that type of attachment didn't interest me, and when other girls talked of such arrangements it was easy to see they were rife with complications. Often the lovers were jealous, and those who were not presented other issues – including a suspicious vested interest in the girls' earnings. I was glad to be free of such entanglements, and having sworn them off at a young age, I'm surprised to be tempted by them now.

To my delight, I find Cohen outside in his yard, sitting in a wicker chair in the shade.

"How did you get here?" I ask.

"I am blind, not lame. I held on to Deirdre's arm and she guided me."

"I'm glad you decided to come outside. It's a beautiful day." I instantly regret my words, for he can obviously not see the beauty, but if he is perturbed by the phrase he doesn't let on.

"It's good to be outside," he says. "I was hoping you'd come."

"Any news?"

My heart races, and this time it's Aristotle who is the distraction from my earlier thoughts of the doctor.

"Your man is free," Cohen says. "Deirdre even saw him. He is busily liquidating the inventory of his store, as he will need more money than he has to pay substantial fines as well as his lawyer's fees. Most likely he will be found guilty but will not be facing prison. What he will face instead is certain ruin as he'll have to sell all his buildings to settle his debts, the fines, and the lawyer. I would say that gambling was by far not profitable for him."

"Ruined?" I ask, taking a moment to calibrate my feelings, which are at present unclear. There is relief in knowing Aristotle will not be going to jail, but also a great deal of confusion.

"I'm afraid completely so. Of course, some wagging tongues say this was unavoidable and that the illegal gambling was a last-stitch effort to turn his fate around. I'm afraid his business endeavors have turned out to be unprofitable overall."

"Oh," I say. "I would have taken him for rather savvy."

Cohen smiles. "Savvy, yes. Apparently your friend is a self-made man with an adventurous streak similar to yours. The gossips also say he himself was a gambler, that his fortune started with gambling gains, and that occasionally he won large sums of money which he loved frittering away on expensive luxuries."

"Such as hundred-dollar prostitutes?"

"There is some evidence to that effect, is there not?"

I take a moment to think about this. Aristotle's enthusiasm, which ebbed and flowed, his occasional expansiveness. Could it have been fueled by the euphoric afterglow of winning a high stakes card game? I am a bit offended and a bit intrigued. Part of me is sorry for him, part of me understands and can relate.

"It would explain some of his… idiosyncratic ways," I say.

"Glad to be of service. So how does knowing all this affect your feelings for the man?"

"I seriously don't know."

"Smart girl. Sometimes it takes a while to understand how one feels and why. It will probably come to you in a day or two, and it will come to you naturally. You might want to distract yourself, in fact. Overthinking can blur your instincts."

"I forgot about the letter to Ernestine," I admit, and he laughs.

"That doesn't matter. It was a decoy. I would much rather leave Ernestine be. Especially since something arrived for us which is bound to be much more interesting and worthy."

He searches his breast pocket and produces an envelope. It has a man's handwriting on its back, meticulous, with just a hint of unbridled energy. The address is in Chicago. I remember writing to him.

"Dear Mr. Cohen,

I was so glad to receive the letter from your charming assistant. I'm glad, after these many years, to remember our acquaintance, of which I think frequently because of the painting of my mare, Luna, which I so treasure, it seems even more now that the beautiful creature it depicts is long gone. Luna with her kind eyes looks upon me daily as I read my paper, drink my coffee, and tend to the dwindling business of a man who has retired and passed on his empire to his sons. Perhaps, as I grow older, I shall even speak to her. Beautiful Luna, with her black shining mane, is a wonderful companion. I'm glad I had the foresight when I was young and in my prime to get you to paint her. Though at the time I did so to impress a lady, and though I balked at the expense once you quoted me your price, I'm very glad now I went through with it. I have made arrangements that after my death, the painting will be donated to the Jockey Club. I was wondering if, perhaps, you might write a few words that could go on a plaque next to it. You probably can articulate better than I can the importance of a horse in a man's life.

Yours sincerely,

Theodore Swift."

Cohen smiles. "That one was quite a ladies' man. Dashing, in fact, and a sportsman and gambler like your beau. Who would have thought, that after all these years, his truest love would turn out to be a black horse named Luna?"

"Do you remember her?" I ask. "Shall we write something to go on a plaque at the Jockey Club?"

"We shall."

My rendezvous with Cohen succeeds in cheering me up. There's something in composing a note about a horse that's bound to add gaiety to even the dreariest day. Before returning to the brothel, I mail the letter to Chicago, then take the extra dollar Cohen has given me and decide to shop for a new book. My steps lead me toward the Strand, and I consider heading for Aristotle's store. I've never been there, and I'm not sure it's a good idea to go now. I'm not sure if it's solidarity, or familiarity, or curiosity that's prompting me in that direction. I decide to take more time to digest my feelings and intentions. But I cannot concentrate on shopping anywhere else, so I stick my silver dollar back in my purse and head back to Mrs. Harden's. If tomorrow I wake up fresh and serene, perhaps then I'll head to Aristotle's to spend it on French soap and other luxuries. After all, what's the harm in helping a friend who needs to get rid of his merchandise?

CHAPTER 26
SPARKS OF LIGHT

The evening brings the visit of the boring young banker. I rise to the challenge of getting him to talk about things that are moderately entertaining. After I'm done with him, I am hungry and tired, and I withdraw happily within these feelings that have an immediate satisfactory solution. Our bodies can be easier to deal with than our minds. I sink into a deep sleep and dream of English Pointers playing on the beach. I awake in deep sadness. And I decide that for once I will allow myself the most fanciful of fancies. I will follow my unexamined feelings, my feelings steering me into the unknown. I will go purchase French soap, cologne, embroidered handkerchiefs, whatever useless silly stuff a silver dollar can buy. I will go to Aristotle's shop.

I put on a pretty day dress, and a hat that is most flattering. I manage to feel excited about the prospect of seeing him, and decide to have the most pleasant disposition, to joke and flirt and bat my eyelashes. Surely in a time of distress, he will welcome a gay distraction. But the closer I get to the store, the more nervous I become. It's as if I am going to see a dead body. I've always been squeamish about those, and never seen one except for Maw Maw. But that's not true. There was also Marie. Marie with her eyes open and that jewel she was so proud of still around her neck. She had seemed alive at first, and I'd wanted to talk to her. The memory is most unwelcome, especially on a morning when I'm already rattled. I close my eyes, stop in the middle of the sidewalk, and take a few deep breaths. The island air is already growing hot, but there's still a hint of a breeze. I let it caress my face and try to find my strength. I will not lose my composure.

Aristotle's store is near the port, in a red brick building two stories high. Despite the buzz of activity on the Strand, the store looks somehow forlorn, as if the shadow of imminent disaster looming over it has driven away all prospective customers. But maybe that's my imagination, and the growing heat is the only thing keeping people away.

The door is open. I step inside. The interior smells like coffee beans, soap, and candy, the same hallowed scent I remember from the shops of my childhood, where I stood behind glass cases hoping for the elusive sweet treat Maw Maw would spoil me with on occasion. I see Aristotle right away. I didn't expect him to man the counter himself, donning a white apron, ready to pour spices from large wooden crates into jars and paper sacks. His dark eyes take me in, and knowing that he's seen me, I have no recourse but to draw closer, approach the counter, a huge smile on my lips, my earrings jingling, as if I were trying to dazzle him like I used to inside the brothel walls, not here in this store full of the scents of my long-forgotten childhood.

"Well, well," he says, and his eyes shine, but his face doesn't look entirely happy. "What a sight for sore eyes."

"I had a dollar to spend, and I told myself I'd call upon you and spend it here."

"That's quite an honor."

"I was hoping for some French soap. And maybe some cologne," I say, batting my eyelashes. "But I might as well also buy some candy. This store, it smells just like…" I stop before I say something I must not. After all, I should keep up the pretense of having grown up in Paris, not Louisiana, and who knows what stores in France smell like? "Why, it smells delightful. It makes me want candy. So yes, French soap, cologne, and the best candy you have."

"Is that it?"

I look down. "I wanted to see you," I say, not having to feign the shyness I'd been hoping to use as an artifice.

He walks around the counter, stands just inches away from me. "If I put the Closed sign on the door, would you come to the back with me?"

I look at him, and before I can consider, a huge smile blooms on my lips. I giggle like a young girl being propositioned for the very first time.

"What's in the back?" I ask.

"A store room," he says. "Stables. And a room where my friends and I would gamble. But there's this one wall, in particular, that I'm thinking we might make use of."

I smile, but I hesitate. I think of the hotel room I'd imagined, my fantasies of being with the doctor. This is different and somehow better. More dangerous too. Because it's Aristotle, and with him I know things will be most exciting. In fact, I can feel myself melt just looking at him. But I prolong the moment, just to tease him, to tease us both with the suspended possibility.

I wait perhaps a heartbeat too long because an old lady wanders into the store. She asks Aristotle for hazelnuts for a cake. He weighs them for her.

"I'll pray for you," she says putting her old gnarly hand on top of his.

"That's mighty kind of you." I notice him tipping the scale slightly in her favor. Perhaps he needs to gamble because he gives his wares away. The old lady takes her time and I wander the aisles looking at confections in tall glass jars. My impatience and anticipation are pulsing in my veins. Finally, I hear the little bell of the front door closing. Aristotle hesitates with his hand on the lock. His eyes meet mine. I smile.

"All right," I say. "Show me that wall." And just like that, I'm just a girl, a girl whose heart beats faster when a man grabs her hand, a girl who sneaks into the back of a store, who is afraid of getting caught as her lover hikes up her skirt for a few stolen moments of passion. It's fast and intense, both familiar and new. I've never done this before, I wish to say, but obviously I have, so many times I've lost count years ago, but not like this, not just because I wanted to, not with uncertainty and trepidation and whatever else might be mixed in with this swirl of feelings. Afterwards we embrace, and I find myself hanging on to him.

"You could have told me," I say.

He disentangles himself from our embrace, straightens out his clothes.

"Take whatever you'd like," he says, as he passes back into the store.

I follow him, slightly dazed. He flips the sign back to Open, then unlocks the door. Not knowing what to say, I pick out a few bars of soap, a small bottle of cologne, a bar of chocolate. The bell rings again, and two ladies enter the store. They both need rice and coffee, and as Aristotle chats pleasantly with them, I pace back and forth.

"Are you ready, Miss?" he asks, as the ladies busy themselves looking at an assortment of candles.

He takes my soap, cologne, and chocolate, and wraps them, adding some choice pieces of candy, also a fashion magazine. He's brushing me off, and yet he's trying to make a gesture. Awkwardly, I place my silver dollar on the counter. He waves it off, and I realize the kindest most gracious thing to do is to accept the gift and go. I blow him a kiss from the doorstep, and he blows me a kiss in turn. His eyes look sad and the sadness stays with me.

I allow myself to do the unthinkable. For more unthinkable than sneaking with a man to the back of a store and letting him do for free what I normally charge a small fortune for, is crying real hot tears, and letting the blind artist I am meant to comfort console me.

"Now, now," Cohen says, and his old hand brushes mine. "Let it all out, it's good for you."

Despair flows out of me as if a pipe burst somewhere in my soul. I didn't even know I held so much of it. The flood seems endless, relentless, tears asking for more tears. Cohen pats my back. "Sounds like you've needed a good cry for about a decade."

Between sobs I tell him everything about my encounter with Aristotle. I don't censor our brief passionate encounter against the wall in the back of the store. Through my tears, I see Cohen smile, his face lit up by something akin to recognition.

"You are allowing yourself freedom," he says. "Well done. We get to our purest selves when we follow our instincts. Let yourself feel the things you feel."

"But I don't know what I feel," I say. "Except sadness. I feel a lot of sadness but I don't know why."

"Sometimes it's best not to analyze the feelings, just to feel them."

"I don't like it, though. I feel like I'm being prompted to do more, but I don't know what. And it's all so confusing... He wanted me but he also shut down completely, wanted me gone, but at the same time gave me a gift. Why?"

"That's easy, my dear girl, and if you were thinking straight you'd understand it perfectly. He'd rather you see him as a savior than a victim."

I cover my face with my hands. "I should not have gone there."

"Of course you should have. It's quite possibly one of the purest things you've ever done."

"I'm not sure pure is the word," I say, laughing through my tears. Though there was something wholesome about the store, perhaps something hidden in that scent from long ago, the memories of Maw Maw and my childhood, the gesture I caught Aristotle making when he tipped the scale in favor of the old lady. Something in there is interlaced with feelings I rarely allow myself to recall. Feelings so pure and cherished they hurt me.

"I don't mean purity in the sanctimonious sense. I mean that was a moment when you were really being yourself," Cohen says, and his words unsettle me as much as the scent of the store and the general experience of it did.

"That's a strange thought."

"It is. Especially for someone like you. We all have trouble shedding the personas we construct. We all pretend to be people we're not in order to succeed in society. But you, my dear, you've taken this pretense to another level. Maybe this is why you like this young man. Have there been other times when you were more yourself around him? When you felt free to be your true self?"

"I need to think about that," I say. For I know, I've put on a show for Aristotle many times. I have outdone myself in performing for him. But something of what Cohen said struck a chord in me. I have experienced sparks of something in Aristotle's company that is rare and different and freeing. It's hard to separate the elation of being admired, wanted, lusted after, from the joy of purely being, and I cannot properly articulate these thoughts, but there is a release, a freedom, and an ease I usually find in laughter, when laughter comes so naturally it surprises me, and this tiny glimmer of magic, this frisson of serendipity has sparkled between Aristotle and me like an elusive firefly.

"How about you?" I ask this not only because my mission is to get Cohen to open up, but because I'm genuinely curious. The firefly is here too, in this room with me and this man for whom I feel no desire but definitely friendship. "Have you had people with whom you felt like you were free like that?"

"It's what I've searched for all my life. It doesn't happen much, even for those of us who invest time and work and money in learning to be free."

"So you purposefully set out to work toward achieving everything I practiced all my life to counteract?"

"Smart girl," he says. "Yes, I've spent a lifetime unlearning habits and artifices and trying to allow myself to be free, to loosen up, to follow my instincts. If you look at my paintings you can see it. There's a certain rigidity I've fought for years to let go of. If only I had had more time. I was only beginning to allow myself to strive less for precision, more for feelings. You know, when *La nouvelle peinture* made its debut in Paris, people made fun of the Impressionists, but it truly was a big leap forward. The best thing we can do is let go of the ways we were taught and simply try to capture the light."

"But you do that. It's what I saw in your paintings downstairs, it's what mesmerized me."

"You have not seen a lot of art, have you?" he asks in a surprisingly kind voice.

"I don't think I paid much attention," I admit.

"That's why you see the light. Your thinking is not tainted by too much knowledge, too much education and expertise. But I wish you had seen the work of the Impressionists. I wish you had seen Monet's paintings, so you'd know what I'm talking about, that kind of looseness and surrender. They literally tried to capture the impressions of things rather than the things themselves."

My mind goes back to the fleeting image of the firefly I imagined earlier. I close my eyes and for a second I see it, a spark of light in the darkness. "You're talking about paintings, and I asked about people," I say. "Who was the person who made you feel most free?"

He laughs. "I was always more interested in paintings than people. But in this case, the two are connected. If there is one painting that truly captures my purest essence, if there's one painting where I allowed myself full freedom, well, it's tied to a person with whom I felt like I could shed all the pretense and be my most authentic self."

"Who was it?"

Cohen's smile strikes me as something from far away, a memory of a different time and place. "I will tell you. But not today. Suffice it to say, that these things are magical, but they are intense. Being one's true self can be scary. Some people get a small glimpse of that magic and it's too powerful for them. Some people would rather hide. Don't be one of those people, Aimée. You're stronger than that. You're stronger and braver and at some point putting on mask after mask gets old."

"My real name is Yvonne." I don't know why I say it and I immediately regret it. "Don't tell anyone," I add hastily, though usually it's what I say when I do want people to tell, and the irony is not lost on me.

"I won't. Thank you for telling me, dear girl. You never sounded like an Aimée to me, too precious, too contrived. And it seems now I owe you a secret. Next time you come, I will tell you a story. For now I hope you feel better, and that you have some interesting things to think about."

I do, indeed, leave feeling lighter. I take a few detours on my way back to Mrs. Harden's, enjoying the sunshine though it does feel mighty hot now. I don't know yet if I'm the kind of person brave enough to be myself, or if I even want to be. And I don't know if Aristotle is either. Isn't part of our dance hiding from one another? I once saw a girl in New Orleans perform an elaborate show, where she was supposed to shed various veils, yet she never did completely. She glided on a small stage to music that was as mysterious as her veiled figure itself, and we only occasionally got glimpses of her naked flesh, an arm here, a thigh there, once even, a buttock round as a ripe peach, a breast that seemed hard and inviting like an apple, the curve of a feminine belly, the elegant shape of a neck. It was all rendered more enticing because of its elusiveness, the veils that never were completely shed making each body part more tempting than if the woman had revealed herself to us fully nude. I wonder if our true selves are like that, mesmerizing because they are hidden, the occasional sparks magical because of the deep darkness they stand in. But then, again, I wonder if the authentic joy I should concern myself with is the one of the person observing these sparks, or the one of the person emitting them. Who am I without an audience? Do I care more to have someone stand in awe before me, or for myself to experience the joy of being truly and completely aflame?

CHAPTER 27
INSOMNIA WITH ORCHIDS

The next day brings a treat: another meeting with Brighton, another overnight visit. Once again, there's a fresh cake preceded by a rather sparse supper, though this time I'm pleased to find an actual cooked meal left behind by his servants, not a meager improvised repast of sardines from his pantry. Brighton himself is more interested in the cake, which we eat in our silk pajamas in his bedroom. There is a lightness to our banter, as we are more at ease with each other than before, and yet I feel like I have carried a shadow into this beautiful home with its white draped furniture. Or maybe the shadow was already here and we are both dancing around it, Brighton and I. There is my sadness over Aristotle, which I fight to push to the back of my mind, and there's my knowledge of the man who came in quietly like a thief in the night, though this was a home where he was not only welcomed, but expected.

I will not ask nor allude to my knowledge of it, but I suspect Brighton is expecting his midnight visitor again tonight, that part of the lightness of our visit has to do with his anticipation of seeing this man. Is the cover of night, the secrecy, part of the appeal? Or would the two of them delight in each other's company just as much if they were free to openly love one another in the sunshine? Perhaps they would delight in it even more, but these are things I cannot ask.

I am not paid to see what needs to remain unseen. I'm paid, instead, to accomplish the impossible, or at least try. Brighton seems just as tense under my touch, but he doesn't pull back when I guide his hand to my breasts. "So soft," he says. "Quite wonderful, darling. You are more lovely than the loveliest work of art. But it does nothing for me. Absolutely nothing."

I'm not as stung this time around, though there's a moment when I do indeed feel the sharp sting of tears approaching. Brighton carefully buttons my pajama shirt, as if dressing a doll, then kisses my forehead. "Don't be cross," he says.

I take a few seconds to compose myself, then we each help ourselves to more cake as if nothing of note had happened. I am mindful to feign sleepiness earlier than last time, to slip into my room, turn on my light, then turn it off, as if it were a signal. I lie in my bed in the dark, the light throw cover pulled up to my chin, and listen for the creak of stairs which I'm not sure I can hear or not. I feel like crying and I don't know why. For a girl who doesn't cry, this is a lot of emotion over the course of only a few days.

The orchid on the nightstand doesn't help. I can make out its elegant silhouette as my eyes adjust to the darkness, and it reminds me of the man who has given me one of my own. I wonder what Aristotle is doing, if he's sleeping alone. Who else would he be sleeping with above his shop, now that he's lost everything? I imagine him staying up late, counting and recounting his money. Does he regret the house he can no longer buy for me, the two English dogs?

I try to picture the doctor too, with the girl he said he visits once a week. Which of the two rooms would I like to be in right now? One of these two men I will see on Sunday. The other I might never see again. Unless I decide to go back to his store. But wasn't our last encounter goodbye? What would it mean if my visit was not once-in-a-lifetime, an exception from well-established habits, but perhaps the beginning of a new one? And what habit would that be? Giving away my favors for free?

The next morning I awake drowsy from crying, but the coffee Brighton has left for me is strong and plentiful. Like last time, I drink a cup in bed, then one on the back porch, overlooking the garden, listening to the waves. There's a serenity to the lush greenery of Galveston Island, to the elegant gliding of butterflies and the circling of pelicans above, that's hard to resist. If you spend enough time in quiet contemplation outdoors, it'll seep into your soul. I drink my coffee slowly, savoring each sip. I let the breeze and greenery bring me peace and joy. When I feel light like a butterfly, weightless like the breeze, and carefree like the grackles whistling their morning tune, I go back inside, wash up, get dressed, and walk in the still fresh morning air, not toward the brothel, but toward Aristotle's store. I try to chase away my trepidation, try to remind myself of butterflies and coastal birds and the light of this barrier island, which has the power of shining through our darkest moments. Or so I hope.

The little bell rings as I let myself into the store. Like last time, the scent of my childhood greets me: spices and soap and powdered sugar. Confections beckon from inside glass jars. Bolts of fabric wait on shelves. The store smells as wholesome as Maw Maw's linen closet, as wistful as a jar of cookies only opened on special occasions, as tender as her hand caressing the top of my head when I'd been good and was about to get a treat.

"May I help you?" comes a feminine voice. I turn to see a thin girl who doesn't look to be more than fifteen.

146

"Is Aristotle here?" I ask.

"He's in the back." For a moment we stand there taking each other in. I wonder if she'll help me or if she's bound to be suspicious.

"Could you please tell him Aimée is here to see him?" I ask in my most polite voice. She's still looking at me like I'm a curious apparition, but without malice. I wonder if there's anything inappropriate about my appearance, except my dress being too elegant for a morning shopping expedition.

"I'll be right back," the girl says. In her wake, there's nothing I can do to still my beating heart. Is it good or bad that I can't see Aristotle's face when she gives him the news of my being here? When he finally strolls toward me, his eyes are warm and he looks genuinely happy to see me. I smile as he takes my hand and kisses it.

"What a pleasure," he says. "I see you've met Minnie. She's my niece, and kind enough to help me."

"I hope this isn't a bad time," I say.

"There's never a bad time for you to stop by, Aimée. Would you care for some coffee?"

He guides me toward a room in the back, an office with papers and account books strewn everywhere. My mind goes back to the vision I had of him the night before, going over his ledgers. He motions for me to sit in a large armchair across from the desk, and goes in search of coffee. When he returns, he leaves the door open, and I realize it's a concession to Minnie, so that she won't suspect anything untoward in our get-together. And knowing that we'll do nothing but drink coffee and talk makes me more nervous than the prospect of a more illicit kind of visit. It saddens me too, as if I'm suffering a loss, the loss of something I wasn't aware I wanted, a special channel of communication between us closed for now. I lower my lids and take a sip of the coffee he's brought, a generous cup topped with milky foam. I encounter a flavor that brings me back to my childhood the way the scent of the store did when I first entered. Chicory! The memories are overwhelming.

"You like?" he asks, seeming amused. "My Maw Maw always made it like that, in Louisiana."

"Mine too," I whisper, and just like it did the other day with Cohen, the confession is followed by immediate regret. "I'd missed it. Your store smells like my childhood."

He smiles the warmest kind of smile. He doesn't point out he knew the Paris story was made up, but his eyes on me look knowing, and I'm more aware than before of how ridiculous I've been. It isn't just Brighton who could immediately see through that story, it's probably everyone. If they pretended to believe it it was only because, like a shiny bauble that isn't real, the story played into the make-believe of the brothel, enhanced the dance of desire and seduction.

147

"I'm glad you came back," he says.

I smile and wipe the milk foam off my lip. "I like being around you," I say. "It's… It's different. Like a part of me coming to life that just wants to play."

"That's well articulated." He sits across from me at his cluttered desk. He has the air of a man with not a care in the world, but I know better. "I'm afraid a bit of amusement is all I have to offer at the moment," he says, taking a long sip of his own coffee. "It's not a position I'm comfortable finding myself in."

The air is thick at this admission, and I look away. But then I meet his eyes and smile. "It's all I ever have to offer, really. Apparently some people find it quite valuable."

At this he laughs loudly and the tension is broken. "You've elevated it to a real art form, dear lady. This is the first good laugh I've had in ages."

I smile at him. "Glad to be of service."

"How come you're out so early?"

"Not all my engagements last late into the night. I quite enjoy mornings, actually. Especially here in Galveston. It's such a beautiful place."

"So you've said before. Have you been farther West, where there's nothing but farmland and sand dunes?"

"Never."

"If you can spare an early morning, or even an evening," he says, "I'd love to drive you out there. It would have to be this week, before I sell my horses. It's a pretty sad state of affairs, when a man has to part with his horses, but since I have to do it, I will, and I'd rather take them on one last adventure first. I'd like to take you on an adventure too."

"I'm free on Sunday," I say, though I know I'm meant to take a beach walk with the doctor.

"Sunday is a good day."

"Could we go Sunday evening?"

"We can, if you don't get scared when we ride back in the dark. You don't strike me as someone easily frightened."

"I'm not," I say. "And sometimes it's worked to my disadvantage."

"Well, that's another thing we have in common." He stands to collect my empty cup, and as he does, he touches my face. For a moment, his finger caresses my jawbone, brushes over my lips. His callused skin is rough, and yet it feels like being kissed without actually being kissed. My breath catches. Then he is gone, and when he returns, I know it's time to head back into the store. He guides me, his hand resting briefly on the small of my back, then retreating as we step into his niece's line of vision.

"Let me make you a bag of treats," he says, putting on an apron. "Did you like these as a child?" he asks about a familiar roll of wafers wrapped in wax paper. I can almost taste them dissolving on my tongue, can almost smell them behind the wrapping paper. I smile and nod, and he drops several rolls into a bag.

"When I was a little boy," he says, fishing for a few more packages, "my friends and I would play with these. We'd pretend they were communion wafers."

The girl at his side covers her laugh. "Did *Maman* know?"

"Oh, my sister was furious when she caught us! She has a fine sense of humor, my sister, but not about anything religious."

I wonder how she'd feel about you introducing her daughter to a whore, I think. But I chase the thought away and focus instead on Aristotle and the bag of treats he's making for me.

"How about chocolate cream bars?" he asks. I smile the brightest kind of smile because those were a rare treat when I was little. He drops a few into the bag, then moves on to the next display. The girl excuses herself to go to the back and look for a bolt of fabric she'd promised to show a client. We are, once again, blissfully alone.

"Cherries?" Aristotle asks. I laugh. Maw Maw didn't allow me to have those, because she'd heard there was brandy in the liquid center. "Forbidden treat," I say, and he places several into the bag. Candied almonds follow, nougat wrapped in wax paper, licorice lozenges I never liked but which always made reaching into the bag more of an adventure, a pink fondant confection, hard candy coated in powdered sugar, and soft luscious gummy drops for contrast.

Once the bag is full to bursting, Aristotle ties it expertly with a ribbon and hands it over. Though candy is hardly out of my price range, I'm elated at the unexpected gift. He must like the joy he sees in my eyes, because this time, when he smiles, his eyes don't look a bit sad. I undo the ribbon as if performing a strip tease, reach into the bag, grab a soft green gummy drop and place it between my teeth. He laughs.

"See you Sunday," he says. "Come in the early afternoon. I need to introduce you to the horses before we set out."

"I'll come as soon as I finish my morning meal," I say. "I tend to breakfast around noon."

CHAPTER 28
A SWEET CONFESSION

I saunter away, floating on happiness. The day is still young, and in my joyful state there is one place in particular I want to go to, and one person in particular I want to share my feelings with – and my bag of candy as well. Of course, I'm ashamed of deciding to cancel my outing with the doctor in order to go on an adventure with Aristotle, but how could I resist? I have only one night of freedom each week, one precious night, and I wish to squeeze as much enjoyment out of it as possible. Surely there must be a polite way to reschedule my walk with Tarner. And Cohen knows the doctor. He'll probably be able to advise me. Though of course I'm embarrassed to admit my predicament to him, and the lack of delicacy with which I cast our mutual friend aside.

But Cohen, happily munching on the sweets I brought, his lip coated in powdered sugar, laughs when I admit to my flightiness. "You followed your instinct," he says. "That should tell you something. Civilization has conditioned us to overthink things, but sometimes our purest desires come out when we allow ourselves to be spontaneous. This is obviously what you wish to do. You might tell Tarner that something unexpected came up, and that you need to postpone your walk with him. It wouldn't even be a lie. Besides, what do you want with Tarner anyway?"

"A distraction?" I say honestly, and Cohen laughs.

"Are you drawn to him?"

"Sometimes. I don't know. Yes, maybe. He was very chivalrous when we met, and—"

"I would assume he's not your client."

"He can't afford it, no. Also... I sometimes get the sense he disapproves. Though he frequents a girl too, just not one that's as expensive."

"Men and their hypocrisy," Cohen says.

"I don't feel so much that he judges my moral character, but rather that he finds my occupation risky."

"It is risky, though, isn't it? Yes, I'm assuming a house as expensive as yours affords a certain standard of protection, but..."

I wish I could laugh off his concerns, but Marie's lifeless body flashes before my eyes. Weren't we in one of the best houses too?

"It's preposterous that anyone should feel sorry for me. I have a more interesting life than most, and I'm a woman of means. As to the occasional dreadful thing that might happen... In a house such as mine it's an aberration, whereas in many so-called respectable homes, a woman might suffer violence every day."

"Unfortunately you are correct."

"Tell me the story," I say, wishing to distract us both, "of the woman who made you feel yourself. The one you alluded to last time."

"Yes," he says, "her. But first you must give me two gumdrops." He holds out his hand.

"Two?" I say, laughing and searching through the bag of treats. "You drive a hard bargain."

"The story is worth it. She was some lady. In some ways you remind me of her. And you have actually asked about her before."

"The Paris showgirl?" I ask, abuzz with excitement. I place all the gumdrops I can find into his palm.

"The very one. She was quite something. And I'm sorry, dear girl, when I alluded to her portrait not being very special, I'm afraid that was a flat-out lie. Her portrait was the best I've ever done. So good, in fact, it piques me to think of it. Not being able to produce anything else quite as alive has haunted me ever since."

He sticks three gumdrops into his mouth at once, winks at me, then takes a moment to gleefully suck on them like a child.

"I remember first meeting Odette at a party," he says. "We barely spoke. It was a night of many people and she and I were both engaged in conversation with patrons that held the keys to our respective futures. I remember pinpricks of electricity going through my fingers as I first shook her hand. I dismissed it as one of those nonsensical reactions our bodies sometimes have with other bodies, the type of static that means nothing. But when my eyes met hers in the crowd, I felt something similar. It was most disconcerting, so I looked away. I concentrated on the evening's goal, which was to entertain one of my collectors and his intended wife, to discuss a portrait with them and secure a much-coveted commission."

"It was weeks after that that I received word from Odette. She, too, wanted to commission a painting and asked about prices. I did something calculated that I did often in those days, when my fame was just beginning to rise. I took my time writing back, and then it was only to let her know I was booked through the summer – a half-truth meant to enhance my fame, though in this case it also had the ulterior motive of avoiding a meeting with a woman whose presence I found overwhelming.

"She wrote back insisting, pressing me for a price. I decided this time not to reply at all. Maintaining mystery and an aura of unavailability was important to creating my fame. People were starting to pay more while feeling privileged that I accepted their commissions. But I couldn't stop thinking about her. And so, one night, against my better judgement, I sent my footman to inquire about her show and to get me a ticket. I couldn't sleep the night before. I considered not going. The bizarre effects this woman had on me were most disconcerting. But I did go.

"The show was not a quality production, not by far. But she shone. There was something mesmerizing about her, and I took comfort in noticing that the rest of the audience felt it too. I was not alone in my reaction to her magnetism. How else would you explain the rising ovation given by a full house to a mediocre show with a trite and trivial plot and dancing that was nothing short of ordinary? Flowers were thrown on stage, and I watched as a large arrangement of orchids was placed into her arms. Then I remembered the rumors that had reached me at that party where she and I briefly crossed paths, rumors of a wealthy lover who was subsidizing her luxury lifestyle, a different one from the one who had passed and left her the apartment on the Boulevard Saint Michel. I wondered if that was who would pay for her commission, and in that moment my curiosity got the best of me. I wrote to her that night with insincere compliments about her show, and quoted a price that was nothing short of absurd. She wrote back the next day and agreed to it.

"My first visit to her apartment on the Boulevard Saint Michel occurred so soon after the show, the large arrangement of orchids had not even wilted. The flowers greeted me in the vast hall with tall ceilings, parquet, and crown molding. They stood before a mirror, elaborate, like a woman's hairstyle in days gone by, but much more alive, and a stark reminder of the presence in her life of that other man who had the means to give her things I couldn't. Normally I would have the person whose portrait I painted come to my studio directly, as there I had my easels and all my supplies and could get to work straight away. But my curiosity about Odette was such that I needed to observe her in her own surroundings. Or so I told myself.

"She came to greet me wearing a pink kimono, and once again that spark of electricity coursed through me when I touched her hand. Her attire was informal and nonconformist, but I had to remind myself this was a woman I had already seen naked on a stage, and who would probably choose to disrobe for the portrait.

"She led me into a large sun-filled salon. More parquet, more crown molding, tall ceilings, and tall windows revealing the type of cast-iron balconies I so love in Paris. In the center of the room, another flower arrangement captured my eyes, this time roses, more resplendent even than the orchids. It was obvious this woman was admired and cherished. She showed me the place where she wanted to hang the painting, and told me about her vision for it — something most immodest and in rather poor taste, Venus being born of the waves, but in her likeness.

"My initial impulse was to dissuade her and have her settle on something more refined, but her enthusiasm was contagious, and what I loved best was that, while being very much enamored with it, she was also able to laugh at her own idea, to see it as both ridiculous and sublime. 'I am a showgirl, not a duchess,' she said. 'There is no need for subtlety here, I'd rather err on the side of provocation. And don't be afraid of bold colors. I want the painting to command the viewer's attention. Like a flamingo! Imagine a flamingo in my salon, with its bright feathers, its thin stalks for legs, and that misshapen beak. It would be most unsuitable but also most interesting and unforgettable. It takes a person with a most alive spirit to appreciate a flamingo, and it takes the same type of person to appreciate me.'

"She served mint tea but also champagne, along with the most exquisite Moroccan cookies flavored with rose essence and adorned with almonds. She told me about a trip to Morocco with a past lover, about the food and the souks, the spices, and how overwhelming to the senses it had felt. She talked about how French society had such a penchant for restraint and understatement, but she loved abundance. Her greed for life and all it had to offer was alluring. I told her I needed to capture that in her portrait, that I needed it to be not just a likeness of her, but the sensation of her, her spirit.

"Her sessions sitting for me were different from any I've had with my other subjects. To get us in the mood, we'd drink champagne and talk for hours. When I drew her, it was later, after she left when, still intoxicated with her, I drew from memory. At first all we did was talk. She loved to look at my other paintings and we had long conversations about art, about spontaneity, playfulness, and the things I wanted to capture in her portrait. It wasn't until later that I became her lover. Our connection transferred well from our long conversations into the realm of passion. We were so absorbed with each other that I forgot to paint. It was like we had both forgotten it was the primary purpose of our acquaintance.

"It was one leisurely afternoon after we had enjoyed champagne and a brief but satisfying lovemaking session on the divan in my studio, that I went to my easel, while she was still stretching lazily on the daybed, and drew her in fast, furious strokes, added paint as if in a trance, and within less than an hour had created the painting I'd been thinking of for an entire month. When she got out of bed and came to look, she was mesmerized, but she also struck me as a bit frightened.

"'Am I that way?' she asked. Her face looked pained.

"It wasn't that she didn't like it. She loved it, and she insisted on throwing a lavish soirée to have it unveiled. But she confessed an unease about the portrait. She said the woman on the canvas was not her, but some idealized version of her, someone she'd never be: prettier, freer, happier, more fulfilled.

"I think it brought on some kind of existential crisis. Who am I? Who do I wish to be? That kind of thing. So I offered what I thought she wanted. I offered to take her on a trip to Morocco. She said she couldn't go, the theater needed her, her lover the count wouldn't excuse her absence. I offered a weekend on the Riviera instead, and we compromised. We ended up going mid-week when she had no shows. It was a beautiful two days. Her glorious smile on the beach, her joy splashing in the waves, the decadent breakfasts on the terrace of our villa. But I made the mistake of getting swept away in the moment. I asked her to marry me and leave the count. I was starting to enjoy success and money. I could not offer her the riches her benefactor did, but I was beginning to see the possibility of a life of moderate luxury and unending adventure."

I smile, nibbling pensively at one of the chocolate-covered cherries. "Your adventures, though. Not hers. She probably liked having her own adventures."

"I see that now. I see that she loved the stage. Had we had more of a chance to discuss things, I would not have insisted she abandon her dancing. Just the count."

"But you wanted her to follow you, and she was not a follower."

"You're wise, my friend. And I was young and I offered the wrong things. I do think I would have understood, even then, that she wanted, needed to keep dancing. I did not want to take that away from her. I only meant to take her away from the life with the count, and all the sacrifices and pretense that involved. I felt that if she allowed herself to be with someone she truly loved she could become the woman in the painting. It was the count and the others like him, her generous sponsors, that cast a shadow over her light."

"But you wanted to change her, to mold her to your liking. To make her into the woman in your painting."

"Perhaps. I remember her saying those things herself. Funny that you should understand her so well, and I so little."

"So what happened?"

"We fought, and she left. All she understood was that I wanted her to give up her own self to become my muse. I didn't understand those things until later, but would have understood them had she talked me through it. We could have started over. I could have stayed in Paris. Or we could have gone somewhere else where she could have danced. I could have put her through some fancy dance school, or she could have done it herself if she sold that beautiful expensive apartment and let go of some of the constraints of her life. Then again, I see it now... She took offense at me wanting her to do better than the type of dancing she did. Perhaps she was right. Perhaps I didn't fully respect or appreciate her. Perhaps I felt enchantment but not real love. I might have not made her the best offer, or made it in the best possible way, but in that moment the world was open to us, wide open, and the possibility for building our own happiness was there, but she slammed the door shut and left."

"Did you go after her?"

"I did, but in Paris she wouldn't receive me. I wrote letters she wouldn't reply to."

"What happened to her in the end? Did she become a great dancer?"

"No. And I'm not saying this out of spite. The sad thing is, nothing happened. For as long as I followed her career and stayed abreast of news of her, nothing changed, at least not dramatically, in her life. She danced in the same theater until she retired. The same type of roles. She stayed with the count for a few more years, then her next lover was a wealthy businessman. She stayed in the apartment on the Boulevard Saint Michel. She retired eventually, spent her life in cafés. If she had regrets, I never heard about them, and I suppose I'd rather not. There comes a day when all you wish is for the person you thought you would be happy with, to have been happy without you."

"But you still think she would have been better off with you. You think she could have been more herself than the self she chose."

"I know she didn't love the count. She told me so repeatedly. But she loved the comfortable life he offered. As to her dancing... Perhaps I'm wrong and maybe unfair, but any artist requires new challenges and growth. I think she had more talent than she pushed herself to display. The place where she was... It was comfortable, known. I offered her a leap into the unknown, a new adventure. I think there were more layers to her as a dancer that she could have discovered."

"Yet she had made a nice life for herself."

"She had. And a nice life is nice. But is it enough?"

I sit in silence as I contemplate his question. "I always thought so. In fact, her life, like mine, sounds more than nice. It sounds like there was quite a bit of adventure, quite a bit of luxury too."

"Luxury becomes boring after a while. So does having the same adventure over and over. At some point we all need something more, something higher. Those of us who are given gifts need to constantly find better ways to use them. You're young, of course, and your life up to this point has probably not been easy. But one reaches a moment, dear girl, when simply waking up in a nice room and drinking good coffee and wearing fine clothes and even throwing the occasional party is not enough anymore. Of course, since regrets never did anybody no good, it is kindest to wish Odette never reached that point. But having known her the way I knew her, having seen how she carried her inner light, I cannot help but wonder about it. I cannot help but think that she was destined to do more, to be more, but she was afraid to take a risk."

"Would the count have been angry if she left him?"

"Undoubtedly, and it would have had some repercussions. No more flowers, but maybe also no more star roles at the cabaret. Still, I believed that there were other roles out there for her, roles to secure through her own merit, without a wealthy lover's protection. And there were also opportunities to hone her craft. There was more than that one cabaret in Paris, and definitely more establishments throughout the world."

"I've never really traveled," I say.

"Maybe you will, dear girl. Maybe you will. It's a whole beautiful world out there."

"Where else have you been, besides Paris?"

"Monaco," he says. "Spain. I couldn't bear to go to Morocco without her, but I did go to Spain and Portugal. And I did go to Italy. And Greece. That was perhaps my favorite. Seeing the wonders of antiquity, then seeing the beauty of the Greek Islands... Those aqua blue waters, nothing like Galveston, dear girl. Think aqua blue like a jewel, and then perfectly white houses on hills. Such surreal beauty! Such magic!"

"Did you paint there?"

"A lot. And I sold every single piece. I used the money to prolong my journey. I went to Istanbul, saw the palaces and mosques, and the Grand Bazaar, ate grilled sardines on street corners, grilled mussels filled with rice and drenched in lemon juice, sesame pretzels shared with high-strung seagulls as a boat rocked me across the Bosporus. From there I sailed to Venice. It was magical, a city on water. Someday, I hope you get to see it."

"Did you ever fall in love again?"

"A few times. I don't believe we're meant to live that only once. It maybe wasn't as intense as with Odette, the feeling of being purely myself wasn't as present, though I got enough glimmers of it where I was happy with other people too. I'm not saying it only comes once in a lifetime. I'm just saying it's precious and hard to come by and you need to pay attention. But I'm not trying to tell you what to do. I'm just an old man sharing his life experiences with you. Just an old man who likes to talk."

I smile, satisfied, because not long ago, he was an old man who only wanted to be quiet. I'm happy I could draw him out, but I want to hear more.

"Your life story is fascinating. Have you ever considered writing a book?" He laughs and I immediately become aware of my contretemps. "I mean, telling your story so somebody else can write it."

"I've been approached by a few would-be biographers, but nobody I cared enough for to actually want to talk to them for hours."

"What if I helped?" I ask. "I'm not good enough a writer to write a book, nor would anyone be interested in publishing my writing. But perhaps I could write down your stories as you tell them to me, give my notes to the biographer, and then make sure they don't write things you don't approve of."

He laughs. "That's a lot of work. A big commitment."

"It would be entertaining for me. I like listening to you."

"Let me think about it, dear girl. Let me think about it."

CHAPTER 29
THE HORSES

Back at the brothel, before getting ready for the evening, I hastily pen a note to the doctor with my apologies, telling him something came up for Sunday, but that I would like to talk to him soon. I include in the letter, because I cannot wait, my idea of helping Cohen get his biography written. I feel like the doctor would be happy to learn of such a prospect, and hopefully he might have time to call on Cohen and convince him. The thought makes me happy, and as I prepare for the evening, I am in a most excellent mood.

Unfortunately my client is tedious and cantankerous. And much as I enjoy getting men to talk and have a good time, it occurs to me that some, unlike my friend Cohen, are not worthy of the effort, because despite a lot of masterful prodding, they have nothing interesting to say. I have to remind myself several times that I'm being paid handsomely for my services and my company. Yet despite myself all I want is for the evening to end.

When Saturday night comes around I find that I practically ache to get rid of my client – who wishes to drink a lot and stay with me until the wee hours. I find myself pouring more brandy for him, just so he'll fall asleep. When he finally does, I give one of the servants some money to make sure the man makes it home safely. I myself bathe with great care, eat like a wolf, and sink exhausted into my bed, enjoying the sweet anticipation of knowing that the next day I won't have to entertain anyone. Instead I'll get to ride out to a wild unspoiled beach in the company of Aristotle and his horses.

The next day, I awake earlier than expected. I call out for Sarah to bring my breakfast and eat it in a hurry, then ask for her help with getting dressed. I arrive at Aristotle's store before noon, hoping that he'll be happy to see me earlier than expected. The scents of soap and candy envelop me like an embrace. It's like slipping into a different world, one coated in magic and sunshine.

Aristotle's eyes smile as he places the Closed sign on the door. "Since you're early, how about another chicory coffee before you meet my horses?" I sit in his office, where the same mess of papers and accounts greets me, and he brings two cups of steaming *café au lait*. I savor mine, like a cat that's been given milk after a long deprivation. It tastes like my childhood, like those long-ago days when someone actually cared for me and wanted to spoil me with no ulterior motive.

After the coffee, Aristotle takes my hand and leads me to the back of the store, outside, then to the stable. The scents of hay and manure greet me, and the whinnying of the big elegant animals, their velvety muzzles coming out of the stalls as if curious to see who the unexpected visitor is.

"This is Lucky," Aristotle says, stopping before a speckled horse. "And this one here is Queen of Spades." A black mare extends her neck, waiting for his caress. "Yes, I named my horses after what some believe to be my supreme vice."

"Are they friendly?" I ask.

"Very much so. I hope you're not afraid of horses." He extracts two shiny apples out of a satchel hanging outside the stalls, and hands them to me. I hold one in my flattened palm, offering it to Lucky. His muzzle is gentle and warm. I'm tempted to give him the second apple too, but I know that as two leading ladies in Aristotle's life, Queen of Spades and I will have to make friends, so I better not give away her treat before we're even started.

I'm more hesitant about her, and she too seems to eye me with suspicion. Am I projecting my own insecurities onto a horse? Determined not to let any hesitation show, I wipe the second apple on my skirt and step toward the mare, holding it out. Instead of going for the apple, her large head with dark knowing eyes approaches my face.

I will myself not to be scared, not to back down. Her lips touch my cheek. I can feel her warm breath on my skin. She smells of dried hay, of the stables, but it's all mixed with a sweeter, balmy scent, which I recognize to be her pure animal essence. Not knowing what to do, I raise my left hand and scratch her neck. The large horse head leans into me, her cheek against mine. I inhale her scent and decide that I like it. There's warmth and comfort in smelling a creature like this up close. I wonder what she makes of the way I smell, what messages her big horse nostrils are conveying to her about me: cologne and powder, expensive dress, lots of artifice, but underneath it all, a real woman, warm and full of joy. Is she still in there, that woman? Can I strip off all the other layers and find her?

I keep scratching, and after a few moments, Queen of Spades bends down and grabs the apple with the top of her lips. I am now no longer scared and am starting to like this moment of affection with an animal so big and yet so gentle. I place a kiss on her forehead, and she bends her head as if to receive it.

"She loves you," Aristotle says.

"I love her too," I say, giddy as a child.

He takes my hand and leads me into the horse's stall, an enclosure that's a lot bigger than I thought. There, he hands me a brush. "She likes this. I think she'll be in heaven if you do it." He shows me how to run the bristles through her mane and along her body. We stand there, man, woman, and horse, enjoying the pure joy of the moment. Aristotle's hand guides mine, and Queen of Spades seems to be relishing the process, as far as I can read a horse's body language. "Look at her ears," Aristotle says. "See how relaxed she is?" He lets me brush her by myself for a while, then pulls me back, and before my amazed eyes, Queen of Spades rolls onto her back and kicks her legs up in the air. I burst out laughing, then carefully sit next to her, caressing her, as she does a little dance of joy I have seen puppies do before, but never horses.

By the time we leave the stables and go back into the store, looking for supplies for a picnic Aristotle suggests we might take to the beach, I have hay in my hair. We pause in front of a mirror next to a display of straw hats, and we both laugh as he picks the golden strands out of my messy bun. "That won't do," he says. "Come upstairs for a second."

I follow him up a narrow set of stairs. He pushes open the door of a room with tall ceilings, where piles of books stand around an unmade bed. The room smells a bit like the store. That wistful mix of French soap, coffee, and candy permeates everything in this building. But it also smells like Fougère Royale, and shaving soap and shoe polish, and underneath it all, like Aristotle's own skin, a sweet scent not too different from the essence of Queen of Spades. I look around, take in the bed and books, more papers strewn around the hardwood floors, a nearly finished bottle of brandy among them.

In a corner, there is a basin for shaving, and next to it, shaving utensils, a comb, and the Fougère Royale I'd smelled on him so many times. Three pairs of leather boots are lined up against the wall, and a travel trunk lies open next to them. I've never been inside a man's room before and this one, in its state of dishevelment, seems more personal. Aristotle is getting ready to leave this building, and I want to know where he's going. I inhale the scent of shaving soap and leather, the lingering notes of nostalgia from the store downstairs, and I'm seized by both longing and loss.

He takes the pins out of my bun, and my hair falls loose onto my shoulders. He glides the comb through my hay-strewn tresses, as if I'm Queen of Spades, the black mare that so enjoys being brushed.

"Do you really have to sell your horses?" I ask. "Isn't there a way around that?"

"It's not so bad," he says. "I'll see them every day. My friend is buying them. And he offered me a job at his stables."

"Oh! Here in Galveston?"

"Just down the street."

His hands continue to go through my hair. I reach for the bottle of Fougère, open it, and take a whiff. Overpowering sweetness gives in to fresher notes – lavender and moss. "That sounds like a good arrangement," I say.

"It is. I'll go back to being a mere stable hand. But I'll be near my horses. And it's how I started anyway."

"I remember that story." I think of him as a little boy, carrying buckets of feed and water, cleaning the stables, working until his hands grew so callused they never recovered. To distract myself from this vision, I dab a little bit of the fragrance on the back of my neck.

"If you like it, you can have that," he says.

"Thank you, but I just want some of the scent on me. Though what I truly wish is that I could bottle the scent downstairs, in the store. I wish I could bottle it and take it with me."

"Me too," he says, and now I'm afraid I've made him sad, that he'll withdraw, close up on me like he's done before. "The scent is my favorite thing about this store."

"Mine too. It reminds me…" I trail off. "Never mind. I'm afraid I'm getting sentimental."

"What's wrong with being sentimental?"

"It tends to get in the way of my work."

"I thought Sunday was your day off," he says, smiling and smoothing the hair out of my face. I feel like I'm going to melt.

"It is," I say, ecstatic with the freedom of it. I bring my lips to his. Our kiss is gentle and tentative, because although we are two people who have already exchanged many kisses, many embraces, and countless passionate moments, this is new. This quiet room uncharted territory, this tenderness an unexplored continent lying vast and wondrous at our feet.

Later, before we leave the room that from now on shall be imprinted in my fondest memories, I walk around barefoot, reading the titles of books. Probability, Blaise Pascal, Analytic Probability Theory, Science of Probability.

"So there is science to gambling?" I ask standing in the middle of his piles of knowledge.

"Lots," he says. He's sitting on the bed putting on his boots. "And I love reading about it. But at the end of the day, it's mostly about trusting your instincts."

I crouch down to open one of the books and come across some complicated math. "You understand this?"

"I do," he says.

"And it's useful?"

"More interesting than useful."

"You ever win big?" I ask.

"Every time I came to see you." We both laugh. He's now swiping a brush across the surface of the boots, as if a trip to the beach requires extra shine, and he looks unbelievably handsome in the late afternoon light, more handsome that I thought him to be when I first met him. It's as if his features have improved as my fondness for him grew.

"What other books do you have?" I ask.

"Things about horses. Everything on how to care for them, how to train them, illnesses they might have."

"Gambling and horses."

"They're somewhat related. There's nothing as magical as betting on a horse. Have you ever been to a race?"

"No."

"If you'd like to go, I'll take you. I can't exactly afford the best seats at the moment, but I promise we'd have a good time."

With that, we descend to the store to look for provisions for our picnic. Aristotle wraps cheese and salami in white wax paper, grabs a bag of bread, a small jar of olives, some cutlery, napkins, a small bottle of wine. He places it all in a picnic basket. I watch as he attaches Lucky and Queen of Spades to a small carriage.

It's still hot out, but once we reach the beach, a merciful breeze makes the fading sunshine bearable. We ride out slowly, following the coastline West. The city recedes behind us, and the landscape turns wilder – tall sand dunes, and yellow flowers growing lush between them. The air tastes salty, and the horses advance slowly, as if enjoying the leisure ride as much as we are. I don't know how long we ride, perhaps an hour, but when we finally stop, we're on a deserted beach, with nothing but the sand dunes and a bunch of sea birds for company.

Aristotle helps me down, then spreads a blanket on the sand. The heat has mellowed, and the light holds that hallowed glow of nearing dusk. He unhitches the horses and ties them to a tree behind the dunes. I climb up there myself to see and discover a landscape that's surprisingly green.

"This is so beautiful," I say.

He smiles. "Wait until you get in the water."

"I can't swim."

"You don't have to. We won't go far, and I'll hold your hand."

I take my shoes off and wade with him into the warm waves. It's supreme decadence to feel the sand between my toes, to get to put my bare feet in the water, no stockings, no bathing shoes standing in the way of this beautiful sensation. There are no bathing machines here, no bath houses, no police hidden in the dunes to sanction the behavior of loose women. The water feels warm and velvety. It's like walking into a giant cup of tea that's only starting to cool. I lift my skirts and step in deeper, to where the water rises to my mid-calf. Aristotle squeezes my hand. "We won't go farther than this, but doesn't it feel good?"

He tells me about riptides, though the water right now is peaceful and soothing, nothing to be afraid of.

"I've always wanted to take off my bathing shoes and actually feel this," I say. "It's so wonderful!"

"We could take our clothes off," he suggests, "and lie down in it where it's not deep."

"What if somebody sees us?"

"Ain't nobody here. Besides, you've never struck me as shy."

And so we lie down naked in the warm salty water. I look up at the sky and something eases up in me.

"It's been a long time since I've felt this free," I say.

"I would have thought you feel free often. I always saw you as that kind of person. It's one of the many things I like about you."

I smile at him. Here is a man who understands me. Someone who sees me the way I want to be yet accepts me and likes me the way I am.

"I used to feel free," I tell him. "Utterly and completely. But not so much anymore. The things that made me feel free, all the excitement and adventure, the feeling that I had a say in my own destiny, it's all... I don't know. Everything is different and recently I've started feeling confined."

"What changed?" An image of Marie descends upon me like a patch of darkness. I turn my face away.

He doesn't press. I've liked that about him from the very beginning.

"Don't you have money saved up?" he asks. "You could leave."

"I've thought about it. I don't know that I have enough to live as I please. Though sometimes I wonder if I couldn't be content with simple things. Then there's the problem of Mrs. Harden. I'm afraid she'd make my life difficult if I tried to leave."

"I've never liked that woman," he says. "But don't let her intimidate you. She might withhold your last week's pay, but she probably wouldn't even do that. Madams are not interested in having enemies all over town."

"She's holding something over me," I say, and my voice cracks.

"That dreadful thing you don't want to talk about?" His eyes search mine, and once again I turn away. I am both touched and piqued that he hasn't forgotten I'd once intimated that I have a dark secret.

"Let's please not talk about it," I protest. "It's too dark and this day is too beautiful."

The sky is now blushing like the petals of wildflowers. Pelicans are flying above us as the waves crash gently over our naked bodies.

"All right, darling, but if you change your mind... Whenever you are ready, I'll listen and I'll try to help you. I might be broke, but I still have an Ace or two up my sleeve, and I'm good at calling a bluff, in case that lady's bluffing. I always thought there was something untrustworthy about her, something not quite right about that house. I wanted to take you out of there, though I didn't think you would come."

I laugh. "I didn't want to at first. When you mentioned buying me a house, I was at first going to say no."

"I could tell. There is a difference in you when you're honest and enthusiastic, and when you're pretending. You're an excellent actress, Aimée, and I'm sure most people can't tell, but I can. At least some of the time."

I feel my face color. Red, like the blushing sun.

"I thought I was doing a better job giving you your money's worth," I say.

"Always excellent, darling. And I actually liked you even better for the small imperfections in putting on a show. I liked your rebellious streak too. You wanted to be free, not beholden to anyone, even someone you liked, and I could tell you liked me."

"You know I did. I do. And the better I know you, the more I like you. But the house scared me and I don't know why."

"So what made you reconsider?"

"It was a good offer. I would have asked you to put it in my name."

"I would have."

The sun gives off a last glimmer of radiant golden light, an invitation to think about all things magical and unexplained. "That's not what made me want it in the end. I couldn't bring myself to want it, as advantageous as it was, until you mentioned the two English dogs."

"The Pointers?" he asks.

"Can you imagine them? Running through the water."

He laughs heartily as if completely thrilled with my answer. The sun is dying in a crimson bloodbath. I have a sudden impulse to get up, to run and splash. He chases me as if I were an English hunting dog myself, an English hunting dog running wild. We finally collapse into the wet sand, laughing. "If what you wanted most were two English dogs," he says, "darling, I can get you two English dogs even as a poor man."

"What are you saying, Aristotle?"

He smooths the hair out of my face, kisses me again and again as the crimson sky fades into an unexpected peaceful shade of purple.

"I don't know yet. But there are possibilities."

We ride back in the dark. A huge yellow moon illuminates the water, and Aristotle explains how staying on the beach provides an easy path back to town. Sand scratches my salty sun-kissed skin, sand inside my dress and in my hair. Yet with the crashing waves and the hoofbeats of the horses as lullabies, I fall asleep against Aristotle's shoulder and awake only as we reach Mrs. Harden's. My heart sinks at the sight of the house, with its lights still on, and faint music still coming out of the parlor windows.

"We're here," Aristotle says. "Unless you'd like to spend the night with me above my shop." I smile, temptation itching more than the grains of sand against my skin. "Don't go back in there. I'll make you chicory coffee in the morning." There are few things I want more than I want that coffee.

"I can't," I say. "I wish I could, though. This was the best day! Thank you."

"We'll have more," he says. But will we? As I walk back into the house where I am paid a fortune to delight and entertain wealthy men, the window of my freedom seems narrower than ever.

CHAPTER 30
NOT IN THE MOOD

The next day, I awake alone in my own bed at the brothel. My skin tingles from salt and sun, my body is sore from running around with the illusion of freedom, and sadness has me enveloped like a fog that even coffee can't disperse. This would be an excellent day to rest. Instead, I'll have to get ready to entertain again, and Mrs. Harden summons me to her office before I even get a chance to finish my second cup of courage.

"Your hair looks a fright," she says, as soon as I enter. "Are you turning into Medusa?"

I smile despite myself, for my hair is a fright indeed, but on the nape of my neck, the faintest trace of Fougère Royale still lingers.

"I will wash it. I was at the beach yesterday."

"You better not get freckles."

I let her stinging tone slide. "Why did you wish to see me? Is it about tonight?"

"It's actually about last night. You were out late, weren't you?"

"It was my day off," I respond, trying not to sound challenging or defensive. "I went to the beach with a friend."

"Not just any friend, but a male friend. One who seems very much interested in you."

"I can see men in my free time if I want to."

"Not my clients! That particular gentleman needs to come here and pay if he wishes to enjoy your favors."

"That particular gentleman is my friend," I say. "I have one day off. I may do with it as I please."

"That does not include fraternizing with my clients outside of business hours."

"He's no longer a client."

"Let me show you something, Aimée. Something that will deter you from being this argumentative in the future. Perhaps it might remind you to know your place and be grateful for my protection."

From a drawer of her bureau, she pulls out an envelope. My stomach veers into a dizzying abyss. I know before she even opens it, what it contains. I draw in air and remind myself I am, first and foremost, an artist. As Marie's young face and my own long-ago chubby-cheeked smile greet me from a piece of paper, I force myself to meet Mrs. Harden's eyes and look amused and a bit puzzled.

"I heard that one of these girls met an unfortunate end," she says.

I shake my head as if not understanding. "We all know there are risks, Mrs. Harden. I don't really take chances. And I do feel safe in this house. Though the one time I encountered a violent client nobody came to my rescue."

She narrows her eyes. "Uncanny resemblance between you and the other girl. Don't you find?"

I shrug. "Maybe a little. She looks fatter, though."

"Funny, one girl was found dead, and another girl who worked with her that night is rumored to have cleared out her belongings and disappeared. Around the time you showed up here running from something. I wonder what the police would make of such a coincidence, that mixed with your resemblance to this younger, fatter sidekick to the dead girl..."

"I would think we'd rather not have the police in here. Unless they come in an unofficial capacity and we all pretend they're not the police?"

"I don't think this charade is necessary," she says putting away the picture and locking the drawer. "You understand what I'm telling you. Now go get ready for tonight, and I shouldn't even have to say it, but you won't see yesterday's gentleman again."

I wish to contradict her, but I'm afraid my voice will tremble. Instead I say nothing, let the silence settle in. When I do speak, it's to inquire about the evening's client. Though I don't want to know anything about him. I'm too tired to entertain. Too tired and not in the mood, and Mrs. Harden's threats and her unreasonable request are the final drops in an already full bucket. The picture I just saw, the picture I wish did not exist, fills me with dread.

But that girl in it, that chubby-cheeked young thing, is a far cry from me. Recognizable to Ruby and Mrs. Harden maybe, a striking similarity that sparked Ardoin's interest, but would she really warrant attention from an officer of the law? Would the madam really show it to the police? Would there be an investigation? The men who were there that night in New Orleans were too powerful to allow that. And what can Mrs. Harden have to win from ruining me? I can see how she would profit from keeping me here, but if she were to lose me anyway, having me ruined might serve as a cautionary tale to her other girls, yet not the type of tale that would get them to cheerfully perform their work.

I wonder if perhaps I can barter for the picture. If I can buy it from her. I tally up my money in my head. But Mrs. Harden doesn't deserve more of my profits than she's already gotten. I will not let her have it. I will not let her best me.

I bathe, have Sarah wash and comb my hair. The salt seeps into my bathwater, like tears. The Fougère Royale washes off too, teasing me with yesterday's memory as it evaporates. Did that day really happen? The store and the horses, Aristotle's room, his bed, the beach, it all seems like something I've invented, or something out of a novel. The familiar pain of Sarah lacing me up jolts me back to reality, yesterday's sunshine squeezed out of me with each powerful tug.

The corset is so tight I can barely breathe, the fragrance on my wrists and in my cleavage nauseating. It's all more oppressive than usual because I'm tired. But I'm also starting to feel sick. I know how to reign in my physical impulses, know how to smile and feign having a good time, know even that if I ignore my malaise it will eventually disappear. But I'm not sure I want to discipline myself into performing my role right now.

Tonight's client is a bear of a man, and I can imagine his large body crushing me. The feeling is acute and more stifling than the cruel whalebones of my corset. A stubborn streak erupts inside me. I don't want to smile at this man and make small talk. I don't want to kiss him. I don't want his hands on me, his body next to mine, his warm breath in my face. I don't want to pretend that his proximity brings me pleasure. I don't want any of it, and most of all I do not want to bend to Mrs. Harden's will.

"Please excuse me for a moment," I tell the bear. "Enjoy another drink. I'll be right back."

I step out of the parlor and make my way up the stairs. In my room, I rummage through my drawers, through my trunks, until I find what I need. Sarah knocks on my door. "Mrs. Harden sent me to see if you're all right," she cries, urgency in her voice. I open the door, almost bump into her, a fake smile on my lips. "I needed a pill for my headache," I say. "I'm going back in there now."

I glide down the stairs, smile at Mrs. Harden as I slip back into the parlor. She gives me a warning look. I resume my place next to my client. I see him looking at Ruby, and I think it's just as well. She too is looking at him, and I figure the big bear of a man is probably attractive to her. He might have been attractive to me too under different circumstances. Big burly men sure make a girl feel dainty, but tonight I don't wish to make myself want this giant. With a little effort, I know I could, but something unbending inside me that I didn't even know was there refuses to play along. It's like there is a bar of steel at my core, unyielding and a little frightening, but also holding me upright with a welcome kind of strength.

"Would you like another drink?" I ask the bear-like creature, then shimmy to the bar, ask for a julep, specifying it's for my client so they would know not to give me the sugar water reserved for prostitutes. Out of the corner of my eye, I see Mrs. Harden watching me. I smile at her and give a small curtsey. I bide my time as the bear drinks his julep. I wait until he's on his last sip, then ask if he'd like for us to be alone. We slip into a private room, and there I pretend to suddenly notice his empty glass. There is a bottle of liquor on the end table, but I'm betting on him wanting another julep.

"Make yourself comfortable," I purr. "I will get you another." And with the empty glass in hand, I step into the long empty hallway. There is nobody here, no Mrs. Harden, no Sarah, no Ruby. I do not walk into the parlor, where the bar is. I walk instead toward the back door. My heart races as I unlock then open it, it races as I step into the back yard, cut across it, steal into the dark alley where I pray to a God who's probably turned away from me forever that I shall not encounter drunks, vagrants, or other dangers.

I run, run to the side street, run as fast as I can, and my heart doesn't stop racing until I'm far enough away I know it's unlikely they will find me. I run to what has become my favorite house on this island, run to the back door, knock with urgency. A light flickers on, then more lights. I wait for what seems like an eternity. Then Deirdre, the servant, wearing her sleep bonnet, opens the door and lets me in. I stumble into the kitchen, set down the empty julep glass, and stand there looking at it in disbelief at what I've done.

Deirdre gives me a glass of water. I notice a man I haven't seen before, wearing a sleep shirt, standing beside her.

"It's all right," she says to him. "Go back to sleep, Andrew. I know her. She's the lass who comes to read to Mr. Cohen. She's good people." The phrase hangs in the air like a promise. I know I don't look like good people, decked out as I am to entertain. But the man bows his head in greeting, then retreats.

"I thought I could come here," I say. "I ran away. I didn't know where to go. I thought Mr. Cohen wouldn't turn me away."

"No, no," Deirdre says. "You did good. Mr. Cohen is sleeping now, but I'll fix you a room, and in the morning he'll be tickled pink when I send you in with his coffee and correspondence."

"Are there new letters?" I ask.

"Ay," she chuckles. "Two new letters. You and Mr. Cohen will have a lot to talk about."

Her big green eyes, which always struck me as sad, are fixed on me, but I notice no shock as she studies my most improper evening gown, no obvious wish to retract her statement that I am good people. If there is judgement she hides it well. Or perhaps Deirdre judges the world in a different kind of way, a way that allows a girl such as myself a modicum of goodness.

"Are you sure you're all right?" she asks. "Did somebody hurt you?"

"No. Nobody hurt me. I'm fine, Deirdre."

"Well, thank goodness for that. You hungry?" I shake my head. All I feel, deep in my bones, is exhaustion.

CHAPTER 31
IN THE LIGHT OF DAY

In the room Deirdre makes up for me, I take my money purse out of my bosom. This and my bank book are all I've taken. My fingers tremble, and the fears in my heart grow sharp. But I am hoping that the previous two week's wages which I've yet to be paid, and all my fancy dresses, which will probably fit Ruby fine, my baubles and other little luxuries, will be enough to deter Mrs. Harden from looking for me.

I am bone weary from the night before, but in my guest bed in the unfamiliar room at Cohen's house, sleep eludes me until the night starts fading into day. When I finally awake, the sun shining through the crack in the heavy velvet drapes is hotter and more powerful than the morning sun, so I know it must be past noon. My first thought is that I'm not at the brothel, and that thought brings both delight and terror.

The fear of Mrs. Harden's retaliation is real, but my curiosity and excitement over what a day spent entirely in this house might hold is stronger. I rise out of bed and open the window, as this whole house needs much more air than it's been getting, then put on yesterday's dress and make my way downstairs. I catch a glimpse of myself in one of the mirrors, and realize I look unmistakably like a prostitute in my evening attire with its lowcut bodice and provocative emerald color. I know Cohen can't see me, but if she didn't already suspect it, it must be plain to Deidre that this was my occupation. Poor Deirdre, who let me in without questions, made me a bed, and called me good people. Will she be disappointed when faced with evidence of my sinfulness in bright daylight? Though, of course, the darkest thing about me, the one thing I truly regret, is not visible, but buried deep inside.

"You're up," Deirdre says, as I step into a vast sunny kitchen. "I wanted you to surprise him with his breakfast, but I didn't have the heart to wake you."

Last night's julep glass sits washed and sparkling on a clean dishrag on the counter, like a reminder of where I came from, but also hopefully a promise of redemption.

"Want some coffee?" the girl asks in her thick brogue. In the afternoon light she seems almost cheerful.

She pours the dark liquid into a large cup for me, offers warm milk, with a nice froth of cream on top. I sit at the table, and she lifts a white napkin off a plate of biscuits. "I don't know if these will still be warm. Let me pop them in the oven."

"It's all right," I say. "I don't want you to have more work on my account."

"It's no bother, Miss. You seem like you could use a warm biscuit. I've been there myself."

She sets a plate in front of me, cutlery, a clean napkin. She lights the burner under a pan of something I assume to be gravy. I hold my breath so my stomach won't make distasteful noises. I'm ravenous after skipping last night's meal.

"We're all running from something," she says. "When I left Ireland and came here, there was a man there, had a claim on me. My Mam and Da made me marry him when I was just fifteen, but he was not a good man. When my baby died, I sold my wedding ring and bought the cheapest fare to America. Almost died on the ship, but here I am."

"I'm so sorry," I say. "About your baby."

"Thank you, Miss. Babies die, you know? My point is, I know what it's like to run away."

She busies herself by the stove, and soon enough, there's a plate of warm biscuits with gravy in front of me. I set upon them like a wolf.

"That was good. Thank you."

"Ay," she says. "Now I will give you his letters, and you can go see him. I told you were here so he could have some joy early in the morning. He looked like I had given him a Christmas present. Can't wait to see you. After you talk to him for a while, I shall draw you a bath."

"Thank you. But there's no need to wait on me, like…"

"Like I'm the servant in this house?" She laughs. "But I am the servant, Miss, and glad to be of service. I'm devoted to Mr. Cohen, and so is my husband, Andrew. We're here to serve on him, and so we're here to serve on you. Now you go do your own work in reading to him and making him come to life, and I'll be happy to be doing mine."

She hands me two letters and a newspaper, and I ascend the stairs and push open the door to Cohen's room.

"Good morning," I say. "Or rather, good afternoon."

"Yvonne!" he cries out. "I've been waiting for you, dear girl. Whatever happened, I'm so glad you knew to come here. I never told you because you didn't seem ready to leave, but this house is your house."

Tears roll down my cheeks, and I collapse into the chair by his bedside. "Now, now," he says. "Tell me what happened. Last I saw you you were getting ready for a beach excursion with your young man."

Between sobs I tell him how magical my day with Aristotle was, leaving out some of the more intimate bits, but going into detail about the two horses.

"That sounds like a wonderful day, dear girl. So was it hard to return to your normal life after that?"

"It was terrible. Unbearable, almost, but I can make myself do most things if I set my mind to it. I was going to carry on, much as it didn't feel right. I was going to carry on, and only hope that in my free time I still had this type of enjoyment to look forward to. I was so tired the next day, too, bone weary, all that sunshine, the salt water, but I could pull myself together and put on a good show. I can get over feeling tired when I need to, I can get over feeling blue, I can put all things out of my mind and concentrate on my client. But then Mrs. Harden called me in to scold me. She knew I'd been with Aristotle and she said that he was a client – though frankly he can't afford such luxuries anymore – and that I wasn't to see him again."

"So you told her to shove it?"

"I couldn't. She threatened me. There is this thing, this awful thing I did in my past life, which she knows about, and which she holds over me. She threatened to expose me if I didn't stop seeing Aristotle. I tried to act like I didn't know what she was talking about. I even... Aristotle said something about how a gambler knows when someone is bluffing, so I tried, in my way to call her bluff, and suggest she wouldn't want to talk to the police considering her own occupation."

"That's a good point. What happened then?"

"I carried on as usual but I couldn't do it. I got ready and met the client, and... It's not really that I couldn't do it, but suddenly I so violently didn't want to. The night ahead of me seemed like such a farce, such an ordeal! I just didn't want to make myself go through with it. So I escaped to my room and got my purse and my passbook, then I pretended to go back because Mrs. Harden was on to me, led the client to a private room, and went to fetch him another julep. Except instead of going to the bar, I slipped out of the back door and I ran and came here. Deirdre was so very kind to me."

"She's a good girl, my sweet Deirdre. I'm glad you came here."

"Me too. Thank you. But I'm afraid Mrs. Harden will find me. I'm afraid she might be spiteful enough to make good on her threats."

"What can she win from it?"

"I don't know. Set an example in case other girls decide to leave?"

"Girls come and go. I don't see that she could win much by having relationships with them based on fear and threats."

"I left my dresses there. And she has wages left to pay me. Maybe that will appease her?"

"Or maybe you need to claim what's yours. My manservant, Andrew, Deidre's husband, could accompany you back there. Or we can send him alone to get your things."

"Then she'll know where I am."

"Yvonne, dear. Do not show her that you're afraid. Besides, what is it that you're afraid of? I know you don't want to talk about it, but what does the woman hold over you? If I know what it is, I can think of a way to help you. I might be an old blind man, but as you saw, I still have connections. I have some money too."

"As do I. I've made some money in my day, and I've saved a great part of it. I could probably buy Aristotle his horses."

Cohen laughs. "The things you think of, dear girl. I doubt he'd like that, this young man of yours. Leave him the dignity of helping himself. And let's think of ways to use your means to help you. What terrible secret are you running away from? What does the woman have to blackmail you with?"

Can I tell him? I'm tempted, so tempted. For he is wise and I know he cares about me. Would he scorn me if he knew what I'd done? Or would he patiently advise me? I decide that I trust not just his wisdom, but his good heart, his fondness for me, our friendship. He's told me his secrets. I might as well be brave enough to let him learn mine.

"A picture," I say. "It's me in New Orleans, when I was just fifteen, just starting out. It's me and another girl. Another prostitute. We were friends, but really we were rivals. That other girl died, Mr. Cohen. She died, and the way it happened, I'm very much to blame for it."

"Did you kill her, Yvonne?"

"I did not. But the way it happened, nobody would believe me. It's why I ran away. I knew they would pin it on me, and the worst part of it is, I was to blame, my greed and my vanity, and my foolishness. It wasn't by my hand that she died, but I was there and I will always feel guilty over how I acted. I could have saved her, and I failed to do so."

"Tell me exactly what happened."

And then it pours out of me, the dreadful story, the secret I've been holding onto all these months. It pours out of me, entrusted to my friend. Will he still care for me once he knows the truth?

176

CHAPTER 32
THE DREADFUL TRUTH

In a way, I'd been longing to tell this story, longing to revisit experiences and places in which I was a different girl and Marie still alive. A time of innocence long lost. A time before we were rivals, when we were children, then joyful young girls up to lots of mischief.

Marie and I were friends growing up. Our families were not exactly poor, but not comfortable either. We lived on the outskirts of New Orleans. I was the youngest of seven, Marie the youngest of five. It's probably why we ran wild, why our families didn't pay much attention, why the small freedoms we sought out early on, our acts of rebellion and bravery, went largely unnoticed. We'd skip school and ride the streetcar into the city, not paying the fare, and when we returned home at night nobody asked where we'd been.

The only person in my family who seemed to care about me was Maw Maw. I spent summers at her house out in the bayou, and those were my favorite times. But Maw Maw died the summer I turned fifteen, and my parents sold her little house to pay off their debts. They didn't even let me keep her cat.

I spent a lot of time with Marie that year, getting into trouble. I felt alone and bereft and I needed distractions. Marie was not a friend that could ease my sorrow, not the comforting sort of friend. But when we set out on adventures, I would forget that Maw Maw was dead, that I was alone in the world, and that the world could be a sad and cruel place indeed. I learned that it could also be a playground.

After Maw Maw died, I stopped going to school. My mother had a cousin in New Orleans, and through her, she found an apprentice position for me with a dressmaker. I loved fashion, and loved New Orleans, so the prospect was one of the few things that cheered me up. Marie begged for an introduction to the dressmaker too, promised to be the most industrious apprentice, promised to be the most courteous, helpful, and pleasant houseguest for her own relatives in the city.

In truth, neither of us was interested in learning to sew. We were, instead, captivated with some of the clients. The best dressed, most beautiful young women who spent fortunes on rather outré gowns Marie and I both secretly admired, were young women the seamstress, Miss Adèle, instructed us to be courteous but brief with on account of things she would rather not discuss. We were never to displease these well-paying customers, but we were discouraged from having long conversations with them. We were instructed instead to let Miss Adèle deal with them in person while we ourselves retreated to the back of the shop, where stifled by the smell of mothballs, we carried out boring tasks – endless hours of stitching. What vexed us most, was that we were most curious about these glamorous women, but were kept so far from them we could not even overhear the conversation.

It seemed everyone from Miss Adèle to my overly religious aunt, conspired to turn my life, and Marie's too, into one of dull and quiet drudgery, devoid of any color or joy. I shared a shabby little room with another distant cousin, one who worked as a shopgirl during the day and counted rosary beads at night. She frowned upon my habit of reading novels and was most displeased with my curiosity about the women I saw at Miss Adèle's. She said she abhorred helping such women in the shop where she worked, and that I had to be careful, as the city was most sinful and girls like me could easily end up losing their virtue. As she spoke, I'd have to look away from her red fingers, chafed from years of drudgery, for my aunt, in return of a meager room and some stingy portions of food, abused this poor relation as if she were a servant. I could easily foresee a future where I would fare no better, and that was a prospect more frightening than the devout cousin's warnings about sin.

I'd have to find a way to improve my life. Yet all my money was spent on the novels that kept me up late at night, there were holes in my one pair of shoes, and my meals, much like the devout cousin's, consisted of portions far smaller and less attractive than what was set on my aunt and uncle's plates. Still, it was better to share a musty room with a zealous fool in the city than it had been to stay home with my mother and sisters. At least my life had some potential for adventure. And if I really did become a dressmaker, I could perhaps afford nicer accommodations one day. But would I be able to wait that long?

I only wished Marie and I were in the same home, but we were not. Still, there was comfort in our parallel lives. We exchanged stories of our privations in the households of our respective relatives, and whispered about the further indignities and unfair treatment bestowed upon us by Miss Adèle. In all honesty, we were both rather indolent apprentices, and Miss Adèle had much cause to complain about us to our aunts and even issue repeated warnings that she might send us packing.

We lived for the occasional free evenings when we escaped the scrutiny of our families and went for walks in the Quarter. Young men noticed us, especially when we were together. We'd bat our eyelashes, we'd flirt and tease, and get them to buy us ices and other treats. This led to severe admonitions from our scandalized aunts. There was talk of us being sent back home. But all the warnings we received were merely hot air, so we grew bolder in our scandalous behavior.

What we loved best was to flaunt Miss Adèle's instructions not to spend much time with the glamourous young ladies that visited the shop. There was one girl, in particular, a tiny brunette called Clarissa, who was voluble and chatty, and whom we both loved helping. One afternoon, Clarissa came in while Miss Adèle was off to a fitting at a client's home – something she did grudgingly for the best-paying matrons. Alone in the shop, Marie and I were thrilled to have the opportunity to talk to our favorite customer at length.

Miss Adèle found the three of us chatting and laughing, and though she was most polite to Clarissa, after the young woman left, she scolded us more harshly than she ever had before and asked to speak to our aunts. This time we both were punished, not just reprimanded. In my meager little room shared with the zealot, I had to go to bed without supper, while in her own house, Marie got into such a heated argument with her own aunt, that she was asked to pack up her things and return home to her parents.

"You belong at Madame Rouge, not in a respectable household," her aunt called to her as Marie gathered her shabby dresses and other accoutrements. So Marie took her carpetbag and instead of getting on the streetcar to go back home, she presented herself at Madame Rouge's, saying she was a friend of Clarissa's.

I was shocked at first. But Marie waited for me around the corner from the shop one day, wearing new shoes and a dress I recognized as one Miss Adèle had charged Clarissa a small fortune to make. We agreed that we would meet secretly on occasion. She took me to Café du Monde and bought us *café au lait* and beignets. She took me to stores too, bought me trinkets and ribbons, paid for my shoes to be resoled.

Her stories from her new life were both fascinating and a bit repugnant, but I couldn't help wondering if sleeping with various men was really that much more disgusting than handling piles of dirty laundry as my devout cousin saw herself forced to do in order to placate my aunt. Marie was buying pretty dresses and eating fine meals while my eyes strained, I was bored out of my wits, and I unwittingly pricked my fingers with needles.

One unseasonably cold winter night, as I lay on my lumpy bed, swaddled in blankets yet still shivering, for my aunt was as stingy when it came to heating our room as she was when it came to meals, my hostess and protectress came barging into my room demanding to see the soles of my shoes. The devout cousin jumped out of bed and tried to shield me from the blows that followed.

"Did your friend pay for this with her dirty money?" my aunt screamed, clawing at me. "Your uncle says you were seen together, you lying ungrateful girl! Did she give you money? Do you know what she does to earn it? Is this how you repay me for taking you in and taking food from my own mouth to feed you? Bringing shame upon my house?"

She yanked at my hair, clawed at me, and I barely escaped her clutches, as the cousin tried in vain to appease her. "Shut up, you unworthy leech," my aunt called at her, pushing her away. She chased me down the stairs and into the street. "Come back, you fool, you're gonna catch your death!" she screamed, but I ran into the night, the freezing pavestones under my bare feet less off-putting than her blows and the rage in her voice.

I didn't know where to go. So I found my way to Madame Rouge's, where Marie, dressed in a stunning red velvet dress, was still up. She fussed over me, and so did all of the other girls. A servant drew me a hot bath. The cook warmed up stew and rice, and when I was too shook up to eat, soaked tender cornbread in warm milk. Madame Rouge herself fed me. She smelled of vanilla and looked more beautiful than any creature I'd ever seen. Each spoonful approaching my mouth was accompanied by cooing and caresses as warm and soothing as the food itself. After I'd eaten to her satisfaction, Madame told me I was to sleep with Marie in Marie's bed, where the sheets had been changed while I was eating.

The next morning she came to wake me, bringing chicory coffee and fresh biscuits with butter and strawberry jam. She wore a pink silk wrap with emerald green peacocks embroidered on it, their eyes glimmering crystals, the most beautiful thing I'd seen. Sunshine danced in her auburn hair. Her skin was white like fresh milk, her fingers soft, like the touch of a butterfly. Her voice, though, was her most charming feature, like honey, with the occasional hint of spice. I was transfixed. I wanted to be her, for how could anyone be this lovely and this warm and not be utterly delightfully happy?

She told me I was welcome to stay as long as I wanted, that nothing would be expected of me. She didn't try to talk me into becoming one of her girls, but she slowly seduced me into wanting that lifestyle and all the teachings and knowledge that came with it. I never liked school, but learning from Madame Rouge was different. I felt like I was being trained to be an expert in human emotions, a cross between an actress and a physician for the soul.

She encouraged my passion for reading novels, gave me money to buy them, discussed them with me at length. She helped me practice my posture, my dance steps, the way I spoke certain words, my facial expressions. She had dresses made for me, bought me fragrances, helped me choose the ones that suited me best. She told me funny anecdotes about men and their passions. It was all new and fascinating, and once I finally got to practice what I learned, she praised me and made me see the power of my talents.

I didn't learn until much later that Marie had been paid handsomely to recruit me, and the resentment I experienced when I did learn it had nothing to do with feeling duped, because I was not duped. I made my own choices. I chose Madame and I delighted in her choosing me. The only person this delightful creature, my role model and protectress, preferred to me was Marie. This fueled my jealousy of her, which I soon discovered was mutual.

It was ironic, of course, that as our friendship turned into full-on loathing, we were trapped in a scheme of Madame's that had us working together. There were a series of clients that requested the two of us. We had perfected an act where we performed as a duo. Under the clients' greedy gazes, we undressed each other slowly and lasciviously, drawing out every move, every gesture. We'd even kiss, which invariably reminded me of the kisses we'd practiced on each other before we started kissing boys.

This went on for years, our rivalry, our so-called friendship, our double act. Marie always seemed one step ahead of me, her dealings with clients more complex and sophisticated. These included evenings with men who wanted something different, often something bizarre and a little frightening. Sometimes they requested her services away from the brothel. Marie said she liked going to clients' houses, that she relished the additional mystery.

She told me about some of the sumptuous homes she'd been in, some of the restaurants, the hotels. Her life seemed more interesting than mine, but there was the occasional undertone of darkness. I would not have wanted to go to the places she went, I would have been afraid and horrified. She laughed at me if I expressed this. "You silly goose, these are just games people play." She acted like she was superior because she was braver, more curious, more adventurous. I stopped showing my true reactions to her stories. I had already learned enough to be a good actress. I didn't want her laughing at me. My vanity couldn't take it. But what piqued me most was the growing complicity between Marie and Madame, a complicity that excluded me. If I wanted not to be left out, I needed to learn to push my limits.

So one day when Marie purred like a kitten, "Yvonne, would you care to accompany me and Mr. X to the Hotel Monteleone this Friday night? We shall dine with a friend of his in a fine restaurant first, and they will pay us double if we're open-minded about the encounter," I did not express reservations. Mr. X was one of the clients she'd told me about who scared me. She once told me that in the middle of lovemaking he'd put his hands around her neck and choked her, not playfully, but rather hard, hard enough for her to black out. She said the sensation was intense and that it was a way to add a primal element to the act, talked about how the French referred to an orgasm as a "little death," and said all this with such an air of superiority that I didn't dare act shocked.

Still, much as I wanted to dine out and spend the night in a hotel, much as I wanted to be paid double, much as I wanted, above all, to be an equal of sorts to Marie, to make as much as she did, to be praised and rewarded and fussed over by Madame, I did not want to spend a night with Mr. X and his friend, especially away from the brothel's protection. But my pride wouldn't let me say it. So I spoke to Madame privately, told her of my fears.

Madame, too, laughed at me. Perhaps this shook me more than Marie's disdain, for I was hungry for her approval, and left forever craving the affection she'd lavished on me when I found my way to her house barefoot and shivering on that cold winter night. Now, to coax me into compliance, she patted my hand and spoke to me softly, yet not as tenderly as she had in my early days in the brothel. There was more spice than honey in her voice these days.

She told me these were prominent New Orleans men, that they were paying a small fortune for the outing, and that they wouldn't do anything to harm us. It would be terrible for their reputations. She said choking was something some people liked, that women liked it too, asked for it even, because it could intensify pleasure. There was no saying that the men would do that, it might have just been something Mr. X tried on Marie once, but if they did do it, I was to lie back, relax, and enjoy it. "I'm trying to further your education, my pet."

"If you really feel frightened, we will agree for you and Marie to have a safe word. A word that, if spoken by either of you, will alert the other one to immediately end the evening and leave the premises, or, if that's not possible, to call for help. You'll be in a hotel, so there are people downstairs who can help you should you be in danger. There are people in the hallway, in the rooms next door. Worst case scenario, you scream and someone comes to your rescue. More refined, of course, would be to discreetly approach the concierge and tell him about your distress so he can solve it in an elegant manner, without causing a scandal that could upset our clients.

You are to understand, Yvonne, the code word is not to be used unless you truly fear for your life. If one of you screams without it being truly necessary, I shall skin her alive. But obviously, if there's real danger, scream and save yourselves. You understand that's a preposterous scenario, but better safe than sorry, *cher*. I shall talk to Marie about this privately as well. Now, let's think of a word you normally wouldn't use in conversation, a word that can work as a code word to alert your friend that you need the evening to end."

"Butterfly," I said. Little did I know, that word would haunt me forever.

I was a fool. Instead of being more alarmed after my talk with Madame Rouge, I felt more certain that I was overreacting. I focused on the money and on my curiosity to see some of the places Marie went to that I didn't get to explore. I focused on my toilette for the evening. I was resplendent in turquoise silk, but Marie, in a jade green dress, upstaged me. Her skin was positively glowing, and a jewel I knew to be real hung low into her décolletage. That jewel reminded me to quell my apprehension and forge ahead. If I were half as daring and as worldly as Marie, I could maybe replace my fake baubles with real jewels too.

We met our clients at a restaurant where we were led into a private dining room full of mirrors and crystal chandeliers. The room was dark but for the glow of candles. Two men waited for us there, dressed in black suits. We each sat next to one of them, but it was obvious from the beginning they were more interested in Marie than they were in me. My ego was bruised, but I kept my smile on.

There were fresh flowers on the table, and the food was plentiful, resplendent. At first, I focused on the feast and tried as best I could to be the type of audience the men needed as they lavished attention upon Marie. Raw oysters were brought in on platters of ice. I loved their briny taste, their delicate texture, but I had barely enjoyed my first few, barely tasted the silky crab bisque before me, when Marie pronounced, with a cruel sparkle in her eyes, "Look at these two oysters next to one another. Why, Yvonne dear, don't you find they look exactly like a butterfly?"

She stressed the syllables of the last word, looking me straight in the eye, the corners of her mouth raised in a mocking smile. It was hard to maintain my composure. There had been many a meanness that had passed between the two of us throughout the years, but surely this was one of the most unforgivable ones. She was going to mock me and my need for a code word all night, I knew it.

To add to my discomfort, which I struggled not to show, once having downed some cocktails and partaken of a white powder they did not share with either Marie or myself, the men grew coarser than I would have expected high society men to be, and their jokes and general conversation were of the utmost vulgarity. Marie laughed at their unpleasant remarks and tried, as best she could, to turn the conversation around so that it was me, and not her that became the target of the most unsavory remarks.

She laughed shrilly at their comments, and at some point began slipping ice chips down the bodice of my dress, a spectacle the two men found agreeable. I shivered, the chill almost painful, but I tried to be a good sport and laugh along with them, then to entice Marie to search for the ice chips, her hot lips following the frozen bits, melting them against my skin. I feigned enjoyment at this, the way I usually did, but then she bit me, bit me hard. I called out in shock. The men shouted with laughter. I jerked my body away, but Marie's fingers clung to my bodice, and the lace and silk ripped. She laughed out loud, covering her face with her hands, and I could tell she delighted in having ruined one of my favorite dresses.

"Oh, no," she said, "little butterfly, I'm so very sorry! Now why don't you go fetch us more ice?" She shook the nearly empty ice bucket, and I gathered up my torn dress as best I could, and left the private room. I had a sudden urge to run out into the street and never come back. In hindsight, I wish I had done that. But I thought of Madame, thought of the money and the praise, thought of Marie and how I wished to wipe that mocking smile off her face, how I might yank at the necklace holding her precious gemstone in retaliation.

I asked a waiter to please bring more ice to the private room, and I myself slipped into the washroom, where I splashed cold water onto my face, looked at myself in the mirror, and tried to see something other than the silly girl Marie and the two men enjoyed poking fun at. When I reentered the private room, Marie was sitting on one of the men's laps. She smiled an evil smile when she saw me. "Why, look at this, the innocent little butterfly has returned. I thought we had frightened her off."

I made myself overcome my revulsion, made myself climb onto the other man's lap, made myself move and glide in such a way as I had learned was most effective, drawing out desire yet steering clear of offering the possibility of its fulfillment. But this was not a pleasant task. The men talked about rather vile things they'd done with cheaper prostitutes and how, given the money, Marie and I would surely be willing to allow such acts, as after all, a whore was a whore and the price was just a technicality.

I was by no means an innocent girl. I did the things prostitutes in the finer houses did, and I enjoyed some of them very much. I knew what men liked, knew how to tease, but also how to deliver. I was good at giving and receiving pleasure in different ways, ways some self-righteous people would say I'd burn in hell for. But what the two men were talking about was repulsive, first and foremost because there was a sort of meanness to it I was not used to. In my experience, most clients were kind to me, and grew kinder still if I showed myself not just willing, but enthusiastic. These men were of a different sort.

Marie continued cooing and teasing, but her voice shook slightly. For once, even she seemed ill at ease. I considered uttering the word. I considered saying it again when we left the restaurant and waited with the two men for a carriage. We could have left them then, disappeared into the protective cloak of the crowded street. We could have turned around and walked away. My lips almost formed the syllables, but the word wouldn't come out. How could I say it, when Marie had mocked me and continued to do so?

"Let's show this butterfly a good time," she said, as we entered the carriage. I almost ran away then, but part of me still held on to my vanity, my desire to compete with her, my eagerness for the large sum of money and Madame's praise.

The hotel room was large and ornate, overlooking the Quarter. I would have loved being there, if it were with anybody else. But this group was sinister, and when one of the men locked the door, I considered opening the window and screaming. I bit my lip recalling how Madame had threatened to skin me alive. Marie poured drinks for us all. One of the men took out the vial of white powder they'd used at the restaurant.

"I want some," Marie whispered in her most seductive voice. The man sunk his index finger into the powder, then approached Marie, inserted his finger into her mouth and moved it around in a way she seemed to enjoy judging by the sounds she was making. With someone like Marie, it was hard to tell. He repeated the gesture and she moaned like she was in ecstasy, but then much to my horror, he removed his finger from her mouth and slapped her hard across her face. "Greedy bitch," he said. I thought I saw Marie's face briefly grimace before she gave a shrill laugh, as if she welcomed the unexpected violence.

I needed to get out of there. I needed to get Marie out of there too. I needed to get help.

"Would you like me to bring some ice?" I asked, having a sudden saving thought.

"Oh, yes," Marie purred, having apparently regained her composure, though the man had grabbed her by the hair, and I could see a pale line around her scalp-line growing even paler. "Ice would be excellent. Go get some ice, little butterfly."

Did she speak the last word differently this time? Was she distressed or was she still mocking me? I could not tell. But as I took the metal ice bucket and left the room, she whispered one more time, in a husky tone she sometimes liked to use, "Butterfly." It's the last word I ever heard her speak.

I stood in the hallway clutching the bucket to my chest, trying to assess the situation and my best course of action. I remembered what Madame had said about discreetly approaching the concierge and asking him for help without causing a scandal. But did the situation warrant it? Marie was used to unconventional clients. She took such things in stride. She would laugh at me forever, begrudge me the lost wages and lost clients, and who knows, maybe even the lost opportunity to have a twisted kind of thrill. I, on the other hand, had not agreed to being subjected to ridicule and violence. Or had I? I had agreed to entertain gentlemen who might get a little rough, maybe, but what were the acceptable limits?

This was not the kind of amusement I wanted to sample. This was not the type of seduction I excelled in. But was I a fool for being so easily scared off despite the outrageous sum of money we'd been offered? Madame had assured me they wouldn't hurt or endanger us. It was, as Marie said, a game.

A rough, dirty, and unsavory game, as far as I was concerned. This was Marie's territory, not mine. As far as I knew, she enjoyed this type of thing, would brag about it tomorrow. But what if she didn't like it? What if she had repeated that word as she saw me go, because something about the men's actions, maybe that unexpected slap, or the way the man grabbed her hair, had awoken her fears that tonight was not as harmless as other similar games she'd played?

Then again, men had slapped Marie before, and they'd done other things I wouldn't have enjoyed no matter the sum of money. She laughed about these things and said that sometimes the pain enhanced the pleasure and that, as long as they were willing to pay extra and were careful not to scar or bruise her, she saw such eccentricities as an added bonus. "The stranger things they like, the more money you make, silly goose!"

I walked down the corridor, walked down the stairs to the lobby. Was Marie up there praying for my help, or was she having what she'd later describe as an interesting time? Did she truly enjoy these things? There was not enough honesty between us for me to know for sure. Perhaps she merely liked to brag in order to shock me. Perhaps she was grinding her teeth through it all while mentally counting the money she'd make. If she was scared, how was I to know? Why had she used our code word so many times to mock me? What kind of perverse game was that? Did she just love tormenting and humiliating me, or was this part of throwing all caution to the wind and scaring even herself? My anger burned so hot, I was afraid it would melt the ice, once the bartender obliged and filled up the bucket.

"Would you like a drink, lovely girl? On the house," he said, and I set the ice bucket down. Although Madame had taught me to stay away from drink in order to always retain control, I accepted the liquid courage. It came in a crystal glass, and was dark, translucent amber. The bar was dark too, discrete lights casting a reddish glow onto the faces of the patrons. It felt both forbidden and safe to be in there. The bartender winked at me, and I smiled, feigning nonchalance, normality. I looked at myself in the mirror above the bar. I had pinned my torn dress with a safety pin, and it showed a shocking amount of flesh, yet covered enough too. It was obvious I was no decent woman, but at least I looked like a beautiful and expensive one. A composed one too. My ability to feign being well at ease filled me with pride and bolstered my ego, restored some of the damage done by the two men upstairs and Marie's mockery. I would not be this easily undone.

I drank the liquid fire in my glass and it fueled my vanity and my ambition. I would not be intimidated by Marie. It was she who was stupid for mocking our safe word, and joining the two men in tormenting me as if she herself was anything more than a plaything to them. The bartender topped off my glass. He was attractive. I enjoyed smiling at him, enjoyed letting him undress me with his eyes. I took a long, languorous sip, relishing the intoxication. Did I have the time to drink more before the ice chips in the bucket melted? Before they all wondered where I was? They probably thought they had scared me off. They were probably laughing at my expense. Or more likely, they had forgotten all about me. I was not an essential element of their ensemble.

Perhaps Marie thought she'd get all the money herself, or perhaps she was cross because they would refuse to pay such a steep fee if one of us had jumped ship. I dropped one of the ice chips into the amber liquid in my glass, watched it melt, took my time sipping the intoxicating concoction. It tasted bitter on my tongue, with just a trace of sweetness. Let them wait. They'd be more shocked when I returned, and perhaps they'd be thoroughly spent by then, with not much energy left to torment me.

My drink was strong, and it grew more delicious, more intoxicating with each sip. The edges of the room blurred, my fear and apprehension dimmed too. It all struck me as laughable now, and I had half a mind to run back upstairs, push open the door, and greet treacherous Marie with "Hello, butterfly!" The thought of it actually made me giggle. The bartender gave me a look, shook his head as if scolding me. An intoxicated girl of the night in his bar was not a desirable spectacle. But his eyes were playful. He had black eyes, long-lashed and intense. I imagined letting him kiss me, letting him undress me. But he was working. And so was I.

I set my empty glass on the counter. I waited a heartbeat hoping he'd refill it. "Thank you," I finally said, stood up on wobbly legs, took hold of the ice bucket, and headed for the stairs. In front of the door, a sudden wave of sobriety caused me once more to hesitate. The silence of the room seemed ominous. It was as if nobody was inside. Not just because I couldn't hear them, but a distinct lifelessness emanated from the other side. My hands on the ice bucket hurt. I held it away from my body and turned the doorknob to reveal an empty room. The bed shone white and huge. "Marie?" I called. Had they all left? Were they done with their dark amusements? Had I stayed gone too long?

But in my heart I already knew before I saw it with my own eyes, that the truth was more sinister than that. I set the ice bucket down. I stepped through the open door to the bathroom. Marie was sitting in the bathtub, half naked, her eyes open wide, the jewel in her cleavage shining its cruel indifference. "You scared me," I said. My first impulse was to laugh, but she didn't laugh with me. Understanding sank over me like the ice chips I could still feel numbing my fingers.

Her features didn't move. I don't remember if I screamed or not, but if I did, it wasn't loud. I touched her, shook her. Her skin felt cold, but was it because she was dead or were my hands numb from the stupid ice? I remembered something I'd read, dug into my purse for my hand mirror, held it to her nose. She wasn't breathing. Her hair was wet, and even as I fetched the ice to try to somehow revive her, I realized that the two men had had a similar idea.

She was in the bathroom because they'd tried using cold water to make her come back to. They'd left her there because they knew she was dead. I sat on the floor, put my head in my hands, forced myself to breathe, forced myself to think. All I could think of was that I shouldn't be there when Marie was found. I grabbed the ice bucket, closed the bathroom door behind me, closed the room door too, put on the sign that said "Do not disturb," and walked as calmly as I could down the corridor where I deposited the bucket in front of someone else's door.

It was late when I crossed the hotel lobby. Not many people were there to see me, but the doorman gave my semi-exposed chest a look that made me regret not having tried to find a back exit. I was afraid to take a carriage. I was afraid of everything, even my own shadow.

I entered Madame's through the back, crept upstairs while the whole house was sleeping. I packed two carpet bags with my favorite dresses and baubles. I thought of Marie's jewel, regretted not taking it, but selling it would have been dangerous, keeping it in my possession even more so. If I was lucky perhaps whoever found her would be tempted to steal it, and they would later become a suspect. The men had been too smart to take it, and I figured I should be too.

As soon as the bank opened, I withdrew all my money, closing my account. I was on a steamer leaving New Orleans before Madame and the girls awoke and before any housekeeper would have dared knock on the door of a hotel room with a "Do Not Disturb" sign on. I should have perhaps run farther than Galveston, but knowing the two men who were in that room that night, knowing how much they had to lose if they were associated with Marie's death, I was almost sure they would arrange for it to be written off as an accident. They didn't know I returned with the ice bucket. Nobody knew except perhaps the bartender if he'd put two and two together once news of the dead girl reached him.

This is my story, my dark secret, the shadow that's followed me to Galveston, the shadow I've attempted to drown out with sunshine. I lay it all bare for Cohen. I tell him everything. I trust him not to turn me in. But there's no guarantee that knowing all this he will still think highly of me. Though as I speak I learn that unpacking my baggage of darkness, unfolding each of its compartments in the shining sun, chases away much of my fear and guilt. As I speak, the unspeakable ceases to be so. I release my secret and learn that perhaps I'd overestimated its power.

CHAPTER 33
THE GREATEST LUXURY

"Now that you know it all, do you hate me?"

"No, dear girl." Cohen squeezes my hand. "There's nothing to hate. You might be blaming yourself entirely too much."

"I could have saved her. I should have tried."

"Yet to your knowledge she was not asking for help, but making light of the very notion of it. Chances are, if you'd gotten the concierge to intervene, everyone would have been embarrassed and appalled, your madam would have kicked you out, and you would have had to leave New Orleans under a cloud of shame anyway."

"But Marie would still be alive. I would give anything for her not to have died."

"Because you cared about your friend despite it all?"

"She was no longer my friend. She was despicable in the end. But her death is still tragic. It was preventable and I wish I had acted instead of hesitating."

"You might not have saved her anyway. I don't think, from what you told me, those men set out to kill her. It was an accident. Either the roughness went too far, or she had a heart attack, maybe because of the drugs, maybe unrelated. Whatever it was, it sounds like it happened in an instant and that moments before she was engaging in the unsavory encounter of her own free will."

"I know that I stayed gone too long," I say.

"You stayed gone long enough. You must have a special guardian angel, for it was lucky you were not there when she died. Those men would not have wanted you to witness it."

"Why do I feel such crushing guilt over this? Sometimes I think it's because toward the end I loathed her so. It's as if my jealousy and other vile thoughts materialized and caused her death. But I never truly wished her

189

harm. Still, I feel like she will haunt me forever. Like I will never escape her memory and all the guilt."

"The human conscience is complex, Yvonne. Be glad for your feelings, they show your heart is not hardened. You also probably feel guilty because your instincts told you what to do, and you did not listen. You let the madam and Marie talk you into something you didn't want to do, then you stayed in a situation that was unnatural to you because you doubted yourself. You're getting much better at living your truth, my dear. But in the story you told me, you were not being yourself. It's funny, I was listening to it, and imagined you much younger, not the self-possessed woman I have come to know."

"I felt that way around Marie, at times. It's as if in her presence I reverted to being my most awkward self, a younger and less knowledgeable version of myself, more insecure and more impressionable. I didn't like that version of myself. I didn't like who I was that night."

"Except in the bar. You were yourself in the bar."

"Because she wasn't there. But... but I stayed there enjoying my drink instead of helping her."

"You needed that drink. And you probably could not have helped her. All you could have done was gotten yourself into more trouble."

"I resented her so much in those moments. I resented her, and then she died."

"She frankly sounds pretty vile. Which doesn't mean she doesn't deserve compassion. In time, what you will come to learn, is that the only way to right this wrong is by not perpetuating this type of mean behavior."

"But I have," I say. "There is a girl at Mrs. Harden's who was a competitor of sorts, and I'm afraid I was pretty vile to her. We were competing over Aristotle's attention, and the things I did to manipulate her and get her out of the picture, they reminded me of Marie's behavior toward me. I didn't mock her or purposefully try to humiliate her, but I did make sure she exited our tableau as soon as possible."

"Oh, women," he says.

"I realized afterwards, this is a cycle I do not wish to repeat. I do not wish to be Marie."

"It might be easier to break this cycle once you are outside of the brothel."

"Perhaps."

"And more than that, what I believe is that the way we right some wrongs and better ourselves in the grand scheme of things, is by helping others. Think about it, dear girl, you might have failed to be the friend Marie needed – though goodness knows she wasn't an easy one to be a friend to – but you were able to do for me what the poor doctor has tried and failed for years to accomplish."

I smile despite myself. "Are you back among the living, Mr. Cohen?"

"More than that, I'm enjoying quite a few aspects of my life. And I'm seriously considering that book you want to help me with."

"You're not saying that just to cheer me up."

"No, dear girl. If you had a bit more time, which now it appears you do have, I would love for you to become my official secretary. I cannot, obviously, pay you as much as your madam did, but I'm not nearly as exploitative."

"You're offering me a job?"

"If you'll consider it. It would be twenty dollars a month plus room and board for however long you decide to stay here. If you choose to live elsewhere, perhaps with your young man, though I would love to have you stay here for a while, and I think it might be good for you, I would pay you fifty. I'm well aware you used to make that much in an evening, but you will find the demands on your time and person to be much gentler. I would expect for you to address correspondence and take notes for a few hours a day, four days a week, let's say after lunch and no later than five or six. Surely you see how that arrangement would give you a lot of freedom."

"I would do it for free," I say.

"Oh, Yvonne!" He shakes his head, laughing. "What did I tell you about receiving money for your writing? Don't scoff at people paying you for it. And don't scoff at the twenty dollars either."

"I know I'm spoiled."

"You are and you aren't. I think you're beginning to understand that there are luxuries greater than what you've so far enjoyed. Freedom is, after all, the greatest luxury."

CHAPTER 34
A WOMAN IS NOT A HORSE

After my talk with Cohen, I set out for Aristotle's store. I feel lighter now, lighter and freer, emboldened by my confession and how it was received. If Cohen can know my darkest secret and still care for me, Aristotle probably can too. Especially since Aristotle is not that pure himself. There's a sweet kind of intimacy to knowing each other's faults. But I'm still afraid too, the leap of faith before me like quicksand threatening to swallow me whole. When was the last time I trusted someone other than myself? Of course, I trusted Cohen just this morning. I trusted Deirdre last night to let me in. But the acceptance I'm hoping for from Aristotle is deeper. Still, there's a tingle of happy anticipation too, the joy of seeing him, of laughing with him, of telling him I'm free of Mrs. Harden and no longer bound to a house to which I have to return every night.

I say a silent prayer that the girl is not there, his niece helping him out. I wouldn't like for her to see me in my evening dress. My prayer is answered. I find Aristotle alone, and his eyes light up when he sees me. The store, too, embraces me like an old friend, its scent reassuring, as if I'm entering a realm where I am safe, accepted, even cherished.

"My darling lady, what a surprise!" Aristotle kisses my hand, and the sweet gallant gesture contributes to my feelings of confidence.

"And I've quite a surprise indeed. There is so much I need to tell you."

"Me too," he says. "I have some news you will enjoy. In fact, I was about to write to you."

"It's a good thing you didn't, because my address has changed. I left Mrs. Harden's yesterday."

His face lights up. "You left?"

"I did," I say. "I will never make that much money again, but from now on I will do as I please."

"You have run free, darling!" He looks at me like I'm the most marvelous of marvels, Christmas with all its cheer in the middle of a long hot summer. "Congratulations! And what about the threats you were afraid of?"

I look away. "That part, unfortunately is still unresolved. I may, in fact, need your help."

He grabs my hand firmly in his, flips the closed sign on the door, and leads me to his office in the back. "Sit, and we shall talk. Is it too late for coffee? Would you care for something stronger?"

I shake my head. There is no remedy but to start talking. His eyes, fixed upon me, encourage me. I look away, mostly, as I talk, but every now and then I look back at him, as if to make sure his warmth toward me has not dimmed. At some point, as I hesitate, he grabs my hand across his desk and holds it. I carry on. My voice breaks a little. I didn't realize how uncomfortable it would be to tell him about my double act with Marie, how the parallels with what happened with him and Ruby would sit between us like an abyss.

"The world is full of immature idiots," he says as I tell him how irresistible Marie and I were together, how in demand we were, how much money we made. "You obviously know that men are fools, and unfortunately you have seen that I'm one of them. That was me being juvenile. You understand, though, that at some point something changed."

"For me too," I say. "And it was different with you and Ruby than it was back when I was performing with Marie. I was jealous of Ruby in a whole different way, and I'm not proud of it."

"I could tell you were jealous, and I liked it. Can you forgive me?"

"You know I have. It was a stupid game, and I played along too. I like games and I was toying with you just as you were toying with me."

He smiles. "We're very much alike, Aimée. And games are easier than being honest. I didn't know it would bring up the past in such a way for you."

"I tried not to let it. I'm good at controlling my emotions. This story I'm telling you, it's like a ghost that I kept exorcising over and over, yet it always comes back."

I tell him about Marie's special client, his proclivities, and my hesitation when he requested we both entertain him. Aristotle's face darkens. I tell him about Madame and her assurances, the code word she helped me pick, and my experience at the restaurant, Marie mocking me by abusing the code word, the ice chips in my dress, my desire to abandon the party.

"You should have left," he says. "The moment she spoke your secret word out loud, that's the moment she betrayed you. That's when the deal was off. She didn't respect the terms. You should have run back to the brothel and told the madam you couldn't work with difficult clients with a girl you didn't trust."

"I should have," I say. "I wish I had. Everything would be different then. But I was confused, I was intimidated, and I felt stupid for being afraid. I let her have such power over me, let her ridicule seep in, to where I doubted myself and my instincts. I should not have gone back to that table. I should not have gone with them to the hotel. But I did."

"What happened at the hotel?"

"She acted like she was having a good time, but they were rough with her. I didn't know what was a game and what was pushing the limits. She repeated the word but I thought she was still mocking me. She said "go get us some ice, butterfly," then she whispered the word as I was leaving the room, but I don't know if she meant for me to get help or not. I thought she was still making fun of me. I didn't know what to do, I didn't know if I should alert someone, or simply leave and never come back, or toughen up and go back in there and play their stupid games and get the money. I didn't want to, but... I went to the bar to ask for ice and the bartender was making eyes at me. He poured me two drinks on the house and I stayed and drank them. I didn't know if I was drinking them for courage to leave or courage to stay. In the end, I took the ice bucket and went back upstairs."

He winces. "Aimée!"

"I know, I don't know why I did it. It was my vanity, my fear of Marie mocking me forever, my fear of Madame's wrath perhaps, my pride in not shrinking away from a challenge, my foolishness. Or maybe I was destined to go up there. Maybe it was my punishment for all my jealousy and loathing, maybe it was Marie's revenge for not helping her."

"Was she dead?" he asks.

"Yes," a tear rolls down my cheek as I tell him. It's the first time I allow myself to cry for Marie. Crazy, misguided Marie! My once-upon-a-time playful friend and confidante! "The men were gone. They had tried to revive her in the bathroom, then they'd just left her there."

"What did you do?"

"I put the do not disturb sign on the door. Then I went to the brothel and collected my things. I left before anyone woke up. I came to Galveston, stayed in a hotel, and reinvented myself as a French girl."

"Which nobody believes, by the way. How much of this does your new madam know and how?"

"She has a picture of me and Marie together, when were about fifteen. There is a client from Louisiana who knew her. She knows the other girl in the picture is dead. I guess she must have learned it from him. I don't know if she knows about me being there the night she died, at least I don't know if she knows for sure, or if she simply connected it to me having a secret that drove me to flee New Orleans, that drove me to pretend to be someone else."

"It's probably the latter, if I had to guess," he says. "And you probably can convince her that she stands to lose more by exposing the picture than by returning it to you. My guess is those two men are powerful enough to have the girl's death declared an accident and any investigation closed."

"Or they could have tried to pin it on me."

"Too complicated. A dead prostitute in a New Orleans hotel is more likely to have been killed by her client than by another prostitute. She's also likely to have died of an overdose, which could be dismissed as an accident."

"Wouldn't hotel records show we were all there together?"

"The room must have been booked under one of the men's names. But witnesses could claim to have seen the man leave the hotel before her time of death. I doubt, in any case, knowing the weaknesses of law enforcement in New Orleans, that a lot of energy has been put into solving this case, and I'm quite sure that anyone trying to stir up trouble by reopening it would make more enemies than friends."

"I hope you're right."

"It might not even matter if I am or not. As long as we convince your madam that I am. I can be quite convincing. Would you like me to talk to her?"

"You would do that?"

"I'd love to, darling. Let me help you. We can go there together, and I promise we will get all your things, but first and foremost that photograph."

"And the money she owes me," I say. "I was going to let her have my last two week's wages, but she doesn't deserve to keep my money."

"That's a small fortune, darling. Don't let her have your money. Don't let her have any more of you than she's already had."

"I won't. I want to go back there and confront her. But maybe not tonight?"

He looks at me and smiles, squeezes my hand, which he's still holding. "All right. Tonight we'll celebrate. You're a free woman, and I have a little bit of good news of my own."

I return his smile. "What is it?"

"I'll tell you over dinner. How about I cook for you?"

"Cook for me? That sounds exciting!"

"It's canned soup, an omelet, and yesterday's bread. But I will open my last bottle of champagne for you, and I will feed you the last of the confections you like. And tomorrow morning I'll make you coffee with chicory the way you like it."

"Sounds like a dream," I say. "I've wanted for a while now to spend a night with you, a whole night."

"You can spend every night with me from here on out," he says. "I'm afraid it'll be above a stable as of next week, but I shall always make you coffee."

"You want me to come live with you?" Panic creeps in, as if the offer forces me to navigate something unknown and dangerous.

"It won't be the house I promised you, but if you'll have me, yes. I want you with me every night of my life, Aimée."

"Yvonne," I correct.

"I might always call you Aimée."

"That's fine," I say. "May I see the horses?"

My heart, aflutter with excitement mere minutes ago, feels different now, as if his offer has darkened the light mood I had briefly allowed myself to enjoy. The truth is, I want to be with Aristotle every night of my life too, even above a stable. I want him, I want his morning coffee, his sleeping body in bed next to me, his horses downstairs, his books littering the room, and the bottle of Fougère dwindling away until it's all gone. I want it all and more. But something about the prospect frightens me, as if a different kind of danger than losing myself in the temptations of the brothel lurks in the kind of warmth that envelops my soul in the presence of this man. What scares me about the warmth I cannot tell. Is it that it might be deceiving like so many other things too good to be true? Is it that it could be snatched away at any moment if I am not careful? I think of Cohen's house, more solid ground beneath my feet, of the paintings and letters, the small salary he promised, of a whole wealth of lessons to be learned. I possibly could have it all, Aristotle each night, chicory coffee each morning, and Cohen's correspondence during the day, but something tells me to pace myself, to proceed slowly into this newfound freedom, to let in happiness bit by bit, prolonging the process and taking my time to learn about myself and others.

Aristotle kisses me on our way out back to see the horses. He kisses me and I know that, despite my hesitation, my story made him care for me more, not less. Still, there is apprehension inside me, a nagging fear that giving myself to him too freely, too completely, would cause the passion between us to dull. How am I to keep the fire stoked long-term without burning myself? Is either of us even capable of sustained affection? And what about my other dreams, my other interests? I can't yet articulate what these are, but I dare hope that even outside the confines of the brothel, my curiosity will take me down some adventurous paths, perhaps not ones filled with lust and other men, but places, instead, for my mind to go, new discoveries to be made.

I pull away from him. "The horses," I whisper.

We feed apples to Queen of Spades and Lucky. I brush Queen of Spades' mane, have her once more roll over for me, in a gesture of supreme surrender. Sadness pierces through the happy moment. Will I ever become as trusting and loving as this beautiful creature? Is it even necessary? A woman, I figure, is a different being from a horse, her needs more complex and more nuanced. Perhaps I could be content with being fed and brushed and given the opportunity to bring joy to the person I love best, but there is more to me than that.

"I know you'll see them every day," I say. "But I wish you didn't have to sell the horses."

"It's what I wanted to tell you. I was going to tell you at dinner, but I might as well tell you now. I managed to sell enough of my wares and get a good enough deal for this building. I won't sell them, after all. I will go work for my friend at his stables, and he'll give me a substantial discount on their boarding. I will be able to keep them as my own. You've brought me good luck, Aimée. At the very least, you've inspired me to try harder to find a solution." He takes me into his arms, and I allow the simple joy of his affection to wash away my many fears. "I think you're good for me," he says. "I will try to be good for you too."

We eat by candlelight. We drink champagne and consume the last of the sweets. We make love slowly, leisurely, and I manage to cast aside my fears and apprehensions and enjoy it. The feeling between us is warm like melting caramel, and for once the warmth doesn't scare me. Peace of a kind I am not used to fills my heart. I lie awake in my lover's arms and relish in the newfound joy of these emotions, in the luxury of allowing them to wash over me completely, to engulf me, to fill my soul and the room and the night and the Island. But awash in my ocean of joy and tenderness, I cannot fall asleep. Even imagining the two English dogs sleeping next to us, their muzzles gently shaking with whatever dreams hunting dogs might dream, doesn't help. I watch the moonlight glide in through the tall windows, and I wonder about what tomorrow might bring, about the future, and about whether allowing this ocean of caring into my soul might eventually drown me.

Somewhere in the night, I must drift off, for when I awake the room is bathed in daylight. I slip into my dress and go downstairs to find Aristotle in his office peering over his papers. As promised, he makes me chicory coffee. I've enjoyed but two intoxicating sips when he asks, "So what are your plans now that you're a free woman, Aimée? Will you come live with me?" He looks at me expectantly over the piles of paper on his desk.

"I want to, Aristotle, but…"

"Where will you stay then?" His voice is so imperceptibly different that someone less attuned to nuance might not catch the trace of bitterness in it.

"I'm staying with my new employer, Mr. Cohen. He used to be an artist."

"You've left the brothel in order to be some other man's mistress?" There's not so much accusation as disappointment in his voice. I would have bristled at an accusation, but disappointment breaks my heart.

"No," I say, trying to sound gentle yet not defensive. "I'm not his mistress. I'm his secretary. He's hired me to carry out his correspondence."

"If that's what you wish to call it." His cynicism hurts. I remember the confidence I admired in him before, the confidence that was a source of generosity and kindness. Has his loss of fortune depleted it?

"Aristotle, the man is old and blind," I explain patiently. "Before I was brought there by a friend to try to read to him and cheer him up, he was terribly depressed and I tried to help him. I started writing letters on his behalf and this activity has grown into a bigger and more interesting project. He's been a friend to me. A true friend, and nothing more. He has encouraged me repeatedly to come see you. He has encouraged me to be myself, and he has offered me the opportunity to stay on and help with the writing of his biography. He will even pay me. A laughable sum, compared to what I used to make, but it's attractive to be paid for this type of work. It's most interesting, more interesting even than my life before."

"If he's a platonic friend and you truly are helping with correspondence, then you can live with me and help him with his letter writing during the day."

"Because you're jealous?"

He sighs. "Because I need you." His eyes on mine burn with longing and the kind of vulnerability it takes strength to show. Is this what caring requires? "And also, yes, because I want you for my own. I have for a while now, and you know it."

"I know," I say. "But I'm tired of being a courtesan. All my life I've been paid ungodly sums to cater to every whim, smooth every wrinkle of discontent, do everything in my power to please and appease. I will not do it anymore. Not even for you."

"I'm not asking you to do that. If anything, my loss of fortune should put your mind at ease. I'm not trying to buy your favors in exchange for a house."

"But if I didn't come to live with you as a courtesan, what would I be?"

He hesitates. I see it on his face. My mind goes quiet, waiting. What am I hoping for? What am I most afraid of?

"I suppose what I'm asking you to be is a poor man's wife."

I look at him but can't read his expression. Nor can I be certain of my own feelings. Fear mixes with something warm and soothing, like the cornbread Madame fed me the night I met her, and yet a ripple of discontent vibrates through the crystalline waters of my peaceful sea.

"You suppose? Well, I suppose neither of us is certain of anything. Why not wait?"

He smiles a painful little smile. He gets up and walks to the window, looks outside. I stand up too and stand next to him, but it's one of those rare moments when I don't know what to do with my body. Should I draw nearer, reach for his hand?

"I know, my dear, it's quite a shabby offer," he says, turning to face me, the sadness in his smile reaching his eyes. And yet he looks at me as if my presence next to him both pleases and amuses him.

"It's not," I say. I touch his face, hoping the tender gesture can speak better than my words. "Not in the least. It's lovey, actually. But such a union for two people like us... It seems risky."

"I am a gambler," he says, his smile warmer now, more playful. "And you're a brave woman."

"We've both been reckless. But our lives are not a game of chance."

"Everyone's life is." His callused hand caresses my cheek, the way it did that day I came to see him when his niece was here, the day we had coffee in his office and he suggested we go on an adventure, the day I truly opened myself up to all of this, whatever it is. I hold on to the tenderness of the gesture, hold on too, to the feelings it stirs up inside me. I'm working up the courage to lean in for a kiss, but he steps back to his desk, and gestures to my chair and my abandoned breakfast. "Finish your coffee. I think your former madam should be up by now. Time to get your things."

"Are you sure you still want to help me?"

"It's not conditional, darling. You need to learn to trust me and trust that I care for you. You might even need to learn to trust yourself and trust that you care for me."

"You know I do," I say, piqued with myself for my uncertainty, my many fears, my lack of faith in my own ability to sustain anything other than a charade.

He reaches into the drawer of his desk, and pulls out a pistol, which he clips to the inside of his belt.

"You're not thinking of shooting her!"

"Absolutely not. But better safe than sorry."

I look at him and weigh his devotion against my own. "What you said earlier," I say, my voice trembling slightly. "Can we talk about it later, when I feel more composed?"

"So you might reconsider?"

"I didn't say no."

"You sure as hell didn't say yes." He laughs, shaking his head. "But for today let's focus on the more immediate problem of the madam."

I take comfort in the light I see in his eyes, his genuine good humor seemingly returned. I don't know what the future might hold, but my instincts tell me that in this moment I can trust this man, that I can go with him to Mrs. Harden's and have the confrontation I both dread and anticipate. I don't know if we'll be successful in eliminating her threats. I don't know if she will let me have my money or my dresses. And I don't know, above all, if Aristotle and I will be able to navigate the storms of a new precarious life together, if my willfulness and my quest for freedom will clash with his need for reassurance, if his frustration and loss will embitter him toward me, or if we're both too wild and free to forge a meaningful attachment. But I do know that I have an ally for my visit to Mrs. Harden's. Will we be able to talk her into relinquishing the damning photo and letting me walk away from my former life? And if so, will Marie's memory and the guilt stop haunting me from here on out? Will a guilt-free Yvonne have an easier time believing that maybe love won't crumble like a sandcastle and slip through her fingers?

CHAPTER 35
CONFRONTING THE MADAM

An hour later we are sitting together in Mrs. Harden's small office. She makes us wait. I know her tricks, know that the minutes slowly ticking by as we expect her arrival are a show of power, a way of driving home the point that we are insignificant while she is important. I have waited in this room before, though never as long as other girls, and never as long as this. As a well-paying customer, Aristotle has probably never waited. This, I know, is a way to underscore his diminished status.

When she finally appears, Mrs. Harden is all effusive energy, a calculated contrast to our long wait time. "Aristotle, what a sublime surprise," she coos. "And Aimée, my beloved dove! I knew you'd come to your senses and come back. And look, this arrived for you yesterday, all the way from France."

She pulls out a white envelope, but doesn't give it to me. Odette! The showgirl has written back! I smile despite myself.

"Now, darling, I will not pretend that I haven't read it, or rather had one of my girls who speaks a few words of French look over it for me. I was worried about you, so I had to. That stupid girl, Ruby put some awful ideas into my head, talking about the other girl in that photo, saying she was found dead in a hotel room in New Orleans, which sounds like a sordid affair, but now I am thoroughly confused, my sweet dove. Did you come here from New Orleans or from Paris? Did you know the girl who was killed or did you not?"

I try to calibrate my response. Not knowing what the letter says that has, as I had once hoped, led Mrs. Harden to believe that perhaps I had a history in Paris after all, I don't know what I should say. "May I please have the letter?" I venture.

"The letter from your lover?" she asks, teasing. "So interesting, Aimée, to finally understand your proclivities, though I must say they're neither that original, nor that shocking. Perhaps somewhat nontraditional, but sapphic liaisons are more common than you think. And men love these types of arrangements, don't you, Aristotle?" She winks at him.

"I think I'd like to see that," he says, and it's his outstretched hand Mrs. Harden doesn't ignore. She surrenders the envelope. He doesn't open it, hands it instead to me. I must see what it says. I unfold the scented paper. "My forever darling," it starts. So Odette addressed Cohen directly but through some lucky coincidence Mrs. Harden thinks it's intended for me. I smile.

"You seem happy to hear from her," she says.

"More than words can express."

"Interesting. Now, will you kindly explain about the other girl, the one rumored to have died in New Orleans? What's the story there? Did you know her?"

I look away.

"Was she your lover too?"

"That was so long ago," I say. "Before I went to Paris. It's a part of my life I wish to forget. An old friend told me she met a bad end while I was still in Europe, and I was not surprised. Can't we forget about her? She was a wild girl who led a dangerous life, and whoever digs up her memory might meet a bad end too."

"How dramatic," Mrs. Harden says, but I'm hoping my words have planted a tiny seed of fear in her heart.

"New Orleans is a dangerous place," I say. "That girl made enemies. We could make enemies too if we call attention upon—"

"And you think this makes you interesting?" She laughs. Perhaps I cannot rattle her.

"No. *Au contraire.* It's precisely why I reinvented myself. Paris is a better background for me. And it's part true, true enough, at least."

"Smart girl. I do think it's attractive to advertise you as a new girl from France. And it's most fortunate you were abroad when whatever happened to the other girl occurred. Best to stay away from the underworld."

"My point exactly," I say, failing to point out that we, too, are part of said underworld, albeit in a different, less sinister way.

"Would you kindly return the picture to Aimée?" Aristotle says. I'm grateful for his presence of spirit.

Mrs. Harden unlocks a drawer, takes out the dreaded picture of Marie and me, gives it to him. He looks at it before handing it to me. "Yvonne and Marie, 1890," is handwritten on the back by Madame Rouge herself. I trace my finger over her elegant lettering. I avoid eye contact even with the imprint of a Marie that once was. In three swift moves, I rip the picture to shreds and stuff it into the envelope with Cohen's lover's letter. Aristotle has a look of supreme satisfaction on his face. Mrs. Harden nods her assent as if I've done her the service of crushing a roach under my shoe.

"So much for that," she says. "Darkness is never good for business." I don't point out that in my previous life I met clients who were willing to pay a small fortune for a night of darkness.

"While you have your drawer open and your account books before you, I do believe you owe Aimée two weeks' worth of wages," Aristotle says. His tone is friendly but firm.

"I'm happy to increase her pay too, by ten percent, and I will get rid of Ruby. But darling Aimée, you cannot ever walk out on a client again."

The silence in the room is laden with expectation. In a most surprising twist of fate, I have the upper hand here, new bargaining power. I could resume my position, enjoy even more money, newfound privileges. Aristotle raises his eyebrows, looks at me expecting my reaction. I know in my soul that he'd resent me for returning to my vocation. But this decision belongs to Aimée, not to Aristotle.

"I am not coming back, Mrs. Harden," I say. "I've come to collect my things and my wages. And to say a proper goodbye. Surely it's nice to leave on good terms, isn't it?"

"Twenty percent," she says. "It's my last offer. Frankly, my dove, it's more than absurd, but you seem intent on being absurd, so —"

"No. I won't come back regardless of the price."

"Aristotle," she pleads. "You've always been a smart man. Enterprising. I admire that. Perhaps you can talk some sense into her."

"I thought you didn't want me to see him anymore," I point out.

Aristotle looks amused. "That so?" he asks. I can only hope the knowledge that the madam forbade me to see him and that I resisted brings him some of the validation he needs.

"Pure miscommunication," she says. "I've nothing against the two of you getting together. But I did not and do not want her to leave with you. Surely that's understandable. It would be a mistake. I was so sorry to hear about your loss of fortune, Aristotle. But surely you can see that it would be a profitable arrangement for all of us if Aimée continued to make good money. Prostitutes have been known to keep a lover."

"No," I say, but Mrs. Harden is not looking at me. She's looking at Aristotle as if the two of them might strike a deal.

"We're not interested," he says.

"She could even have two days off," she offers, "though it's a loss of profit, and you probably won't have much free time and much free energy yourself. Rumor has it you'll work for your friend Aronson as a stable boy, is that true?"

Aristotle's face darkens. "You've heard correctly."

"Will you live with him above a stable, Aimée? Or would you rather be here where you can have all the luxuries your greedy heart desires? You could share in her profit, Aristotle. Girls have been known to support men on the side."

"I'm not interested in Aimée as a source of income."

"How noble of you," she sneers.

"Mrs. Harden, I'd like my money. You may take out an extra fifty dollars to make up for the disgruntled client, but the rest is money I worked for. And I will leave a dress for Ruby. I think that, losing me, you might consider keeping her on."

"How grand of you. But I'm afraid you'll have no dresses to give. If you leave this house you may leave it the way you came."

"I came with dresses," I point out. "And I've earned my money."

"I mean the way you came this morning. You and your stable boy lover can go if you so wish. But Aristotle, darling, have no illusions about it, once a woman is a whore, she'll always be a whore. And Aimée, a gambler will also always be a gambler. You two will be at each other's throats within days, and you will regret this, because once this door closes behind you today, it will remain closed."

"Thank you," Aristotle says, "for your well wishes. At least we're not extortionists and traffickers of live flesh like you. Did you know it's illegal to coerce someone and bribe them into an arrangement where they sell their own body?"

"Enough of this." She slams the drawer shut. "Get out."

"Give Aimée her money, and we'll go upstairs and pack. I might be a mere stable boy these days, but some of my more powerful friends have not deserted me. Perhaps you'd like to avoid the unpleasantness of being taken to court? Or maybe you'd like to avoid an investigation into how you treat your girls? What happened, for example, that night when I came to see her and her face was bruised and you tried to disguise it with dim lights and makeup?"

My heart stops. He saw that? How silly to have thought I'd fooled him. And how noble and generous of him to pretend not to have noticed. Instead, that was the night he first brought up the house. My hand goes out to his. I interlace my fingers through his callused ones and hold on tight. We might both have a hard time getting past our fickle hearts and bad habits, but perhaps, if we survive the tension of navigating his loss of fortune and my newfound freedom, perhaps I will indeed take this man for better or for worse, in sickness and in health.

"You slapped Ruby too, and we all heard it," I say, hoping the tears in my voice come across as indignation.

"Do you want to stand up for some dim-witted hussy who tried to convince me you came here fleeing a murder scene?"

"Funny how you believed that yet covered it up as long as I was profitable to you."

"I think my friends at the newspaper would have a field day with all this," Aristotle says. "And luckily I no longer have a reputation to lose in this town."

"And I never had one," I say. "Is it worth it, all that trouble over a few dresses and books, a potted orchid, and two weeks of my wages?"

"I'll give you one week's wages and thirty minutes to pack your rags and disappear."

"You'll give her all her money," Aristotle says.

"It's the last money either of you will ever see," Mrs. Harden says, rolling her eyes to show she's tired of us. "I'll tell the other madams not to hire you, Aimée. You've got two to three years tops in this business and no prospects here in Galveston. You're older than you claim to be. Your looks are fading. Two to three years tops. Waste one on the likes of him, and you'll be poor in your old age, you little fool."

"Well," Aristotle says, "I thought you gave our love affair a week or two, but now you think we'll last a whole year. Things are looking up."

"You'll both regret it." She pushes the money across the table at him. He takes it, counts it, then hands it to me.

"Goodbye, Mrs. Harden," I say. I'm holding on to Aristotle's hand as we leave the room, and I take comfort in the steadying firmness of his grip.

We make our way upstairs, the sight of the interior of this house so familiar to me, yet suddenly so foreign. In my little room I take in, for the last time, the little luxuries I so relished. My clean white bed, my little window with a view that didn't quite stretch to the water. The magnolia blooms on the wallpaper. The orchid Aristotle gave me.

"I always wanted my own room," I tell him. "Girls have to sleep in the beds where they entertain, but I wanted a clean bed all to myself." Aristotle looks at the tiny bed with its white sheets and fluffed pillows. The orchid he sent me what now seems like a lifetime ago sits on my nightstand next to a pile of the books I didn't have time to read. He traces his finger over their spines.

"They're just novels," I say. "Not science like what you read. But I enjoy them very much, and I never had time for them. You know, sometimes I think the greatest luxury is time. It's what I felt was constantly being stolen from me in this house. There was never enough time."

He touches my perfume bottles, my brush, the baubles hanging over my mirror. His hand stops on the shiny crystal that so mesmerized him during our paid encounters. "You better take this with you," he says. I laugh. I'm throwing books and dresses into a carpetbag, and I take the crystal from him, wrap a lacy blouse around it, and nestle it in a soft spot inside my hastily assembled luggage.

"These silly frocks," I say holding out a dress that's outrageously low-cut. "I paid so much money for all this, and most of what I have is so inappropriate I almost want to leave it. But I guess I'll dress up for you on occasion. Would you like me to do that?"

I bat my eyelashes, my heart in my throat. Will he say that unless I marry him there's no point? Will he remind me that dressing up and playing games of seduction is exactly the type of courtesan behavior I said I'd abandon?

"You know I would," he says instead, and I take comfort in the warmth in his face. This morning's tension seems gone, diffused by our victory over Mrs. Harden, and by the unexpected intimacy of being in this room together – my little sanctuary where no men were allowed, my tiny place of refuge where I tried to enjoy a few blissful hours of rest in a clean bed all of my own.

"Will you miss it?" Aristotle asks, pacing my bedroom and taking in the little luxuries that made up my former life.

"No," I say. "All my good moments here were stolen moments. I felt like I was riding a carousel and it was moving way too fast. I want to wake up and know that the day is mine."

"A carousel," he says, smiling. "That's a charming way to put it. Was I one of the horses?"

"The most dashing one," I say. "The only one that mattered, truly. I always hoped you'd come back around again to take me for a spin."

He approaches me, smooths the hair out of my face. "You liked it, but you wanted the carousel to slow down. And now you're afraid that if it really does and you get to sit there leisurely on your favorite horse, you won't like it anymore. But maybe you will, darling, and you shouldn't be afraid to try it."

We kiss, and it feels forbidden to do so in my little room at Mrs. Harden's, forbidden to have his arms around me in a house where we did so much more than embrace. "Let's get out of here," he says. I look around for what I might have missed. Silk stocking hanging to dry, the French soap I'd bought from him just days ago, my tooth powder and toothbrush next to my wash basin, the tiny metal container where I store my diaphragm. I clutch them to my chest as if they're valued relics.

Aristotle carries my carpetbags, and I carry the pot with the orchid. We laugh as we descend the stairs. There's something merry about our exploits this morning, our victory in securing my money, my earthly possessions, as unsuitable as they are for a life outside the brothel walls, and most importantly, that incriminating picture of Marie and the young girl I once was.

The mood is not broken when, sitting in the carriage holding the orchid, I give Aristotle Cohen's address. I search his face for traces of resentment. I pray that maybe his role in rescuing me from Mrs. Harden's clutches has bolstered his confidence and that he feels good enough about himself and his role in securing my freedom to not resent my hesitation about uniting my life to his in a more meaningful and more binding way.

"It's not terribly hot today," he says, "and the horses had a good breakfast. Do you mind taking a detour by the water?"

I smile. I don't mind one bit prolonging our time together. "That sounds lovely."

We advance slowly, the sunshine a reassurance that on this beautiful day nothing terrible will happen, that the man sitting beside me will not begrudge me my uncertain heart any more than I will begrudge him his.

"I'm so happy right now," I say, trying to channel the brightness of the day into our conversation. "Look what we did! Look what you did, Aristotle! I'm free of that horrible woman and the picture is ripped to shreds! She doesn't believe I was there when Marie died, and in fact, she thinks it's best not to get involved with that story. It was you who planted the seed in my mind that I could dissuade her —"

"Luck played a part too," he says. I can see the water glimmering in the island sun, joyful, as if wishing to celebrate my freedom. "You're afraid to gamble, Aimée, but I think you were born lucky. What was that letter she gave you? The one from France? Who was that from?"

I laugh. "Cohen's old lover. I'd written to her on a hunch. See, I wrote to people who have some of his best paintings, and I'd heard about his portrait of her and I wanted to know more. I'd used my own address because I thought that I was trespassing in writing to her. I never thought that she'd write back."

"But she did. And it made the madam believe you were in fact in Paris recently."

"I must say, I was hoping, when I used my own address that a letter from France would make my far-fetched story a bit more credible."

"Well played, darling, well played! You are both smart and lucky."

"Lucky indeed! I haven't yet read the letter she sent. I can't even understand it without help, but it seems that she wrote a love letter, one directly addressed to him as, "my darling." And Mrs. Harden thought it was for me."

"That's like rolling the perfect dice. It's fate. Perhaps you truly are meant to write this old man's correspondence. Perhaps this is a sign."

"I never thought of myself as lucky before," I say.

"You're very lucky, Aimée. Today was lucky for you."

"I can see why you like this, the twists and turns of chance."

"You like it too. You're an adventuress. And I hope you take heart in this. Take your luck as a sign. Whatever guilt you're carrying over that girl who died, let it go now. It's over. And God or the Universe or Providence or whatever you wish to call it gave you a powerful nudge that you're meant to be free of it and happy."

I smile into the golden sunshine. "Thank you," I say.

"Don't thank me. Take it to heart. Look at this beautiful day, look at the sunshine and the clear sky and the water and remember you're meant to be lucky. You were lucky that night in New Orleans, you were lucky when that letter arrived, and you were lucky many other times. It's a good thing and you deserve it. When happiness comes your way, don't question it, just seize it and run with it."

I smile. Perhaps we can go on like this, keep our dealings with each other light, like a salty breeze providing solace on a hot island day. Though in my heart I know, he's still trying to talk me into it, the leap of faith required to unite our destinies.

"There's something else, too," he says. "I just made a decision. I wasn't sure of it this morning, but I've decided to once more trust my own luck. My friend is going to a race off Island and he invited me to come with him and enter my horses. I thought I was done with all that, but I decided I'll go. If I win big, I might be able to improve my situation sooner than I thought."

"I hope you do," I say, but a warning bell goes off inside me. "When are you going?"

"Next week. Perhaps you'll give me something of yours for good luck."

Against my better judgement, I pull out the envelope of money from Mrs. Harden. He frowns. "No, no. Put that away. A man has his pride."

"I know what I'll give you!" I say victoriously before the gloominess of my faux pas can fully settle over us. "I will give you that sparkling bauble you so loved that night at Mrs. Harden's." I don't add that that was the night he pretended not to see that my face was bruised. "I promise you it's completely worthless," I add in a happy voice. "And perhaps if I wear it for you before you go, that would really be good luck?"

"You sure know how to make me feel better, Aimée. Yes, definitely, I'd like to see you wear it before I go."

He drives me to Cohen's, brings my carpetbags inside, carries them up to my room. I can see that once inside the house, his demeanor changes. He seems more tense. Am I making a huge mistake? Should I change my mind on the spot, throw caution to the wind and ask him to take me and all my possessions back to the store? I remember the race and tell myself not to get swept up in some fleeting emotion. He's not free of his vice, and I myself am complicated and fickle.

"Let me show you something," I say and lead him back downstairs. I open the doors to the parlor, open the curtain wide and let the light come in. Aristotle stands before the paintings that have awed me since the first time I set eyes on them, and for a long time he is quiet.

"I know nothing about art," he says. "But these are really something. I can see how it would be nice to wake up and come down to see these instead of some smelly horses."

"I love smelly horses," I say. I smile, but my heart is hanging in the balance, not only to see if he'll choose me despite my independent streak, but to learn if he is worthy of the love that has sprouted within me for him, if in the end this is a plant I wish to nourish, or one I would rather uproot.

"Thank you for helping me today," I say as I kiss him goodbye.

"Anytime, darling."

CHAPTER 36
CHANGED CIRCUMSTANCES

Later that day, with my limited French with a Cajun twist, I try to read Marie's letter to Cohen. He helps me out as best he can, considering he can't see the words I don't understand. I spell them out for him. Together, we decipher her message, and the more of it becomes clear, the heavier my heart grows.

"My forever darling," she writes. It's this opening line that made Mrs. Harden believe the letter was addressed to me.

"Don't think I ever stopped loving you. Don't think I ever will. For I have thought of you every day since you left Paris. While you were still here I thought of you too and there were moments I reconsidered my decision to not give up my own aspirations to be with you. But no, my love, while it hurt, I know I chose wisely. I know you found my ambitions laughable, my dancing act unformed and unsophisticated. But it was a life I had chosen, a life I had meticulously constructed and sacrificed for. I did not choose mere creature comforts over our love. What I chose, above all, was to leave open the possibility that certain things could happen. You might wonder what those things were and if they occurred indeed, if I've regretted my decision. I did, in fact, regret it every day, but I was grateful for it too. Some life choices are not black and white. Here in Paris I met a great many people. Writers and actors and artists and dancers more illustrious than myself. My life is not as much fulfilling as it is rich. I took a gamble and some would say I lost. But there were no guarantees to our love either. Only limits. I wish, above all, that we had both been more patient, more willing to compromise. You wanted me to roam the world with you when I already had a life in Paris. It was romantic, but required me to give up everything. I've met so many women who did, and they got precious little in return.

I know you will never return and I shall never see you again. I will always love you,

Your Odette."

"Stubborn woman," Cohen says, a crooked smile hung precariously on his lips. But why is the woman always the one who has to yield? I wish I could talk to this Odette. Perhaps she would understand me.

I tell Cohen about my time with Aristotle, about our visit to the madam, about the incredible coincidence that got her to doubt the suspicion Ruby had planted in her mind. I tell him about Aristotle getting her to surrender the picture, getting her to surrender my money, even. And I tell him about Aristotle's disappointment that I did not want to go live with him, about his tentative marriage offer, about my own apprehension at his desire to have all of me.

"It's natural," Cohen says. "He wants you to himself. He's already shared you enough."

"He no longer has to share me in that way. But I still need to have adventures of my own. I don't resent him his interests," I say, though I do realize that it's not entirely true. Isn't the race he's going to something that makes me uneasy? Don't I wish he would stay here and devote himself to me? Is love selfish and possessive? Or is this type of feeling Aristotle and I have for each other not truly love? Was this Odette's woe with Cohen? Had she correctly noted that wanting to own the other person is not truly loving? Had she been more loving herself in setting him free?

I fall asleep late and my dreams are haunted, not by Marie and her death, but by Odette, who chose freedom over a man who loved her but wanted her to become his shadow. The next day I feel melancholic and I decide to cheer myself up by going shopping. I remind myself that while I no longer make a small fortune each week, I do have a lovely home to live in at no cost, a small income of my very own that doesn't require me to do anything I don't like, and savings that some people would kill for. I can certainly afford a new dress.

As I enter Garbade, Eiband & Co, the shopgirls stop and stare. I hear hushed whispers as soon as I turn away. As I'd initially assumed, news travels fast in Galveston. And oddly enough the shopgirls were all more eager to serve me when I was a prostitute than now that I've left Mrs. Harden's and embarked on a relatively respectable path. The obvious lack of enthusiasm with which they attend to me ruins my enjoyment of the wares on display, and I decide to abandon the shopping expedition.

I return to Cohen's to compose letters to some of the writers and editors who had expressed interest in his story. I also pen a note of my own, to Brighton, alerting him of my changed circumstances and telling him that I shall very much like to meet with him as a friend from here on out. I know how much this would displease Mrs. Harden, but there's not much she can do about it, is there? Besides, my action is not motivated by revenge on her, but rather by my wish to preserve my connection with a man who has become a friend of sorts, a man I'd love to confide in about Odette's letter and my own agonizing decision about Aristotle. My doubts too and my fears. I am afraid that for all his joy and his magic Aristotle will never recover from the loss of his fortune, that the setback will crush his spirit, that he will spend his life haunted by the specter of the wealth he once had and had to give up. That he will blindly pursue chance, that he'll want me, a coveted and dangerous woman as his wife, and Lady Luck forever as his mistress.

My sobering experience at the department store underscores my fears, as my own loss of income and status, even as I have enviable savings, stings in a way I hadn't anticipated. I'm used to being talked about, whispered about, occasionally scorned by some righteous matron who will cross the street in order to avoid me. But I'm used to being catered to as well, as a woman of means, albeit a disreputable one. I remind myself that I am still a woman of means, but the allure that came with my money is gone. And so fast, too. How rumors circulate in this town!

I tell myself it doesn't matter. I do have dresses and I have money too. I will find a seamstress who will be happy to have my business. She will alter my dresses, make them suitable to my new life. But Aristotle has lost both in reputation and actual wealth. A fortune he had made himself, through honest work, with a little bit of gambling thrown in. Will he forever chase the specter of his former success? Is this what the race is about that he wants to participate in? Is this why him going to that race makes me so uneasy?

There is a lot I still don't know about this man I've come to care a great deal about in such a short time. I know that gambling can be a powerful vice and I don't know to what extent it has him in its grips. I don't know if its hold on him will now become stronger, as a desperate means to secure a windfall and replace some of his lost fortune. Cohen, even, has warned me against tying my life to that of a gambler. Though ironically, I do understand that a man must be comfortable with taking risks to even consider tying his life to mine.

Mrs. Harden's words haunt me. "A gambler and a whore. I give you a few weeks." What if she's right, and the passion between us burns out like a wildfire leaving nothing in its wake? I know so much about men, yet so little about love. I toss and turn all night, and when in the morning I awake to cramps, the agony of the night makes sense. I remember my tears over Aristotle and his predicament, which I knew nothing of, a month ago, last time the female curse was upon me. How could so much have happened in the span of only one month? Part of me feels like I have been given a new life, while part of me feels like I've torn down everything that's taken me so much work to build.

I take my sense of loss with me to Aristotle's shop that evening. I wear one of my favorite dresses, but my complexion is too pale and my sleepless night shows on my face. I wear the sparkly bauble I promised him under my dress, though I will not be able to give him the kind of sendoff I had fantasized about. Then again, aside from that one time we had coffee in his office while his niece minded the shop, this will be my first encounter with him without physical intimacy. There is probably useful information to gather from a chaste evening, information about our connection and whether our feelings transcend passion.

Even in my bleak state of mind, it's a joy to see him, a joy when he puts his arms around me, when I take in the smile in his eyes, and when his lips meet mine. The store too, envelops me with its scent like a long-lost friend. The scent tugs at my heartstrings, as I know this will be my last time experiencing it. From now on, I shall search for faint traces of it on Aristotle's clothes, his books, his pillows, until slowly but surely it will all fade. Perhaps we'll both spend a lifetime searching for it, pursuing it like the specter of a lost love.

The store is empty. The things I can still smell, the coffee and soap and candy and bolts of fabric all gone. It's surreal to see the shelves and counters devoid of their offerings, surreal to think that Aristotle will surrender the keys to the building before he sets off on his trip, and that, if I ever set foot in here again it will not be his store but something entirely different. Eventually the scent will fade here too. It will be lost forever.

Aristotle leads me to the back, where in the kitchen everything is packed up, but a cast-iron skillet is heating on the stove, and a thick marbled cut of steak is waiting on the counter to be cooked. "I thought we'd make our last night here special," he says. To think that of all things, I was craving a steak. There are potatoes in the oven too, and a head of lettuce, freshly washed, is draining in a colander in the sink.

"Where'd you learn to cook?" I ask.

"A stable boy acquires all manner of skills," he says. "I learned to make decent biscuits and steaks in cast-iron skillets while on the road selling horses. My sister told me what to do about the potatoes and she insisted I take this head of lettuce and make us a salad."

"Where does your sister live?" I remember the story he told me about her. The small wafer candy he and his friends used as a Communion host, the sister's indignation about anyone making a joke out of her faith. The idea of this devout sister both scares and attracts me. Reminds me why even a tentative proposal is a preposterous idea.

"Small yellow clapboard cottage at Eleventh and Ball. I bought it for her in better days. She gives violin lessons to children. I'll take you over there to meet her when I come back."

"Do you think she would want to meet a girl like me?"

"You're a fabulous girl, darling. My sister is a bit rigid, but she'll come around."

"Unlike everyone in this town, apparently. The day I've had." I tell him about my unpleasant shopping expedition.

"They will forget," he says. "There will be new things to gossip about tomorrow. There always are. Just hold your head high and go about your business. You've got nothing to be ashamed of."

"It's ironic that I was never ashamed of being a prostitute, not really, but now that I've left that life behind I'm seen as a pariah."

"Will you be sorry you left?"

"No. Not a drop. It's wonderful to have my evenings, my nights, my mornings to do with as I please. I wouldn't be able to be here right now."

"You'd miss out on a great steak," he says, throwing it in the hot skillet, where it sizzles. I have absolutely no kitchen skills, but I wash my hands and gently shake the water out of the lettuce. I try to imagine Aristotle's sister doing the same. I wonder, despite myself, whether she'd approve of the way I do it. I feel her presence in the kitchen to such extent, I almost reach for the fabric of my dress to pull it up and cover some of my exposed flesh. But no, I will not allow the specter of a woman I've never even met to intimidate me. I've never cared for the opinions of ladies who look down on prostitutes, so why would I care about Aristotle's sister?

Our meal is delicious, deeply satisfying. I feel it strengthening my body and my soul. After we eat, we go say goodnight to the horses. They watch me with big sleepy eyes. I kiss each of their foreheads for good luck in the race, though my heart is still heavy at the thought of it. Aristotle leans me against the wall where we made love the first time I came here. He kisses me.

"I can't tonight," I whisper. "Female trouble."

"Stay with me anyway," he says. "I want to make you coffee in the morning."

And so, I spend the night with him, and we don't make love. We talk and laugh late into the night. When we finally say goodnight, he puts his arms around me, and it feels good. We hold the embrace for a few seconds, then let go. I sink into a deep dreamless sleep, and when I awake in the empty room where all the books have been boxed, and nothing but sunshine dances on the bare wood floors, I feel rested. Over coffee I give Aristotle the sparkling bauble I had promised him. He slips it under his own shirt, and I laugh, because it's such a strange thing for a man to wear. And although our encounter was sweet and comforting and full of laughter, after we kiss goodbye, on my way home I cry as if he were going to war and not to a race. Is it the female trouble or a premonition?

CHAPTER 37
FRIENDSHIP

A day later, early in the morning, I walk by Aristotle's sister's house on Ball. I don't know why I do it, why I'm pulled there of all places. It's a beautiful sunny day, and I'm still giddy with disbelief at my new ability to enjoy mornings. The grackles whistle in the trees, sunlight caresses my face, not having yet reached its midday blistering heat, and the air smells salty and clean. A brand-new day stretches before me like a promise.

By the afternoon, sunshine gives way to clouds, and what starts as a drizzle turns into rain. I've yet to grow accustomed to the unpredictable temperament of this tropical island. Rain here is intense, and showers are gone as quick as they came, like the moods of a capricious client.

That afternoon, despite the inclement weather, the doctor visits us. He is most happy to see me and hear about my changed circumstances.

"My dear Miss Bonnard, I think you've made a very good choice indeed. That is no life for a kind, gentle soul such as yourself." I feel both validated and misunderstood. I smile and talk to him about Cohen's book project. "You've brought him back to life," he says. "You've accomplished what I've been trying to do for years but failed."

"Well, you did save my life, Dr. Tarner, and then you brought me here to Mr. Cohen, so I'd say in a roundabout way you've actually achieved your objective."

"That's a most kind way to look at it." His eyes smile at me, and I respond to his warmth. For a moment I bask in it, and the world briefly stops. Then I remember that much as I appreciate this man, this intelligent, attractive, kind, and generous man, what I feel for him is so different than the type of joy and synchronicity I feel for Aristotle. I might have fantasized about the doctor in the past, particularly when I needed a fantasy to distract or empower me, and there could be an occasional frisson of desire between us – after all, I'm an expert in fabricating such emotions – but truly we're meant to be friends.

"I will confess something personal to you," Tarner says, and I'm hoping he will not express a sentiment at odds with my newfound clarity about my own feelings for him. We sit in wicker chairs on the front porch, and for a moment we are both silent taking in the sound of the intensifying rain.

"My wife succumbed to a deep depression. There was no analysis that could help her, no medicine that could do anything for her but help her sleep. One day she took too much Laudanum. I'll never know if it was on purpose or by accident, but either way, I felt like I had failed her."

"That's terrible," I say. "I'm so sorry. I don't think you should feel responsible, though."

"I did for a long time. I failed to save her." I'm familiar with that feeling, but I don't share this with the doctor. This is his story, his moment to confess and have a friend listen. I already had two people who love me hear me out this week, and I have gained invaluable peace from their kindness and acceptance. "After a while I decided that I had to help others in order to make up for it, not that it could be made right. The most wonderful woman was gone forever, but I figured there were other people out there I could try to help."

"There always are," I say. "And that's a hopeful and most generous thought. Is that why you started the free clinic?"

"It's part of it, yes. But while I love doing it, I felt that it was not enough. When I met Cohen I decided that helping him would be the act that would restore my own inner balance, my own sense of self."

"And you kept at it for years. Until you found something that pulled him out of his state of misery."

"You have quite a talent, Miss Bonnard. Please don't ever take it for granted."

"You are too kind, doctor. Thank you for bringing me here. It opened the door to something different for me. I'm fascinated with Cohen and his career."

"He's a fascinating man."

"And he's become a good friend to me. I'm fortunate to have made some wonderful friends here in Galveston, and I'm glad to count you among them."

There is a flicker in his eye, one I can't catch fast enough to interpret. Was he hoping for more than friendship? And if so, am I a fool to toss a good man out in favor of a gambler? But having turned my back from the opportunity of making a small fortune each night by using my charms on men, I am no longer interested in choosing companions out of practical considerations. The doctor would be a safe bet if I were inclined to look for such safety. I could have a nice, tranquil life with him, living forever in the shadow of a dead woman. I would much rather be his friend. Let him visit his girl once a week if he needs that type of female companionship.

CHAPTER 38
TEMPTING FATE

It rains all night, with only the occasional break. It rains, and I feel lonely, bereft and worried. Like a ship at sea during a storm, I feel untethered. The magnitude of cutting myself off from the brothel and my former life opens up an abyss of fear. I know I'm now at the point where the exhilaration of having made a momentous decision begins to fade, and in its wake I'm finding myself in a precarious fluid state, like the world outside, with nothing solid to grasp. Everything is a question mark, my love for Aristotle, my attachment to him, my hope that he will overcome the loss and defeat he's experienced and not fall prey again and again to the irresistible lure of gambling. Yet isn't he at a race now? Isn't he enamored with luck above all else?

I remind myself that I have not tied myself to this man's fate in any way that is irrevocable and forever binding. I have risked his scorn by maintaining my own footing, however precarious, chosen this home and my own path. What ties me to him is not economic dependence and the grim realities of daily coexistence, sharing a wash basin and breaking bread together each night. What ties me to him are my feelings, and those are in some ways more binding than practical considerations. When have I become this person who allows herself to care, and at what cost?

Unable to sleep, I tiptoe downstairs, and in the glow of intermittent lightning, I take in the light and shadows of Cohen's paintings, their contrast both heightened and dulled by the stormy night. I can make out the thickness of some of the paint, knowing now he created the most striking texture through bold spontaneous strokes applied with a palette knife. His feelings, captured on canvas, even after all these years, are powerful, moving, expressive.

I remind myself I'm here to record this, Cohen's work, his life story, his own bravery in allowing himself to be moved deeply and to create. Whatever happens in other parts of my life, there is solid footing to be found here, in this room, with these paintings, which I've the privilege to learn about intimately, and the self-appointed mission to make accessible to others. This, too, is something I care about, as is my friendship with the blind man upstairs. It's something to take comfort in if the emotional risks I'm allowing myself to take prove ill-advised.

Aristotle may well hurt me. He may well hurt himself, may self-destruct in the way in which brilliant men are often want to do. Not having opened myself up to affairs of the heart before, I cannot measure the vastness of the pain I might be exposing myself to. All I know is I can probably survive it. I am no longer building a fortress around my own heart, but rather allowing my heart to boldly enter into several entanglements it desires. I stand to lose a great deal, perhaps, but there is also the possibility of a joy greater than what my previous life would have allowed.

Lightning flashes once more across the surfaces of thick luscious oil paint, and I lose my train of thought. Or perhaps my thoughts did not make sense to begin with. Perhaps they are the sleepless churnings of an anxious mind, but there is peace and beauty in this private moment too. The thunder outside gives in to a heavy downpour, cathartic, cleaning everything.

I return to my bed and let the sound of rain lull me to sleep. I let go of my worries, and somewhere in the night they transform – half dream, half prayer. Marie sits on the edge of my bed and smiles. "God never hated you, you silly fool. Why are you so easy to torment?"

After that, she comes to me for a few nights, but in each dream she seems less real, more ethereal, slowly fading. I will forget her, just like I wanted to. This is goodbye. One night, she sits on my bed, laughing at me as usual, and I reach for her hand. It dissolves to my touch. "I'm not here, silly goose," she says. "I'm dead, you can't touch me." "I'm sorry," I say, "Marie, I'm so sorry." She shrugs. "Don't take it all so seriously," she says. "What's it like?" I ask. She smiles, touches my cheek without touching it, because her fingers are insubstantial. I can barely see her now. "Stop thinking about it and live your life, you lucky pig!"

I wake up laughing, but then I cry into my pillow, cry for Marie's young life cut short, cry for the times we laughed together and the times we hated each other, cry for our friendship which was as elusive as the ghost in my dreams.

Cohen says it's only ourselves we see in dreams. Marie was never there. It was only me, trying to give my own self a message that eluded me in waking.

A knock on my door breaks the spell. It's Deirdre, and if she's indeed brought my coffee to bed I'm ashamed of myself. In this house, I no longer want to be an indolent creature that needs to waited on hand and foot.

"There is a man downstairs, come to see you. A short stocky man with two hunting dogs."

I throw on my robe and fly down the stairs. The stormy night has given in to a sunny morning and the trees, having shaken off the cleansing rain, stand victorious in the steamy daylight. Nature is breathing anew, salty and abundant, the island breeze accompanied by the whistle of morning birds. Aristotle stands on the porch, straw hat in hand. Two English Pointers, one white with reddish ears, one spotted black and white, struggle to contain their boundless energy and their desire to lurch forward chasing the birds.

"You're back!" I exclaim, embracing Aristotle as if he returned from war. "And you brought the dogs!"

I let their enthusiasm overcome me, their wet kisses, their long energetic tails, their paws on my shoulders.

"Down," Aristotle says. "We have to train them." But I am overcome with laughter and delight, and although the claws are threatening to tear the lace of my robe, I know I'm doing nothing but encouraging the display. Deirdre comes out with a water bowl, and they lap it up greedily. She brings them bacon too, and is rewarded with an assault of paws, tails, and drool.

"Oh, my," I say. "We can't have these beasts in Mr. Cohen's house."

"But we can have them in our rooms above the stables," Aristotle says. I don't reply, but the smile that warms my face is telling.

"How was the race?" I ask.

"I didn't go. I was all set and then thought better of it."

"You had a change of heart?"

"I thought I'd try my luck at this instead."

"Bringing me the two dogs I wanted in the hopes I'll reconsider and come live with you?"

"Isn't it a better way to tempt fate?"

"I'd say it is, Aristotle. And I'd say you win."

EPILOGUE

Our rooms above the stables are not luxurious, but the bare furnishings are a good match for the boundless energy of the dogs. The maid I pay out of my savings is a friend of Deirdre's. She keeps the beasts out of the tiny room that serves as our kitchen, and I delight in their presence in our other, larger room, where my whorish dresses, awaiting her patient alterations, still retain a faint scent of decadence, while Aristotle's many books hold within their pages my most cherished keepsake – the scent of his store.

I will not tell you that we never quarrel. We do, and often, with shouts and the occasional slammed door followed by hours of silence, but we always make up, sometimes through passion but mostly through laughter, that current of magic that unites us. The dogs help as a constant reminder of our joyful bond.

Aristotle's sister dislikes me profoundly. She does not attend our small wedding in Cohen's parlor, and refuses to allow her daughter to do so. Our witnesses are Aristotle's friend who owns the stables, Cohen, of course, Dr. Tarner, and Mrs. Bock – who insists on pressing on me the gift of an old embroidered handkerchief that once belonged to her mother. I'm mildly irritated by the sentimentality, yet find myself unable to part with the tiny rag embroidered with German words for the rest of my life.

I continue working as Cohen's secretary for the remainder of his life. His biography is published three years after our acquaintance, and although it only enjoys moderate success, it brings joy to a handful of people who care about his work, and plants the seeds for a new project, a foundation and small gallery that will make his work accessible to the public after his passing. On an island devastated by the Great Storm, this modest yet meaningful endeavor brings hope of a future that might never recapture the glamour of Galveston's glory days, yet might still hold, for those patient enough to seek it out, unexpected glimmers of wonder.

In his last years of life, despite advancing age and despite his blindness, Cohen takes to accompanying me on walks. We advance slowly, arm in arm,

225

him exploring the ground with his walking stick. As I had learned in what now seems like a different life, people who lose one of their senses have a heightened awareness of the others. In the company of Cohen and the dogs, I too, open myself up to the delights often missed by those of us who fall prey to the lure of the world's outer beauty. Together we smell the salty air and listen to the myriad of sounds of waves and birds and the occasional trot of horses.

Cohen passes away peacefully in his home, with Deirdre, Tarner, and me by his bedside. My mourning over his loss is deep and real, yet I work diligently to preserve his memory for the handful of visitors that come to look at his paintings each weekend.

Five years after the loss of his business, Aristotle Fontenot, now my husband, opens a tiny neighborhood grocery on the corner of 11th and Ball, renting two rooms of a small yellow clapboard house he previously bought for his sister. There is no gambling in the back, and the only rumor surrounding his new, more modest business venture is that his wife was once upon a time a showgirl who danced the cancan in a disreputable club. His sister occasionally brings up these rumors and the chagrin they cause her, but her tone toward me has softened. When I come by the store, Aristotle still loves giving me candy, and I myself love standing in line behind little old ladies and children and seeing him occasionally tip the scales in their favor.

We don't have children of our own – perhaps due to fate, or maybe to the methods I've used in the past to prevent or remedy such an outcome. I cannot say either of us is disappointed. Our lives are rich in other ways, and the love we bestow on our animals, on each other, on our work, and on the few people who accept us as we are is nourishing and deep. Marie must have found peace, or perhaps I have. For she rarely visits me in my dreams anymore. Her appearances are years apart. In time, I come to crave her company, to rejoice instead of startle when I see my long-lost friend. "So you married a poor man who sells candy," she says. "I know," I tell her, "Isn't it wonderful?"

ABOUT THE AUTHOR

Maria Elena Sandovici is a full-time artist and writer living in Houston with her Boston Terrier, Holly Golightly. She earned a Ph.D. in Political Science from the State University of New York at Binghamton in 2005 and taught at Lamar University in Beaumont, TX for 14 years before quitting her tenured position in order to write and paint full-time. Galveston has been a favorite place of refuge throughout the years.

Sandovici has published several other works of fiction, including *Storms of Malhado*, a historical novel set in Galveston.

Made in the USA
Monee, IL
04 July 2023